Well Acquainted

A SMARTYPANTS ROMANCE OUT OF THIS WORLD TITLE

LONDON LADIES EMBROIDERY
BOOK TWO

LANEY HATCHER

WWW.SMARTYPANTSROMANCE.COM

One

"**W**e need a doctor."

I froze at the sound of the masculine voice.

With my back to the entryway, I closed the drawer containing the gauze and straightened slowly.

It couldn't be.

"Miss, can you help us?"

It was.

It may have been six years, but I still recognized that voice.

Attempting to blink away my surprise, I spun and faced the newcomers.

And there he was. So very much the same and categorically different all at once. When I'd known Nicolas, he had been tall and lanky, still growing into his newly acquired height. This version of him—now three and twenty—looked strong and well proportioned. He'd filled out and grown confident and comfortable in his skin. His hair was a little darker. But those familiar jade green eyes hadn't changed one bit.

I did not need this today.

After my previous patient earlier in the evening and the upcoming battle I had with my father, I was ready to be done with this bloody day. I should have turned down the lamps when I had the chance.

But my past was staring me in the face, and I imagined the only reason he'd stopped speaking was due to shock. Nicolas had recognized me alright. Standing by the door, he was locked in place with a confused and vulnerable expression on his face.

With dark whiskers along his jaw and a hint of stage makeup under his ear, Nicolas looked tired. It was getting on close to midnight. He'd likely performed this evening.

I finally noticed the *we* and the *us* in the scenario before me. A small girl stood cautiously at Nicolas's side. She was young, perhaps four or five, with a warm complexion and dark hair similar in shade to the man accompanying her to my after-hours clinic.

Jolted into motion and the required professionalism by the sight of the child— one who resembled Nicolas so well—I gathered my wits and moved toward them. "Hello, Nicolas. How can I help you?"

He jerked slightly and then seemed to recover himself. "It's …" Clearing his throat, he started again. "She's unwell."

I could do this. I would focus on what needed to be done. Investigate a problem. Help a child. There was no place in the clinic for my history with Nicolas. Right now he couldn't be my first love, my first kiss, my adolescent obsession.

My pounding heart and sudden panic needed to recede so I could do my job.

I approached the child as she tucked herself behind Nicolas's legs. While observing her pallor and estimating her weight on sight, I offered a small smile before indicating they should come in. "Hello, there. I'm Eliza." I spoke directly to the girl and ignored the protective shadow at her side. "Would you like to sit here on my table so I could have a look at you?"

With small fingers clutched in Nicolas's brown coat, she looked up to him for direction. He led her forward and into the space before smiling down gently and lifting her in his arms. "Up you go, Angel."

He placed her carefully on the examination table.

"What's your name?" I inquired softly.

After a moment in which it became obvious that the child was too shy to speak, Nicolas offered, "This is Angelica. She's been sick for weeks. It comes and goes. Some nights she's fine and others she wakes up gasping for breath, eyes and nose leaking with no rhyme or reason."

Determined to ignore the large presence in the room, I nodded at Nicolas's assertion and took in Angelica's quick inhales and exhales and red-rimmed eyes.

Nicolas continued as I gathered my stethoscope from my desk and a tongue depressor from a drawer. "She seems almost better now, but earlier this evening, I could hear her wheezes from the other room."

"Angelica, would it be okay if I used this," indicating the end of the stethoscope, "to place here?" I motioned toward my chest. "So I can hear your heart and listen to you breathe." She looked calm but weary, as if she often endured hardship and had grown used to it. "I can even let you listen as well."

I finally received a small nod of agreement. Listening to her rapid heartbeat, I appreciated her slightly elevated breathing but couldn't find any evidence to indicate fluid in her lungs. "Does she often cough during these episodes or have a rash of any sort?"

Nicolas answered immediately, intent on my movements. "Yes to the cough. I've never noticed a rash or skin irritation before."

I nodded and moved to register her temperature. No fever was present. I checked for swelling around her throat or any obstruction to her airway.

I tried to ignore Nicolas's attention and persistent stare by focusing on Angelica when I spoke. "Your nose gets very leaky and your eyes water as if you're crying?"

Her large brown eyes returned my stare as she nodded quickly in answer.

"Are you feeling better now?"

Another bob of her head.

Nicolas jumped in. "It always goes away, but it always comes back again. I'm tired of seeing her suffer and never knowing when these episodes will occur. Is there anything you can do to help her?"

I steeled myself and finally met his regard. "There are individuals who experience bouts of difficulty breathing. They can happen at random or can be triggered by something—dust, smoke, even weather or plant life. But I don't believe that is what's happening with Angelica. Based on her other symptoms, I believe there's something in her environment—her surroundings—that is causing her discomfort. And the trouble diminishes once she's removed from the offending articles."

"Explain," came his terse reply, paired with a frustrated expression. I recognized this in patients and loved ones. When there wasn't a simple answer or immediate cure for what ailed them, people often became upset.

"I believe we can figure out what's causing Angelica's reactions if we isolate the elements in her life. By process of elimination. Attempt to deduce anything that might elicit her symptoms. Irritants can range from food or drink to the fabrics that touch her skin, even nearby smoke affecting the air that she breathes. It will require keen investigation to determine the cause and then isolate it. Noting everything from the time of day, what she is wearing, what she has eaten, and who she's been exposed to."

"Can I lie down? I'm awfully tired." The sleepy little voice interrupted my long and boring adult speech.

"Of course, darling." I indicated Nicolas could pick her up as I led them over to one of the fresh beds. I slid the fabric curtain open so we could see her from across the room but still be able to carry on a conversation without disturbing her.

Once settled, Nicolas gave her a tender kiss on the top of her head. "I'll be right over here speaking to Miss Eliza. I'll just be a moment." A tired nod was Angelica's only response.

We moved quietly through the space, and I offered Nicolas a seat across from my desk. Watching as he settled himself in the chair, I noticed how different he appeared in my dim workspace. He seemed such a large presence on the theater stage. And back when we knew each other, he was so much smaller and younger. It was like looking in a slightly distorted mirror. Nothing was too terribly off— just enough to make me question my instincts.

But he'd always been good at that.

It felt impossible that we were sitting here now, after all this time.

The lamps cast a warm glow over his features but his expression was hard. "I didn't know you'd be here. I thought …" His inability to finish that statement made me realize he was as off-kilter as I was. "I'd heard there was a doctor who remained after hours to see servants and the like. A friend of mine gave us this address and said if the lights were on near the garden entrance, then we were free to seek medical attention."

"That's correct," I confirmed, not that he'd asked a question. Feeling unsteady by Nicolas's unexpected presence in my fairly predictable life, I tried not to stare. I wanted to. I ached to trace the line of his jaw that was no longer soft from adolescence. I wanted to catalog all the changes to his expression, the way his dark hair swept along his forehead and how his cheekbones emerged from the familiar planes of his face. It was like watching time expand to accommodate these new versions of ourselves. Nicolas, a darling of the theater, an accomplished man of the stage, and still the most handsome man I'd ever seen.

And me, a sad observer—a quiet shadow to the light and splendor he cast.

I ran a self-conscious hand over my hair and found several strands loosened from my braided chignon. Nicolas's eyes followed the movement before resting once more on my face.

"How are you here?" he asked.

I could understand his confusion. Nicolas had had no contact with me for the last six years.

But of course I knew of him. Several months ago, I'd been shocked to see his likeness in the newspaper. Below the grainy photograph, an advertisement had announced his role in a popular play, but with a stage name I didn't recognize— Silas Viso. Without completely knowing why, I'd ventured out that same week to the theater to confirm my suspicions. So, I could understand what Nicolas was feeling right now. The unexpected, jarring reaction of your past making itself known in volume and intensity … I'd lived it, too.

While seeing Nicolas here, in the clinic, was a startling development. I wasn't unprepared for his very existence. That's likely what he was struggling with now. The utter absurdity of a chance encounter with someone you never expected to see ever again.

Since that initial shock of discovery, I'd seen him again on stage just last week. And the week before that. And twice more before Christmas, if I was being honest. I didn't know what compelled me to return each time, telling myself after each performance that it needed to be the last.

Nicolas was famous for his role. But it wasn't as if he'd seen my face in the newspaper. We didn't move in the same social circles. As well-known as he may be, Nicolas's community was more closely aligned with the demimonde. And while I was a woman attempting a career in medicine, I was still the daughter to the second son of a baron. People acknowledged me as *lady* more often than *doctor*. I was odd and not well regarded, but my friendships with several high-ranking ladies of the peerage often secured invitations and reluctant acceptance.

My father was a well-respected and beloved physician for the men and women of the *ton*. I was Dr. Richard Finley's peculiar daughter seeking to follow in his footsteps. And while he may currently be very angry with me about the after-hours clinic he'd just discovered earlier this evening, he was still my unabashedly supportive father and mentor. Once I'd proven my determination, he'd dedicated himself to supporting my education. I wanted for a lot of things, but an indulgent father was not one of them.

I didn't know how to answer Nicolas's question. But I knew the response he sought. *How was I here?* In London, years after agreeing to marry his brother and ruining everything. Perhaps he wasn't in contact with his family. When he'd left home, I'd assumed it had been for good. However, it was likely that a letter from his mother years ago could have cleared up the suspicion and confusion I was reading in his expression now. Maybe Nicolas and his family were still estranged … because of me.

I decided to go with the simplest and most obvious answer. "I live here. Father and I practice medicine. The clinic adjoins our home."

His eyes narrowed at my obvious attempt to avoid further details. He could just let it go. I wasn't prepared for this meeting any more than he was.

"You know what I mean," he accused.

I did. Of course, I did. That didn't mean he'd get the answers he sought. He didn't have the right to demand anything of me. And he knew it. That's what had gotten us into so much trouble in the first place.

Attempting to push down all my complicated feelings, I cleared my throat before peeking over his shoulder to check on a sleeping Angelica … his … daughter. The thought caused a pang that threatened to steal my breath, but I didn't let it. I'd spent six years controlling my emotions and keeping secrets. I could damn well prevent this unexpected blow from registering on my face.

Distraction felt like the appropriate way forward. I could divulge some of my life, the parts nearly anyone—besides Nicolas apparently—would know. "We moved to London after—after. Father and I. I've been studying with him and assisting ever since. This is my home."

Nicolas looked thoughtful. "I don't know why I'm so surprised." A small smile emerged and I felt my breath hitch at the sight. "You were always so good at this, taking care of people."

I flinched. It was involuntary, but he saw it. Yes, I'd long been tending the sick and ailing. A sick-bed companion, I was. My career began long before my father's practice in London saw its first patients. Before I assisted with house calls and delivering newborns. My calling started in the countryside of Wiltshire with a chronically ill boy who needed so much more than I was ever able to give him.

Swallowing tightly, I said, "Yes, well. I had a good teacher. Father has been very supportive. I'm lucky in that."

Nicolas nodded slowly. I remembered now that his own father was gone, and the urge to comfort him was nearly overwhelming. Before I considered bringing up the late Viscount Robert Morgan, his son spoke again. "Thank you for looking after Angelica. What can we do to stop the episodes from happening?"

I took his question as the momentary truce or subject change it was intended. Relieved to focus my attention on something manageable, I instructed Nicolas to monitor every aspect of Angelica's life. What to make note of and how often. "And if at all possible, I'll need to visit your home and see where Angelica spends her time. I'll need to determine if there are any toxic substances or everyday items that are in actuality quite harmful to children."

Looking mildly uncomfortable, Nicolas nodded his agreement before blurting unexpectedly, "Are you happy?"

My eyes widened in surprise. "What?"

He ran his hand along his jaw in an exasperated movement. "I asked if you were happy, Eliza. With your life. With how … everything turned out. Is it how you wanted it to be?" It was a dare, a horrible gauntlet thrown down.

That brief respite from our past and our mistakes hadn't lasted very long. My throat tightened with emotion. He didn't get to ask me these questions. He was the one who left.

Before I had the chance to object to his hypocrisy and continued demands, he spoke again. "Because looking at you here and now, you don't look happy. You don't look like the Eliza I know."

I huffed a humorless laugh. He was so very accurate, but he didn't have the right to be. "People make mistakes, Nicolas," I said as if he had made the incorrect assessment regarding my general happiness. But in this situation, *people* was me. And I'd made a lot of mistakes. Many while standing across from this man. "You don't know me anymore," I said defiantly.

His green eyes sparked with irritation. "Don't tell me that. I know you better than anyone. You can't have the childhood and history we have together without having a bone-deep knowledge and connection with someone. It's ingrained. You were a fixture in my life. Someone I knew as well as my own family. We grew up together, Eliza. I know you."

Shaking my head, denial heavy on my tongue, I said, "I'm a stranger with the face of a ghost."

His gaze bore into mine. It was sheer stubbornness that kept my gaze locked on his. The desire to look away—to hide—was nearly overwhelming.

Nicolas rose from his chair then, fists clenched at his side as anger stilted his movements.

It seemed we were at the end of our brief reunion as he carefully gathered a sleeping Angelica in his arms before striding back before me. In a low voice edged with tension, he finally said, "That's fitting. Since you are the woman who haunts my dreams."

Two

"Eliza, are you listening to me?"

With a concentrated effort, I focused my attention back on my father, seated behind his large mahogany desk. "Yes, of course."

I was currently in the study receiving the stern talking-to I'd anticipated. The late morning sun shone through the window and painted a square of light on the bookcase behind Father's head. The spines were highlighted and distracting. However, I needed to focus.

Following a frustrated sigh, he finally said, "You're going to continue putting yourself in danger, aren't you? Jeopardizing your career. All of it."

I could read the disappointment in the weary lines of his familiar face. While I may have considered this line of questioning an utter waste of time, the thought of my father's frustration and disapproval made me vaguely ill. I had no desire to let down the one person who'd supported me no matter what. I'd always loved and respected my father. Following the loss of my mother at a young age, that love and respect had grown to encompass all that we'd both been cruelly denied by her death.

The sudden pressure behind my eyes kept my gaze downcast on the patterned muslin of my lap. "I'm sorry for keeping it from you, but I believe the work I'm doing is important. I would very much like to continue with your blessing. But in the spirit of belated honesty, I do intend to continue with or without your support."

Another sigh was emphasized by a shake of his head. "You do realize the risk of being a woman alone in the clinic, at night, do you not?"

Finding it easier to meet his challenge in this, I finally raised my head. "Yes, Father. I know the risk of being a woman … alone anywhere. Day or night."

With a clenched jaw and a tight nod to acknowledge the truth in my statement, my father relented. "What about three nights per week? Would that suffice? Stay open after-hours, see servants in need of medical treatment, if that is your stubborn will. But do not run yourself ragged every night of the week."

Recognizing the concession in his tone, I thought it best to compromise. My father had been fairly apoplectic yesterday upon finding me suturing the hand of a groom from Randolph House. Never mind that the poor young man hadn't meant me any harm. The simple fact of his presence unaccompanied and unchaperoned at nearly eleven o'clock in the evening made him a threat to not only my person but our reputation and business. I understood that. I really did.

However, the work I was doing for those in service was important to me. Not everyone could afford medical care, preventative or emergent. And those servants for the peerage could not seek that care during working hours. Often the type of care they *could* afford was with improperly trained physicians in very poor and neglected conditions. Staff who sought those types of establishments ran the risk of infection from very minor injuries. I wanted to help people— people who really needed it. And I would keep pursuing my goal. But if compromising with my father helped me reach my aim without his constant disapproval or outright refusal, then that was a negotiation I could allow.

"That is acceptable. I will consent to your terms."

My father rolled his eyes at my formality and leaned back in his chair, resting his hands atop his stomach. "I'm not finished. We will also seek an assistant to remain with you after-hours. That way you are not alone and will have help in case danger arises."

"I'm amenable to that as well. Thank you, Father." I nodded solemnly and clasped my gloved hands together in my lap.

His answering snort made me crack the tiniest smile. "Perhaps Dr. Miles would be interested in your charitable efforts."

And that smile abruptly died a horrific death. "I doubt that."

Now my father was the one smiling. "Nevertheless, we'll find someone to assist you. Until that time, you're not to be alone in the clinic beyond ten o'clock."

I grimaced but nodded. "Yes, Doctor."

Another eye roll for my cheek. "Now, away with you."

I took my leave of Father's study and made my way up the stairs to my rooms, startling slightly at the presence of my lady's maid within. Her ever-present scowl was suspiciously absent, I noted. But not wishing to engage in any antagonistic back-and-forth, I ignored Meg's presence and retrieved the medical text from my bedside table. Planning to spend my afternoon in the front receiving room for Saturday calling hours, I strode toward the doorway.

Meg's voice stopped me in my tracks. "How did your discussion go with Dr. Finley, my lady?"

Turning slowly, I scrutinized her interested expression. Meg was my reluctant employee. I had no idea why she was so hostile and unfriendly toward me. She completed every assigned task with disdain, attended to my hair rather aggressively, and gave off a generally odious air. I avoided her as much as humanly possible, but I would likely never fire her from her position. She probably knew this and took it as weakness on my part and resented me even more. I knew how valuable service positions were in London. Meg had no family and nowhere else to go. Being a lady's maid landed her fairly high on the household hierarchy. Demoting her would only lead to further bitterness, and turning her out was out of the question. I didn't want her to starve on the streets no matter how chronically hateful she was. And when I considered alternative employment opportunities for young women in desperate situations … Well, I wouldn't be able to live with myself if Meg was subjected to that sort of lifestyle.

So, we typically found ourselves at a belligerent impasse.

Her bright expression and interest in the meeting with my father gave me pause. The entire staff likely knew of my discovery and subsequent scolding. But Meg's attention made me suspicious.

With slowly dawning apprehension I accused, "It was you."

"What was me?" accompanied her honey-sweet smile.

My eyes narrowed knowingly. "You told Father about the groom I was suturing. You're the reason I was caught."

"Well, technically, I merely noticed a trail of blood along the stone pavers in the garden. I was concerned and brought the mess to Botstein's attention. He was rather horrified to discover you alone in the treatment rooms with a young man. If he felt it necessary to inform Dr. Finley of your deception, how was I to know? I'm not a mind reader, my lady." She'd completely abandoned whatever mundane task that required her presence in my quarters at this particular time. Meg was right where she'd planned to be.

"Why are you so horrible to me? I have done nothing to you to warrant such disloyalty and blatant hatred."

Realistically, I realized that my late-night tending to the wounded and caring for the sick would not go unnoticed for long. But to have Meg purposefully exact such deception made me … want to … throw her in a muddy lake. *Ugh*. She was the worst.

Meg's features went from amusement to something else entirely—something venomous. "You aren't the only one who wants something more. You take for granted the freedoms you have, and you're going to throw it all away by getting yourself killed late one night in that clinic," she finished passionately.

I stared at my maid in shock. Her blond hair was hidden beneath her cap. Her face was young and unlined. She couldn't be more than eight and twenty. But her bright blue eyes—they were world-weary and resigned. Full of fire, yes. But utterly aged and wizened. She'd always been quick to snap at me, equally short in her responses. I rarely received honorifics in her address—unless my father was nearby. However, she had never spoken to me with such unconcealed contempt and total honesty.

My astonishment quickly gave way to ire. "If you want to blame me for our unfair positions in life, fine. Feel free to carry that self-righteous anger with you to the grave. Although why I am your target alone, I will never understand. I may be blessed by my circumstances, but that doesn't mean I'm diminishing you in yours. I've never mistreated you or belittled you or made you feel anything less. If you wanted more, as you say, how the bloody hell am I supposed to know it." I parroted back her earlier statement, "I'm not a mind-reader, Meg!"

Her face flushed bright with anger as she stormed out.

Oh well. We wouldn't be braiding each other's hair any time soon.

LATER THAT EVENING, I found myself organizing supplies and folding towels in one of the large storage closets in the rear of the clinic. Our work area and medical office were attached to the main house, but the entrance for patrons was through the back garden. Typically, patients with appointments would remain seated in the open foyer until we were ready for them in the treatment rooms. It was all part of the same large space, but the beds for treatment and examination were cordoned off behind curtains and screens.

As I stored the remaining gauze in the bottom of the cabinet, a soft knock came from the garden door. It was before my appointed curfew of ten o'clock but just barely. I'd risk it and claim ignorance of the hour later.

Smoothing my hands down my work apron, I straightened and made my way to the clinic entrance. I certainly wasn't expecting Nicolas to be leaning against the archway.

I'd tried my best not to think about him since he'd left with his daughter the previous night. He'd been so angry with me. And I'd been equally off-balance by his presence. I didn't think I'd see him again, assuming his resentment was such that he'd keep his distance. I wanted to help Angelica but that would be difficult to do with her father angry and uncooperative. Nicolas had been out of my life for so long. I supposed I'd resigned myself to frequent theater visits with no one the wiser. Although, that would likely become a habit I'd need to break. It was too addicting, having safety in anonymity as an audience member, but still feeling the magic of his presence.

And now, there he stood, barely illuminated by the light from the interior. He'd shaved since I'd seen him last. His clothes were fresh and neatly pressed. This was no middle-of-the-night-emergency. This was premeditated. And I didn't know how to feel about that … beyond panicked.

"Can I come in?" His eyes searched my face, letting himself look in a way I couldn't fathom. If I acted on instinct and stared at his beautiful face the way I wanted, I'd never look away. I'd probably do something horrifying, like touch him.

I nodded quickly and opened the door wide. He straightened from his relaxed position and waltzed into the treatment room. Nicolas appraised the space. It was feasible that yesterday he hadn't noticed any details due to worry and concern for his child. That happened with visitors sometimes.

"How's Angelica?" I inquired with genuine concern.

He smiled warmly, one dimple deepening his left cheek. My stomach gave an odd swoop that I refused to dwell on. "She was well when I left her. Staying with a friend in the playhouse apartments."

"I'm relieved to hear it." I led him over to my desk and offered him the same chair he'd occupied less than twenty-four hours ago.

After settling myself, I looked at him expectantly, feeling my heart race at this unanticipated time we'd been granted with one another. Had his eyelashes always been so ridiculously long?

Clearing his throat, Nicolas finally said, "Eliza, I wanted to apologize for my behavior yesterday. I was so startled by your presence. It was so unexpected … I reacted poorly, and I'm sorry. I shouldn't have lashed out at you the way I did. I've since had time to gather my thoughts and I want you to know how very glad I am to see you and to know that you are well."

"Thank you, Nicolas. I'm happy you are well, too." However, I wouldn't go so far as to say I was glad to see him. I was too nervous for that. My hands were sweating and my heart was still galloping in my chest. There were likely medical ramifications of a runaway heart, but I couldn't think of them right this minute.

His smile was so warm and familiar then that I felt a warning prickle behind my eyes. "You look familiar and different all at the same. I can hardly believe it."

I acknowledged the truth of his words with a small smile of my own. How I could simultaneously wish to bask in his presence and hide under this desk, I would never know. But that was the strange dichotomy of regret. You fought the urge to see how your actions played out while also holding on to the slight hope that everything would be all right. It was foolish. *I* was foolish.

"Did you have a performance this evening?" I asked in an effort to keep our conversation forward facing. I didn't want the past sneaking into the room with us.

My question spoke to my awareness of his fame and profession. His knowing look said he'd caught it. He didn't comment on it, however. "Yes. Well, a matinee. I would have come earlier but from what I was told, it would be more appropriate for me to visit when you see patients at night. I didn't want to cause you any trouble." His grin was boyish, both dimples on full display, as if to say *Even if I did cause you trouble, it would be easily forgiven.*

And there came our history, slipping under the crack in the door. I'd forgiven him a lot over the years simply for wearing that smile.

"No, it would have been fine," I assured him easily, unwilling to bicker over something so minor and fall into old habits.

He finally looked away from me to take in my cluttered desk. Stacks of notes and parchment waited for filing and further transcribing.

Bringing his warm gaze back to me, he offered, "I thought I might propose an idea. And you can tell me if you have neither the time nor the inclination." Another grin, this one proclaiming *As if you'd be able to deny me anything.*

But I had denied him something at one time, and we both knew it.

The past was filling the room now, like smoke. Could he not feel it—suffocating and oppressive?

"There are several actors and performers and theater employees that could use the expertise of a good physician. What you are doing here … providing care for servants and staff is so commendable, Eliza. I'm in awe of it. If you were willing to take on more, there are many at the playhouse who would be in your debt." I'm sure the surprise registered on my face. "They could pay you, of course. It's just that with the frequency of our shows and the intensity of the rehearsal schedule, it's hard to make the time to see a doctor when needed."

"Of course, I understand. That's why I'm here so late in the evening. My patients require different accommodations. I would be interested in providing assistance to your acquaintances." And in saying that, I found that I genuinely meant it. There was a whole new group of people I could reach with my efforts. This was an amazing opportunity to help those in need. In addition, going to the theater residence could help determine Angelica's environmental triggers.

"… more like family."

"I'm sorry?" I'd missed whatever Nicolas had said as I spun the possibilities for the future in my head.

"Oh, I said, we're more like a family at the theater than simply well acquainted."

That gave me an odd ache when it should have comforted me. Nicolas had found a new family after I'd driven him from his old one.

"Yes, of course," I muttered, feeling off balance with him once more. Or still. I wasn't sure any longer.

I couldn't seem to put the past behind us for a single conversation while he seemed unbothered by the history between us. His smiles came easy and were genuine. Nicolas was charming and charismatic, as always.

Meanwhile, I feared I would always be a nervous disaster in his presence. Too many years of feeling shy and invisible while Nicolas dominated every conversation, stood out among the rest, and shone in every room.

I seemed incapable of reconciling the past and the present. Would I forever be consumed by the fears of my seventeen-year-old self? How did you look at someone you'd loved without seeing everything that tied you to them in the first place? With Nicolas, it was all a reminder and I'd pay any price to forget.

"Eliza, what's wrong?" I looked up at the concern in his tone.

To my utter horror, my eyes filled. "How do you bear it?" I whispered brokenly.

Nicolas leaned forward and clutched my hand resting on the desk. "What do you mean?"

"Looking at me. How can you stand it? After everything." I took a steadying breath through my nose and willed the tears to recede.

"Oh, Eliza. We were so young. I was an idiot half the time, and I made mistakes, terrible ones. And while I ran from my past … I didn't run forever. I let the memories come eventually. There are some good ones in there as well. It seems as if you've spent the last six years running from yours."

All I could do was stare. If I opened my mouth to speak, he'd know the truth of it —of how very right he was. I'd embraced my pain, relished it. It was the least I deserved. Eliza Morgan, the sad, forgotten widow. I directed my efforts to helping others so that I would never repeat the damage I'd done in my previous life. If I lived without risks now, then so be it. At least I couldn't hurt anyone else.

Nicolas was looking at me knowingly and with a heavy dose of pity that made me bristle inwardly and jerk my hand away. I didn't want his comfort, the warm pressure from his rough hand. I didn't deserve it.

I understood his reaction last night. The anger and the resentment—I'd expected that. But this version of Nicolas exuded only patient understanding and sincerity. What did he understand that I didn't? How did normal people let go when all I did was cling with grasping claws?

"Can we—" Nicolas was cut off by Meg entering the clinic. We watched her escort a middle-aged woman who was in obvious pain, clutching a rag to her hand. I recognized her as the cook from Cassandra's father's, the Earl of Crait, household.

"She came to the kitchen entrance by mistake, my lady. I told her I'd bring her to you. She has a nasty burn," Meg explained.

Nicolas and I stood at the same time. I attempted a smile at the newcomer in need of my attention, but I could feel it fail to materialize on my face. "Meg, take her to the first bed and grab the liniment and the linseed oil. I'll be right there."

"Yes, my lady." My lady's maid's face lit with surprise at the attention, but she moved with purpose and did as I bid her. Imagine that.

When I turned back to Nicolas, he was watching me. "I'll let you get to work. But think about my request for the theater workers. And I promised you could tour Angelica's room. You know where to reach me?"

I nodded, knowing I could send word to him at the playhouse or the adjoining living quarters for the performers. "I'll be in touch. I'm … glad you came by. Goodnight, Nicolas."

"Goodnight, Eliza." His gaze lingered and I felt it touch every part of me. Then he was gone.

Doing my best to compartmentalize and banish the evening's encounter with Nicolas, I took a deep breath and went to see about my patient. After washing my shaking hands, I joined Meg where she'd gathered the supplies I'd requested.

"Thank you, Meg. You can return to the main house," I said, dismissing her. After a moment, I realized her shadow had yet to move across the floor. Meeting her frustrated gaze, I said, "Did you need something else?"

"I would like to remain," came her grudging request.

My confusion was evident, and my patience had worn thin. I felt raw and exposed. Why in the hell was Meg standing there looking at me like that? "Why would you stay?" I was genuinely not comprehending.

It looked like she was chewing gravel, but she finally managed, "I would like to stay and assist you with the patient."

Well.

Meg wore her usual expression: resentful with a full helping of aggrieved scorn. But there was something else, too. It was definitely costing her to ask this of me. To give me this power over her by knowing something she wanted. But it was the same stubborn determination that I recognized every day in the mirror that had me nodding and saying, "Well, get over here and bring fresh gauze with you."

Twenty minutes later, we'd cleaned and dressed the burn on Mrs. Chapman's hand. I'd quietly explained everything I'd done and Meg had listened with frightful intensity. She'd even comforted the older woman as I'd cleaned the wound. Who knew my lady's maid could muster up some bedside manner?

As I shut and locked the door behind Mrs. Chapman and turned down the lamps on my way to where Meg was putting on fresh bedding, I considered something that was, frankly, mad. But I was going to do it anyway.

"You were good with her." My voice carried through the quiet of the space, and Meg paused in her ministrations. "I don't know that I actually need a lady's maid, and you're rubbish at it anyway." Meg still had yet to make eye contact.

Maybe we didn't have to stay in our roles. Perhaps there was a way to move forward and break free from the past. I could take a step to alter this relationship in my life. It might even turn out for the better.

Although, it would likely be an incredible failure. But at least I'd tried.

It was time for a little growth on my part.

So I took a deep breath and waited until I had Meg's attention. "But I could use an assistant."

Three

The sound of the raucous laughter of six women met my ears as I ascended the final stair and made my way down the corridor. A fond smile bloomed across my face. Tuesday afternoons were superior to all other afternoons.

After a quick conversation with my father about Meg's training and tending to a few non-critical patients, I'd packed up my embroidery and made my way to the Duchess of Compton's Mayfair residence. The late winter day was surprisingly dry and not terribly cold so I'd decided to walk the short distance to Fiona's home.

"And then he tripped off the bottom step of the carriage and landed in an enormous mud puddle. It was undoubtedly the largest body of muddy water I'd ever encountered …" Cassandra's loud voice carried down the hallway as the laughter intensified.

I popped my head through the open door. "Describing your latest victim, Cassandra dear?"

A chorus of "Eliza!" rang out and I smiled happily at my friends as I continued into the room.

It had taken some time and consistent efforts of their part but after almost three years of weekly gatherings, I could no longer deny my affection for every woman in this room. They hadn't all been here from the beginning as Jane,

Fiona, and I had, but every new addition to our circle brought more joy, more experience, and further convinced me that genuine female friendships were as necessary as breathing.

"Come sit by me, Eliza. I want to see the apron ye have been working on," Ashleigh requested. I took the open seat to her right and relaxed on the settee. Ashleigh was a recent yet entertaining addition to our Tuesday embroidery salon. Visiting from Scotland, she had been enjoying her time in London for the past two seasons. She was charming and funny and painfully honest in her assessments. I loved her dearly.

I pulled the cream linen from my bag and spread my current work in progress across my lap for viewing.

"Ohhhh, ye've done a fine job there," Ashleigh praised.

"Lovely," agreed our hostess. Fiona was arranged in a nearby armchair, perched delicately on her seat to take in my apron. Earning her approval in anything gave me a warm feeling in my chest. The perfect duchess, Fiona was the ideal for maternal support, well-bred decorum, and kindness. It was her early attention several years ago that eased my way into society, and also provided me the resolve to pursue my goal of following in my father's footsteps.

Following our arrival in London and the end of my mourning period, Father had bid me participate in a portion of the season before settling into the life of a physician. I think he'd hoped I'd find a husband and take the more conventional path for a woman of twenty years. Nevertheless, I'd done as he asked and attended balls and soirees, musicales, and ladies' luncheons. With no sponsor nor any siblings, I'd mostly hidden with my fellow wallflowers, and that was how I'd met Jane—another of our embroidery circle. She'd been unable to establish sincere friendships due to the gossip swirling about her family name. I hadn't known the current gossip nor had I cared. So we'd passed our time together. Fiona had overheard one of our conversations—probably Jane calculating the number of people stuffed to bursting in the ballroom—and introduced herself. The duchess had told me later that she'd known during that first encounter that we'd be very good friends. Despite my shy and quiet nature and the sorrow still hanging about me, Fiona's efforts had succeeded. The three of us—Fiona, Jane, and I—had become fast friends. And then we'd been introduced to the others and our ranks had grown over time.

Our conversations on Tuesdays were rarely ladylike but always humorous. We discussed all manner of topics, but there was reliably at least one Cassandra disaster story.

"I'll have you know, Eliza, I was describing my outing with Lord Cargrove who was victimized by his own big feet. I was waiting patiently on the path while his gargantuan-sized Hessian snagged on the carriage." I smiled indulgently at my friend. Cassandra had exceedingly poor luck with gentlemen. She'd had numerous proposals and was fairly beloved among the *ton*. But now, in her fourth season, the sheer number of injuries and catastrophes that befell her callers was bordering on the ridiculous. Alas. Perhaps this was her year.

Cassandra was still defending her honor. "… and who took the brunt of his fall? Me. That's who. I was covered in mud and god knows what else from my bonnet to my boots. I was speckled like a … a …"

"Moooo," came Ashleigh's helpful rejoinder.

"A cow!" Cassandra finished triumphantly with a slap to her thigh. "Thank you, Ashleigh."

A snorted laugh came from the corner of the room and I noticed Kathleen quickly duck her head. Our shyest and newest member, Kat had clearly unintentionally let her amusement slip for she'd rather do just about anything than draw attention to herself.

I glanced back to Cassandra to see that she'd noticed as well. She gave me a little wink, clearly pleased her outrageous behavior had garnered Kat's delight.

"Eliza, would you like some tea?" Jane asked.

I smiled brightly at my closest friend. "Thank you, Jane."

"Here, have some lemon," she offered.

I'd missed my friend. Jane had married nearly two months ago. It had been an interesting event that had not gone as planned, but Jane and Quinton, the Earl Sullivan and future Duke of Benton, had ended up married as intended and they were both exceedingly happy. For that I was grateful.

I tried very hard not to be resentful. Prior to her marriage, Jane had lived with me temporarily. She'd left her father's home over a disagreement and sought refuge. I'd enjoyed sharing a roof with Jane, and I missed her as our busy lives were leading us in different directions. However, I didn't begrudge her newlywed happiness. She deserved every good thing. And as it turned out, Sullivan was one of those good things.

"Nicely done, Eliza. Are you planning to continue the pattern or make it a mirror image down the left side?" Mary's voice piped up to be heard over the general chatter of the drawing room. She was a very accomplished seamstress, and I felt irrationally proud that she approved of my floral design. Actually, Mary was adept at nearly everything. She was a wonderful companion in every setting, and her beatific features only added to her overall appeal among the aristocracy.

Mary's question brought the discussion back toward our embroidery projects. Jane didn't join in as she fairly despised sewing, but happily nibbled her biscuits instead.

Sometime later, after everyone had showed off their current progress, Ashleigh cleared her throat delicately before looking my way.

I was intuitive enough to know I wasn't going to like whatever made her eyes sparkle thusly.

"So, Eliza. A little bird told me that ye have been spending quite a bit of time at the Collins." The Collins was an abbreviated and common name for the Joc Collins Theater—the playhouse where Nicolas performed several shows a week as Silas Viso.

Unsure as to how Ashleigh had received that bit of intelligence, I endeavored to maintain my neutral expression.

The ladies quieted, likely scenting fresh gossip, and all eyes were now on me.

I took a sip of my lemony tea to both fortify and delay. "I suppose I have taken an interest in the recent comedy featured there. Father feels I should implement a positive work-life balance and encouraged me to use his box at the Collins."

Jane frowned slightly. "I didn't know you enjoyed the theater."

Nervously fingering a loose thread on the back of my fabric, I finally confirmed, "I do. It's just been some time since I was able to visit. I'm glad Father recommended the outing."

"Outings," Ashleigh emphasized without looking up from her embroidery hoop. "Plural."

These women were relentless. A solid distraction would be necessary. "In fact, I should be glad Father is even speaking to me after discovering me with a patient after hours a few nights ago."

"He found out about your nighttime activities?" Cassandra inquired, all innocence.

"What?" Fiona's concern was palpable.

Hell, I forgot she didn't know about the work I did outside of our regular appointments.

I found I had a hard time meeting her eye, but I replied nevertheless. "Father found me suturing a groom from a nearby household. I've been keeping the clinic open late in the evening so that servants can seek medical attention as they are able."

Fiona's brown eyes were troubled. "That's commendable work, Eliza, truly. The service and attention you offer could be life changing for those you help." Several ladies nodded and murmured their agreement. I grew slightly uncomfortable at the praise. Fiona continued gently, "But you have to see how dangerous it is."

"I do," I admitted, fidgeting nervously with the strings once more. "But, to me, the reward outweighs the risk. The people who come—who rely on me—need me more than any marchioness with a delicate stomach or a countess with a headache. My presence is important to the shopkeepers who cannot close their stores to seek out a physician during business hours. I'm needed by maids and footmen and all manner of workers. I'm doing good work. I'm helping people. And if that means I face greater risk as a woman alone at a late hour, then that is just something I'll have to live with."

The concern didn't fade from my friend's gaze but she nodded solemnly once I'd delivered my impassioned speech. "I would tell you to take care, but that would be condescending and imply that you're being purposefully reckless when I know that is not your intent."

"Thank you," I said softly, meeting her small smile with my own.

The jovial air of the meeting had turned abruptly. But hadn't that been my goal? No one was asking about the theater or commenting on my frequent presence there of late. The last thing I needed was for someone to make a connection between myself and the star performer. There couldn't *be* a connection beyond my required services.

I needed to get my interest in Nicolas under control. But that had always been difficult for me. Despite our similar ages, as a child, I'd been drawn to his larger-than-life personality. He'd made every game the most entertaining. His attention was always the most prized. As an adolescent, I'd been both painfully shy and agonizingly aware of his presence. Caught somewhere between desperately wishing he'd notice me and feeling overwhelmed by his attention. Nicolas wasn't someone you could just ignore. He'd had to remove himself from my life entirely before I'd been able to put him out of my head.

I would need to be stronger this time. He had a career, a child, perhaps a wife. Nicolas had an entire life for the past six years that had absolutely nothing to do with me. Except that wasn't true. I'd been the catalyst for all of it. The driving force for this version of Nicolas.

Just seeing him perform made me long for him. He was magnetic and engaging, and half of London agreed with me. I was too practical to be charmed. And too familiar with his lure that I should have known better.

And yet.

Cassandra's next words brought me back from daydreaming about a stage on the Strand. "Our cook was singing your praises, Eliza. Mrs. Chapman had a frightful burn and Eliza patched her up late one night last week. Sent her home with care instructions, supplies, and salve to help with the pain in her hand," Cassandra explained.

The second-hand praise and murmured approval made me vaguely nauseous. It was one thing to stand my ground and emphasize the importance of my goal. It was quite another to have it shone upon me like a spotlight.

Shifting uneasily in my seat, I muttered uncomfortably, "It was nothing. I'm glad I could help."

My fiery red-haired friend eyed me knowingly. If I was lucky, she'd change the subject and relieve me in this uncomfortable situation. "So, are you ready to tell us why you've been spending so much time at the theater?"

Or she would stab me viciously in the back.

Cassandra's blue eyes sparkled.

"Oh! Have ye been attending with Dr. Miles, then?" Ashleigh's question truncated my murderous thoughts. Not an ideal change of subject, but it would do.

"Sadly, I have not. Our paths have not crossed of late."

Mary accepted a new pot of tea from the maid before voicing her question. "So what is your relationship with Dr. Miles? Are you courting?"

I sighed, somewhat resigned. "No, we're not formally courting. We're friendly. Acquaintances, really."

"That's what ye call an acquaintance, Eliza?" Ashleigh asked with wide eyes. "The man would likely marry ye tomorrow."

Scoffing, I said, "I doubt that. We've never even danced together."

"That doesn't mean anything. You never dance with anyone." Jane's statement stopped my friends as they tried to remember a time I'd danced with a gentleman. I hadn't. I didn't encourage that sort of attention nor did I court affection so openly. I wasn't looking for a husband.

"I realize that Dr. Miles is probably on the hunt for a wife. And I don't think … that's me. We have a great deal in common, of course. And he is a handsome gentleman. But I can't see us being more than acquaintances when all is said and done."

"Well," Cassandra began despite the glare I threw in her direction. "If you won't take poor Dr. Miles with you to all those performances at the Collins, you should at least invite one of us. I'd be happy to escort you." The rest of the ladies joined in their agreement and I managed a stiff smile. "And if you won't dance with the good doctor, I'd be happy to take him for a spin around the ballroom. I'm not a discriminate dancer."

Laughing despite myself, I rushed to object. "Oh, no, Cassandra. No need for violence. I'm sure some injury would inevitably befall him. I may not wish to marry the man, but I don't wish dismemberment on him either."

My friends laughed once more and I knew our merriment would carry down the staircase.

"WELL, Lady Sullivan, how is married life?"

My question elicited a lovely smile from Jane as we walked along the cobblestones. The weather had taken a decidedly chilly turn following our gathering. Thankfully, there was no rain or sleet threatening.

Jane and I had said our goodbyes to the embroidery ladies and made our way in the same direction on foot. I was pleased to have this additional time together. I'd missed my friend.

"It's odd to live with someone new and share the same space, but I quite like it. I think it helps that we found Randolph House together. I didn't feel as if he had to make room for me in his established household. We made space for each other."

Our heeled boots clacked along the path while I considered Jane's words. I could see how making a new start as a unit would be preferable to simply being absorbed by one party or the other. That would not have changed my early marriage but it was understandable for someone like Jane whose independence and self-reliance had been ingrained since childhood.

With a genuine smile for my friend, I replied, "I'm happy for you, Jane."

"Thank you, Eliza. How has your work been? Is your father terribly upset?"

I sighed. "He was angry at my deception but more resigned than anything, I think. He's well aware I'm not going to stop in my efforts, but with some compromise we should be on good terms again soon. He's bid me to find an assistant so I'm not alone in the clinic at night."

Jane nodded thoughtfully. "That seems fair. I support any decision that keeps you safe."

Laughing lightly, I countered, "You're one to talk—working at a famous gaming hell. How are things at Piker House?"

Jane launched into a detailed discussion of her latest tasks managing the accounts at her husband's establishment. Their working relationship suited them just fine, and I was once again struck at how a marriage could thrive beyond what London society dictated. Quinton and Jane had found their equal in one another, and they weren't letting scandal or titles or any other thing derail them in their happiness. The development of their odd courtship had been eye-opening last autumn. While it didn't necessarily make me hopeful for myself, it made me hopeful in general.

Seemingly out of nowhere, Jane offered, "I've reached out to Q's parents."

My eyes widened in surprise. I'd known of Quinton's estrangement from the duke and duchess following the death of Q's brother. It had been a difficult time for them all. "Does he know you did this?"

Brown eyes bright and earnest, Jane replied, "No. I'm waiting until I have something to report. We've exchanged correspondence in the last month. All very innocuous. General pleasantries and information about our new marriage."

I frowned slightly over Jane's interference in her husband's relationships. "What made you write to them?"

Our steps had slowed and Jane pulled to a stop before she answered me. "I suppose it was the wedding. Q had hardly anyone to support or celebrate with him. His sister wouldn't attend. And it seemed like a waste. While my relationship with my family is unlikely to improve, Quinton has a mother and a father. If they would just communicate and resolve their misunderstandings … I think we could have a family. He's not only keeping them away from himself, he's preventing me and our future children from having a relationship with them as well. I just don't want Q to look back on his life and have further regrets. This is something I can help with. I want to do this for him—for our family."

If there was anything I could understand, it was regret. But the thought of facing mine left me feeling quite sorry for Earl Sullivan.

"I hope it works out for all of you."

"Thank you. I hope so as well. And I'll tell Quinton soon. I just thought it better to beg forgiveness than ask for permission."

Smiling conspiratorially, I agreed. "Well, Q would forgive you anything so I think you made the right decision."

Four

Two days later, the drone of male voices entirely eclipsed the joy I'd absorbed from the Tuesday afternoon spent with my friends.

I was attending a medical talk at a London colleague's home with my father and feeling exceedingly out of place. The only woman in attendance, I was allowed this concession due to my father's good standing. The dozen or so gathered physicians permitted this indulgence in large part due to my silence. Typically, I refrained from interacting with those assembled because they were horrible bores, but there was also a rather large part of me that didn't wish to embarrass my father. He was well respected and admired. It wasn't his fault I was a woman.

Following the lengthy presentations ranging from the benefits of herbal concoctions and tinctures to the new and invasive treatments for hemorrhagic fevers, I was now merely observing conversations during the social hour. Those assembled in Dr. Paulson's expansive library circulated with drinks and inquired after one another's practices and families. Several took the opportunity to collaborate on patient care. However, I, reverting to my wallflower ways, sipped brandy—no weak lemonade at these events—near a potted plant. Stifling a yawn, I was finding it difficult to remain engaged in my surroundings. Perhaps it was the dreary weather or the muted browns of the stuffy library or just the warmth emanating from the fireplace nearby, but I was feeling weary to my bones.

Quite unexpectedly, I found myself in the company of Dr. Kenneth Miles.

Startling slightly at his appearance, Dr. Miles cleared his throat good-naturedly. "My lady, good evening. I hope you are well."

Eyes burning from too large a swallow, I finally managed, "Yes. Hello. Good evening, Dr. Miles."

His brown coat and tan waistcoat had him nearly blending into the scenery. Perhaps that was how he'd successfully sneaked up on me.

"Did you enjoy the presentation?" he asked without meeting my gaze.

"I did," I replied brightly. "I hope you did as well."

Silence descended. And not the comfortable kind. We were simply standing next to one another, not even making eye contact. Just surveying the space as others talked and milled about.

I thought about my friends questioning my intentions with Dr. Miles, and considered him—as I did occasionally. He was very intelligent. Should I be interested in pursuing a relationship with him, we would have our work in common. He didn't seem to begrudge me my chosen profession. We occasionally discussed medical course of action. I wouldn't say we collaborated, per se, but he appeared to genuinely consider my opinions and work ethic.

Dr. Miles was handsome. With fair hair and blue eyes, his fine physique was quite admirable. But moments like this, endured with little connection to speak of, made whatever fanciful thoughts I considered for a future with this man seem utterly ridiculous. He was frightfully boring. And he made me boring. We were boring together.

For some reason, I didn't feel comfortable being myself when I was around Dr. Miles. And, fine, I knew I would never be the belle of any ball. But I could be quick-witted and a decent conversationalist. There was just something about being in Dr. Miles's presence that leeched all interesting thought from my head.

I was unsure how to dispel this nervous energy. Perhaps I was putting too much pressure on myself. We could continue our acquaintance. I didn't need to enter into any sort of romantic relationship with Dr. Miles. I honestly couldn't see myself ever marrying again. And if that was his aim, I needed to sever whatever strange, boring thread connected us.

Cassandra often wondered why I never took any lovers. If I thought that might be an option moving forward with Dr. Miles, I might consider it.

Perhaps.

I didn't know.

Thoughts of Nicolas chose that moment to intrude. He made me uncomfortable in an entirely different way.

Another throat clearing brought my attention back to the person at my side. "Your father told me of your efforts to provide treatment to the lower classes." My eyes widened. That felt decidedly like disloyalty from my father. I could only hope he didn't follow through with his threat to invite Dr. Miles to join in my endeavor. "Forgive me for saying so, but I fear your caring nature and generous spirit are likely to get you into trouble."

Gritting my teeth at his subtle rebuke, I inwardly cursed my father for spreading our business around. I didn't care if he supported a union between Dr. Miles and myself. This man had no business scolding me. I was a grown woman and in no way under his purview. My actions neither reflected upon nor concerned him.

And yet self-preservation was evidentially not a strength of Dr. Miles because he ignored my hard features and continued speaking. "I wouldn't want you to tarnish the reputation your father has worked so hard to build." My facial expression must have finally belied my mounting ire because he stumbled over his next words. "And—and of course I would never want any danger to come to you all alone in such a risky situation."

No longer scanning the room, I met his wary gaze head-on. "Well, lucky for you, you needn't worry. Dr. Finley and I have discussed matters and reached a suitable solution. I think I should be going. Good evening, Dr. Miles."

I hadn't made it a step before he hissed, "Eliza." My warning glance had him scanning the room before he continued very softly, "I wasn't trying to offend you. I merely wanted to express my concern for the path you seem determined to follow. You and I have a … pleasing association. You have to know I'd like it to develop into something more. So if you will not think about your future and reputation for yourself, consider it … for us."

Maybe he wasn't as boring as I'd thought. He sure had some nerve. "You don't want me to embarrass you should we start courting. Worried about our association? Is that it, Dr. Miles?"

Finally realizing his misstep and that he should tread more carefully, his eyes narrowed. "I'm just trying to look out for you, Eliza. And I think you can use my given name. Why do you insist upon calling me Dr. Miles?"

He was assigning familiarity where there was very little. Yes, we shared common interests and would occasionally converse at these types of events. Most of our interactions had been professional in nature. Of course I called him Dr. Miles.

With a sigh and a forced smile, I sought to take my leave. "Dr. Miles, I do not think I'm ready to have this conversation. I don't know if I will ever be. I'm sorry. Good night."

Thankfully my father had just finished his drink and we were able to make a quick exit. But thoughts of what I actually wanted for my future stayed with me for a long time.

THE FOLLOWING day arrived and I still hadn't decided what to do about Dr. Miles, but I had fortified my position on continuing my outreach to those at the theater. I knew the risks associated with my efforts. However, the good I could potentially accomplish far outweighed the disapproval and warnings I'd faced repeatedly in my pursuit.

So, I decided to take in a Friday night performance at the Collins and leave word with Nicolas about arranging a time to see patients and investigate Angelica's rooms for potentially hazardous materials.

Did I need to attend a performance in order to contact Nicolas? Not exactly. Did I want to see him? That was harder to decipher. Some part of me would always be drawn to him, I feared.

I'd contacted Cassandra and agreed to her offer to escort me to the theater. This honestly didn't feel like something I could do on my own any longer. Nicolas made me feel … too much. It was overwhelming and our history was vast and unwieldy. I needed someone to ground me as the person I was here and now at three and twenty. And Cassandra was that person. We'd been friends for the last two years. She knew only the competent, if a little sad, Eliza—a medical professional with determination and lofty goals. On the other hand, Nicolas succeeded in always making me feel nine and enamored, eleven and besotted, sixteen and obsessed, or seventeen and devastated. There was too much between us. I needed Cassandra and her presence to act as a buffer … or a sacrificial lamb, I hadn't decided yet. Either way, she was quite enthusiastic for whatever the night would bring. Additionally, Cassandra was an entertaining companion and selfishly, it was easy to disappear in the shadow of the brilliant light she cast.

Since my helpful friend was to be my escort for the evening, she'd demanded that I pick her up in my father's carriage. I'd rolled my eyes at this but agreed nonetheless. Her father, the Earl of Crait, had an estate some distance away, so we would need to endure a rather lengthy carriage ride to carry us to the theater.

"So, I've been rather patient with you. I've honored your privacy, but I feel something is troubling you—more so than usual. And whatever it is … these theater visits are somehow tangled up in it. Now you don't have to tell me your past if you truly wish it to remain a secret, but I am here for you, as a friend. And I would like to know the situation I'll be walking into on my exceedingly uncomfortable slippers."

I smiled at Cassandra and her forthright nature. I suppose I hadn't realized my past was so mysterious. Jane and Fiona both knew the general events. I assumed, at some point, they would have relayed the information to the remainder of our circle.

"I didn't realize you remained in the dark regarding my past, Cassandra. It wasn't my intent to deceive you."

"Hush, I know that. But I suppose I wanted to hear your story from you." Her candor was appreciated. "And now I feel as if I've waited long enough. So out with it."

I laughed. The fact that I *could* laugh—with the truth so close and the words waiting on my tongue—proved how very far I'd come.

"I grew up in Wiltshire. I don't know if you knew that. We rarely came to London throughout my childhood, so I'd only ever really known the country and our life there. My father was the second son of a baron and became the doctor for the surrounding villages. My mother died when I was but a girl—I hardly remember her now. But her very best friend, Rosemary Morgan lived at the neighboring estate. She and her husband, Viscount Fritterton, had five children. And I was absorbed into their fold. I spent most of my time at their estate and the surrounding lands. We rode horses and had adventures. The two daughters, Roberta and Francesca, were older than I was and eventually left for London and had families of their own. I spent most of my time with Lady Fritterton's sons— Thomas, Miller, and Nicolas. I suspect I was seen as a little sister for the most part. Thomas, was three years my senior and the heir. He had always been sickly as a child, his whole life really. And I'd always wanted to be like my father. So when Thomas had bouts of weakness and couldn't leave his rooms, I would sit with him. As we grew older, I would read to him and play card games with him. Rosemary, she loved Thomas so much. She wanted nothing more than for him to have a normal life. To find a wife and have a family. I think … she mistook our friendship—for that's all it ever was—for something more. She asked me to marry her son."

Cassandra reached across the bumping carriage and grasped my hand. "How old were you?"

"Seventeen. There had been talk about having a season with a sponsor so that my father could remain in Wiltshire where he was needed. But Rosemary approached me and begged me to marry Thomas. I said I would. Thomas was against it at first. But he finally agreed, for the sake of his family. His youngest brother, Nicolas … he … disagreed with the decision. He and Thomas were very close and he knew that his brother was getting weaker and having more and more bad days. He told us not to marry just to please his family. But we didn't listen. I was stubborn and determined to do what I could for Rosemary. She'd practically raised me, and Thomas, well, he was my dearest friend."

I was watching my hand squeeze Cassandra's so I noticed when she carefully removed it. After pulling two embroidered handkerchiefs from her reticule she passed one to me and used the other to carefully blot her own cheeks. I hadn't even realized I was crying.

"What happened?" came her watery voice.

"We married. And then Thomas died shortly thereafter. Father and I moved to London and I haven't seen the Morgan family again." Well, save for one.

That portion of the story was the hardest to admit. I felt incredible guilt for cutting Thomas's family out of my life. But after what I'd done, the people I'd hurt … it hadn't made a difference at all. I'd been desperate to escape, and somehow my father had known. We'd left his family home and moved to London. He'd allowed me the freedom to run, and I didn't know if I'd ever stop.

"Did you and Thomas … ever become more than friends?"

I smiled sadly. "No. We were content being friends, and honestly, his condition worsened dramatically after we were wed. We never consummated the marriage. Never really planned to. Thomas was bedridden within the month and died six weeks after we exchanged vows."

"Eliza, I am so sorry. I can't imagine going through such trauma." Sandra's eyes were red-rimmed and sympathetic.

I nodded. My story was a tragic one. And yet, she didn't even know all of it.

"Is that why you wanted to be a doctor, do you think? All your time spent with Thomas growing up."

I didn't even need to consider her question. "Yes. I'd always wanted to help my father in his work. But I was determined to help others too. It was always natural for me to be nurturing, and to be Thomas's companion. He made me who I am today. I couldn't help him, but I'll do my best to help others."

"Oh, Eliza." Cassandra's hand was back in mine. "You did help Thomas and his family. You provided endless comfort and support to someone who desperately needed it. You attempted to give him normalcy in a world that felt wildly out of his control. You both went through with the marriage even knowing it wasn't for you or Thomas but you did it out of love for his mother and father. And because of you, Thomas didn't have to be alone."

Cassandra didn't know how difficult the decision to marry Thomas had been. She was making me out to be a martyr, and I was anything but.

"And knowing you as I do, if you hadn't agreed to his mother's wishes and convinced Thomas to marry, you would have felt guilty and punished yourself for the rest of your life."

I wanted to laugh and cry all at the same time. Of course Cassandra would strike true. I'd found my way through grief. I'd stopped mourning Thomas a long time ago. The guilt I carried, the punishment I'd accepted was indeed for the choice I'd made, and how I'd ruined Nicolas instead.

∼

WE NAVIGATED our way through the crush and up to Father's box on the second level. Located on the right side of the theater, we had a perfect view of the stage. The audience was starting to settle below and find their seats as the musicians tuned their instruments. The lamps would lower shortly and the performance would begin.

The Joc Collins Theater was located on the Strand within Covent Garden, just north of the river. It was frequented by the middle classes, working professionals, and members of the aristocracy. Father enjoyed attending and bringing his colleagues and friends. The plays were unifying as entertainment for all patrons as this particular theater tended toward comedy. This specific show had been playing for nearly two months. I should know. I'd been attending far too frequently in that time.

I found myself feeling oddly calm after detailing my past for Cassandra in the carriage ride over. Perhaps I had been holding everything in for too long. The space left behind felt jagged and tender, but not unmanageable.

Anticipation flowed hot in my veins. Nicolas would be on stage soon and I'd have an excuse to swallow him with my eyes. I was expected to watch—to absorb his performance—just like every other patron in the building.

It was like having permission to stare when I'd spent a lifetime looking away.

Once again, here was that strange dichotomy of wanting something so desperately but fearing the repercussions. Perhaps it would be easier tonight after my confession in the carriage. Maybe I wouldn't need to punish myself for my selfish thoughts, to swallow my guilt as if it were my due. It seemed inconceivable, but perhaps I could simply be a woman looking at a man without the cloudy window of the past standing between us.

Cassandra situated herself in the chair to my right and leaned forward, propping her elbow on the railing and her chin in her palm. "You're still not going to tell me why we're here tonight?"

I touched my hair nervously. The elaborate style was so different from the serviceable chignon I typically donned. Suddenly the jeweled pins adorning my curls felt silly considering the serious woman wearing them.

The house lights descended and I slid Cassandra an innocent look as if to say *It's time for the performance and I can't talk right now.*

Her grin told me she wasn't fooled, only momentarily diverted.

Settling away from the railing and back into her seat, we took in the stage as the stringed instruments began their lively introduction.

Effectively distracting me, Nicolas burst onto the stage, larger than life and equally as consuming. As he delivered his opening lines that I could in all likelihood recite in my sleep, his arms swept toward the crowd exuberantly and then his gaze landed directly on me.

Five

Nicolas finished his entire opening monologue without breaking eye contact. Initially my shock and panic kept my gaze locked with his but as the moment wore on, I was drawn into his performance. Enchanted in the way I always was with Nicolas.

As children, I watched him because I was intrigued and wanted to see what would happen next. Nicolas had this unpredictable quality that transformed any outing into an adventure. That magnetism evolved as we grew older. As an adolescent, my curiosity still made me look but it was my body's reaction that had me unable to look away. Nicolas's handsome features had drawn my notice for as long as I could remember. The pounding of my heart and the swoop in my stomach kept my attention. Always on Nicolas.

Well, my chest was thundering now.

As his part in the scene ended, his stare broke and he bounded off stage. I felt a rush of air enter my lungs and didn't realize I'd been holding my breath. The relief was sweet and painful at the same time.

With the tension broken, I looked down at the audience below. No one seemed to be turning in their seats to stare at the odd woman who'd drawn the actor's notice. In reality it hadn't been terribly long that Nicolas and I had been gazing at each other. And perhaps they assumed that was part of the show—the performer's attention focused and unwavering as he delivered his opening lines. I could have understood that reasoning … if I hadn't seen this very same show four times before.

Nicolas had never done that. I didn't know what to think but my body was making the decision for me. Palms sweaty and panic threatening, I took a deliberately slow breath in through my nose. I wouldn't think about what had happened. I would put it out of my head as an odd occurrence and a coincidence. Nothing would come of it.

Slowly Cassandra's face entered my field of vision. Her head was craned in my direction and she was leaning toward me with eyes wide. "What was that?!" she whisper-hissed.

I had the strangest urge to laugh at her shocked expression. I guess I wouldn't be ignoring it after all. There was no way Cassandra would let this go.

After a protracted moment, while I quashed my amusement, I admitted in hushed tones, "I know him. We were acquainted in childhood." After the conversation in which I'd relayed the majority of my major life events, I knew Cassandra was thinking and considering how this new development fit. I should have brought someone less intuitive to the theater tonight. She opened her mouth to undoubtedly ask another question, but I preemptively whispered through gritted teeth, "I will tell you later."

Her eyes narrowed, scrutinizing. "At the intermission."

And suddenly I regretted giving my friend the extra time to consider her next move.

As soon as the actors left the stage for the interim, Cassandra popped up from her seat and closed the privacy curtain to our box. She clearly didn't want any interruptions. I sighed inwardly.

Settling back in her seat, my friend turned to me expectantly. "Out with it."

There was no sense in delaying. She knew nearly everything else. "Remember when I told you that Thomas's brother, Nicolas, was very opposed to our marriage?"

Cassandra frowned, likely not expecting this direction to the conversation. "Yes."

"Well, *that* is Nicolas."

Bright auburn brows lifted high on her forehead. "What? Him? Silas Viso, the actor?"

"Yes," I confirmed. "That's his stage name. His real name is Nicolas Morgan, youngest son to the late Viscount Fritterton and Thomas's brother. He's my brother-in-law and childhood friend."

"How is he here in London performing at the Collins?"

This was the hard part. I let my eyes drop to my lap. My fingers were tangled together, joints straining. "I don't know the particulars of how he came to be here specifically. But after I agreed to marry his brother, Nicolas was upset. He said if I went through with the betrothal and the wedding, he'd leave." He'd said he couldn't stand by and watch me sacrifice myself—my future and my happiness. I didn't see it that way, but his words had hurt and so had the pain I'd caused as a result of his ultimatum. "And he did. He left Wiltshire at seventeen, didn't return to university, and disappeared into London. As far as I know, Nicolas cut off all contact with his family." And *with me*, I left unspoken. It was awful enough that I'd driven Nicolas from his own family, but to feel his abandonment for myself so keenly was selfish and reprehensible. As far as I knew, Nicolas was still estranged from his mother and siblings. The ache from that and the knowledge of my involvement was still painful.

"How long ago was that, Eliza?"

"Six years," I answered, eyes still fixed on my lap.

"And you saw him here at the theater? That's why you've been coming so often?" Cassandra sought to clarify.

Perhaps I didn't know before, but I could now admit that returning to the Collins again and again had been a form of penance and a way to reassure myself that Nicolas was alive and well—more than that, he was thriving. I'd told myself to stop my foolishness, but I found it hard to stay away. Impossible, really. Just like when we were children, I'd been drawn to his light. Consumed by it.

I was embarrassed by my actions. They reflected the maturity of an adolescent girl obsessed and infatuated. "I saw his likeness in the newspaper advertisement for the theater and came to see for myself." I hadn't admitted to the difficult bit —returning so frequently. Seeing the play and Nicolas with it, more than once.

But I didn't need to confess. Cassandra knew. "I see. He clearly recognized you tonight though. Was that the first time?"

"Yes. He … hasn't found me in the audience in past performances. That was new since we'd spoken last week."

"You spoke last week?" Cassandra's words were surprised. I suppose I'd failed to mention that.

"Yes, he found me quite by accident at the clinic. Nicolas had heard about my late-night medical treatment for those in need and he brought in his child."

"HIS CHILD?!" Cassandra's shout had my head snapping up from my lap and looking around in alarm as several men and women glanced in our direction from neighboring boxes.

"Cassandra, shhhhh!"

"Sorry! You surprised me," she said in a low tone. "He has a child?"

I nodded tightly. "A daughter. She's been ill, and Nicolas needed a doctor."

"I hope she's alright."

Conscious of Nicolas and Angelica's privacy I offered, "I'm hopeful and will do my best to help her."

Cassandra nodded in understanding. "And how was it to see him again, after all this time?"

I gave her a flat look. "Not terribly pleasant. He was shocked and seemed … angry, I suppose." Who could blame him? Faced with the woman who destroyed your family. "But he returned alone the following night to apologize for his behavior and to ask me to provide treatment for the performers who are unable to obtain it on their own. And I agreed."

"You agreed to visit the theater to help his colleagues?"

I looked around the space in exasperation. I wasn't explaining this well. "Yes. I'm interested in helping those who are at a disadvantage and have increased health risks, you know this." At Cassandra's wary nod, I continued. "And I need to follow up with his daughter to make sure her condition isn't worsening."

"So you weren't just inviting me to take in a show tonight?"

I huffed a laugh at the conclusion she'd immediately drawn and my reluctance to admit, even to myself, that I'd wanted to see Nicolas. "I suppose I did utilize your companionship with ulterior motives."

"Good," she stated emphatically. "You deserve some ulterior motives."

Stunned, I took in her approving expression. "You're not angry with me?"

Her nose scrunched adorably. "What? No. This is getting very interesting."

Laughing resignedly, I couldn't help but inwardly agree.

Cassandra's face adopted a concerned expression. "Eliza, how did *you* feel seeing Nicolas after so long? Are you alright?"

I didn't know how to answer. All I'd done since being confronted with Nicolas and Angelica in my doorway, was try *not* to think about him and how seeing him made me feel. To be given freedom to examine my emotions felt dangerous. "I don't know, Cassandra. It's difficult. There is so much unresolved between us. So much history and hurt. I just don't know."

My friend's gaze became scrutinizing once more. "Was Nicolas something more to you, Eliza? More than a childhood playmate? More than the brother of your dearest friend?"

My gaze refused to meet hers head-on and I, instead, looked out toward the drawn curtain and the stage. The stage where Nicolas would return very shortly. "You have to understand. The man you see out there, he was always like that. Energetic and magnetic, even as a child. It was impossible to know him and not be drawn to him. I … fancied myself in love with him. We spent so much time together, you see. We grew up together. I was always so serious and staid, and he drew laughter from me like no other. But I was also painfully shy. Nicolas never seemed to notice me as more than a sister. Until one day, he did. He kissed me. I thought I would perish on the spot." Smiling, I thought about that day. The surprise of it. The adolescent joy. But also the feeling that we could be more. That somewhere in all of our history, perhaps Nicolas and I had a future.

I willed away those painful thoughts and continued, "But I tried to be logical and not let my imagination run away with itself. Nicolas was always flirting with every girl from the village. He'd been my first kiss but there was no chance I'd been his. I tried not to let my hopes run wild but then he'd kissed me again. And then not long after, Rosemary asked me to marry Thomas. There were no more kisses after that." Just ultimatums and arguments. Everything had changed.

Admitting my foolishness to Cassandra wasn't the difficult part. However, admitting to myself that I'd loved Nicolas was what had me wincing. I'd never told him the truth. I had been unable to find the bravery or the words, and couldn't imagine he'd have taken me seriously anyway. No one wanted to have their feelings diminished, and Nicolas hadn't done that. I'd done it to myself.

He represented a time when I was young and foolish, considering how enamored I'd been with a boy who was friendly with everyone. It wasn't his fault that I felt special for drawing his attentions. Surely everyone felt that way. I hadn't wanted to fall victim to his charms. I was logical enough to know my affections wouldn't be returned in the same way. Nicolas had grown older and of course I'd been aware of him. My body reacted to his body. He'd been painfully attractive —dark hair, twinkling green eyes, and a burgeoning masculinity that made my young heart race. That was how first love felt—achingly hopeful with constant awareness. Nicolas was in my every thought at sixteen and the wanting had consumed me.

In truth, I resented him for making me fall in love with him. I still did.

And when everything happened with Rosemary and the betrothal to Thomas, I resented Nicolas for making the decision difficult. For making me wish that my life was different, that I could be selfish and beg to marry Nicolas instead of his brother.

Lost to my reminiscing, I felt Cassandra's gloved hand squeeze mine. I turned and offered her a sad smile.

The lights lowered then and the music started, signaling the beginning of the next act and the end of our conversation.

There was nothing left to say, regardless. It was all very much in the past.

IT HAD BEEN SURPRISINGLY easy to settle in for the remainder of the performance and get lost in the story, the comedy, and the showmanship. Nicolas was his usual entertaining self, but he didn't look my way again. It was almost as if his attention at the start of the show had never happened at all. And with time and distance between the odd occurrence and now, I could easily disregard it as coincidence.

As Cassandra and I gathered our belongings and made to exit the box, a young boy—perhaps nine or ten years of age—was waiting for us beyond the curtain. With a short bow, he addressed me confidently. "Good evening, my lady. If you could accompany me backstage, Mr. Viso wishes to see you."

"Lead the way, young sir." Cassandra was positively delighted.

I was less so.

Frowning, I followed in their wake.

The child led us along the corridor to a staircase at the rear of the building. The audience flowed in the opposite direction toward the front doors of the Collins. We entered another hallway and pushed through three sets of doors marked "Private" before I heard voices. After rounding the final corner, we found ourselves on the stage. It was empty of actors and the lights were low. The heavy red curtain was closed, blocking our view from the front of the theater.

Cassandra's steps slowed as she took in the stage where not ten minutes prior, we'd seen the cast performing. She spun in a slow circle, eyes wide and mouth curved in amused wonder.

"This way." The boy drew our attention to the other side of the stage where he was patiently waiting for us. We resumed our path.

Finally turning another corner, we followed the source of the voices to find Nicolas still in the shirtsleeves and trousers from his final scene of the play. His hair looked damp with sweat and black as midnight. He was talking to another performer, Beatrice Martin. She was tall and willowy with blond curls pinned in an elaborate coiffure. They were smiling at one another. Apparently their on-stage chemistry translated to their real lives, or perhaps it was the other way around. Something bitter and entirely unprovoked made my eyes narrow before I forced it away.

At the sound of our approach, Nicolas turned and met my gaze. An easy smile graced his lips as he thanked the boy for retrieving us.

"Did you enjoy the show?" he said, eyes still on me.

"Yes, it was wonderful." I smiled at the other actress who gave me a curious look before retreating further into the theater. The boy had brought us to a backstage dressing area. Mirrors and costumes were scattered everywhere. Wigs and props were intermingled with crates and set pieces.

"Hello, I'm Cassandra Fields," my friend said brightly. I jolted, realizing belatedly that I should have introduced her already.

Nicolas's eyes slid to Cassandra and his smile widened. He took her hand in his and with an expert bow, placed a kiss just above her gloved knuckles. "Good evening, Lady Cassandra."

"This is Nicolas," I announced awkwardly.

Cassandra spared me an amused look. "Yes, thank you, Eliza."

Nicolas's smile was enormous. I felt myself frown in response, uneasy and embarrassed, as if he were mocking me.

"Thank you for inviting us backstage," Cassandra gushed rather unnecessarily. "Your performance was wonderful. The whole cast, really. Just delightful."

Nicolas seemed pleased by her praise. "Thank you. I do enjoy meeting patrons of the theater." And after a pause, "And friends of Eliza."

I felt the need to say something or these two would stand here smiling at each other all night. "Yes, well. I thought it prudent to inquire after Angelica and the colleagues you'd mentioned in need of a physician."

Nicolas's eyes moved back to me and his smile stayed firmly in place. "Yes, of course. Thank you for following up." After a short pause in which I felt too tongue-tied to respond, he said, "We typically have a few drinks following a performance. You should join us." With a quick glance at Cassandra, he said, "Both of you."

"I don't think so," I said at the same time Cassandra replied, "That sounds lovely!"

And that was how we found ourselves in the adjoining private apartments of the Collins' performers. There was a large parlor where everyone seemed to be congregating. Men and women from both the stage and behind the scenes. Nicolas introduced us to other actors, a stage manager, two set designers, and through the crush of those in attendance, children weaved in and out of the gathering. I caught sight of Angelica and another little girl chasing the young boy who'd retrieved us from our seats.

After placing glasses of sherry in our hands, Nicolas turned to us. "Please, make yourselves at home. I'm going to change out of these clothes. I'll return shortly." And with a look in my direction he amended firmly, "Don't go anywhere."

Cassandra took a sip from her glass before staring at me with brows raised. "This is an interesting development."

"I suppose," I agreed. In my imaginings, I would have simply left a note with a theater employee to reach Nicolas following the play. I did not expect to intrude upon a post-performance soiree.

"I'll say one thing. Being your escort has not been boring."

I smiled at my friend, recalling the unusually dramatic events of the evening. She was not incorrect.

"Are you the doctor?" came a voice from behind. The accent was lowborn. I turned to meet the curious gazes of a man and woman.

With a cautious smile, I introduced myself. "Hello, I'm Dr. Finley." It was easier to use my family name. I didn't know if these people knew Nicolas's origins. I wasn't eager for them to know mine.

The woman regarded me impassively. It was the man who spoke again. "Nick said you might be coming round the residence to look in on us."

"That's right," I confirmed easily. And then added unnecessarily, "We're acquainted, Nicolas and I."

The man eyed me momentarily before replying, "I'm Bryce Galway and this here is my wife Caroline."

"It's nice to meet you both. This is my friend—"

"Cassandra. I'm Cassandra Fields." She'd obviously interrupted so I wouldn't introduce her using her title or honorific. These people seemed distrustful as it was. Cassandra was wise to greet them thus. And it was quite natural for Cassandra to try to put people at ease. "We enjoyed the show ever so much. What were your roles in the production?"

Bryce and Caroline were happy to answer, warming instantly to Cassandra. They explained their involvement in set production and performance preparation. Cassandra was a charming conversationalist. She knew when to listen and when to ask pertinent questions to keep the dialogue going. I felt slightly out of my depth, but eternally grateful for my friend's presence.

Loud laughter eventually drew our attention and I could see that Nicolas had returned to the parlor, drink in hand. The small cluster of people surrounding him were clearly entertained by something he'd said.

After a time, the Galways drifted away. Cassandra and I introduced ourselves to other theater folk but they all seemed to retreat once they discovered I was the physician *Nick* had mentioned. This wasn't what I had expected at all. I'd assumed my services would be required or at least not openly eschewed. Nicolas made it sound as if these people wanted me here, and yet it was quite obvious they were distrustful of me and what my profession represented. I was used to people being confused by a woman in my role. Perhaps they lacked confidence in a female physician. It would not be the first time. Either way, I'd planned on swooping in and bestowing my knowledge and expertise. Not only were these potential patients not interested, they were not impressed in the slightest.

Feeling off-balance and resentful after the awkward conversations I'd had, I was in poor spirits once Nicolas finally returned to us.

"Good evening, ladies. Apologies for my delay." His greeting was friendly and his demeanor equally so. Now dressed in a bright white shirt and patterned waistcoat, I could tell his hair had been tidied and brushed back from his face. Nicolas brought with him the scent of fresh linen and something citrusy. My scowl deepened. Dratted Nicolas.

Cassandra glanced at me quickly before speaking. If she was waiting for me to take the lead, she would be exceedingly disappointed. I was too ensconced in my own inner turmoil to make polite conversation with Nicolas. I didn't know if I could manage that on a good day—one in which I hadn't been disregarded completely by a room full of people. "It was no trouble at all," my friend said. "We met some other lovely performers and theater employees."

Quiet descended for a moment between us. I glanced beyond to the people chatting and laughing. A fair number of them were watching me—watching us. Nicolas attracted attention no matter where he was in the room. And I could understand that. He was a charismatic person, charming and funny. He made people feel good. It was quite a thing to be his sole focus. I supposed they were all curious about the two women currently holding his attention.

I quickly looked away from our audience and found Nicolas watching me.

Floundering momentarily for something to say that wasn't *I don't know what I'm doing here* or *I've missed you so much I can hardly breathe*, I finally settled on, "I believe I saw Angelica scurrying through the crowd. Is she feeling well?"

Nicolas smiled in response. "Yes, she's been fine since you saw her last."

"Oh good. I'm relieved to hear it. I would still like to tour her rooms or where she spends the majority of her time." Feeling suddenly nervous about the intimate nature of what I was asking, I took a quick breath before continuing. "I don't want to intrude. Just whenever it might be convenient."

Nodding thoughtfully, Nicolas opened his mouth to speak but several individuals arrived, calling out greetings and slapping him good-naturedly on the back. Introductions were made and curious glances were aimed in our direction, but the trade-off for being in Nicolas's presence seemed acceptable enough for being subjected to mine.

"Quite the show tonight, lad," said the stage manager, Laurence. "I thought we lost you right at the beginning. Just staring off into space, you were."

Chuckles and laughter rang out from those circling Nicolas. His eyes met mine briefly before joining in the amusement. Cassandra was laughing overly loud beside me and digging her elbow into my side. I frowned in her direction but she paid me no mind.

"But thankfully you started spitting out your lines so we didn't have to yank you off stage," Laurence finished jovially.

Nicolas placed a hand on the man's shoulder. "Now, when have I ever missed my lines?"

Several of those gathered started speaking all at once, naming different shows and years and decidedly inebriated states. Nicolas laughed and ceded all of their points one by one, but it sounded hollow to me—as much a performance as what I'd seen on stage this evening. It was confirmed when Nicolas met my suspicious gaze and held it a beat too long. That was fine. I didn't want them to note his odd opening monologue any more than he did. I'd never wanted to be the center of attention.

Except for his.

As the friends continued talking and sharing stories—mostly involving Nicolas in various embarrassing situations—I noticed Angelica on the chase once more. Smiling in her direction, she finally took note of my presence before cutting over.

I bent down to offer a greeting and received a shy "Hello, Miss Eliza" in return before she sprinted off once again. I was happy to see her running and laughing, healthy and in high spirits.

As I straightened to my full height I caught the gaze of someone else. A woman across the parlor, surrounded by people in conversation, but her eyes were focused only on me. Her demeanor was intense and hostile. I could read her scorn even from this distance. She was dressed impeccably with gorgeous dark curls pinned stylishly atop her head and a brilliant emerald green gown. I recognized her suddenly from the stage.

Confused and feeling strangely vulnerable, I quickly dragged my attention back to the conversation happening around me. Nicolas was in the midst of a story about a pub and a three-legged dog. Discreetly letting my eyes drift back to the angry woman over his shoulder, I found her immediately, still glaring daggers at me.

Did she know I was the doctor and that was why she regarded me this way? I was certain we had not been introduced. Or was this woman someone important to Nicolas? Perhaps his ...wife?

As those nearby burst out laughing at Nicolas's conclusion, I turned to Cassandra and muttered into her ear, "I think we should be going." She didn't hear me over the amusement but turned in my direction.

Nicolas must have read my intent because he quickly announced, "I'm afraid I need a word with the good doctor here." And moved to offer his arm.

I looked to Cassandra but she waved me off. "Go, I'll be fine." And then louder for those assembled, "I'm sure someone here has more embarrassing stories to tell me about Nick."

Nicolas rolled his eyes as a loud chorus of men started talking over one another about who would go first. Cassandra laughed delightedly. I knew she would be fine. Between the two of us, she was definitely more equipped to handle strangers.

As my hand wrapped lightly around Nicolas's arm, I noticed the warmth of his body beneath his shirt. He led me from the parlor and down a corridor. "You looked ready to bolt. I thought I'd better show you Angelica's room so you wouldn't be disappointed by the outcome of your visit tonight."

I nodded absently in response, still shaken from the vehemence in that woman's expression.

Is that what he thought? That I only came to the Collins tonight to solve the mystery of his child's illness. Perhaps it was because it was indeed the lie I was telling myself.

The night had been eye-opening. I'd been surprised from the moment the lights came down. It had only grown more and more confusing and strange as time wore on. My reception was quite unexpected as well as the comradery I'd seen between Nicolas and his acquaintances—family, he'd called them. Did he truly consider them family?

Based on the kinship and the joy and the history I'd witnessed in that parlor, he did share more with those people than I ever anticipated. Before seeing his image in that newspaper months ago, when I thought of Nicolas—which I attempted to never allow myself to do—I thought of him alone or destitute on the streets of London. Or worse, dead. I'd assumed that the estrangement I'd instigated had essentially cost Nicolas his life.

But here he was in Covent Garden with a crowd eating out of his hand both on stage and off. I didn't resent him his good fortune, not really. My relief that Nicolas was alive and well … it was nothing short of miraculous. Yet it didn't take away the years of guilt and worry. I supposed that was why my feelings felt trapped as if under water and struggling to break through the surface. Or perhaps they were encased in ice, and I was unable to crack through the layers of pain and history binding me to him.

While my emotions were a disaster and my frustration a living, breathing thing, I knew I couldn't bear laughing in a parlor filled with Nicolas's life that I had absolutely no part in. Leaving that room felt like a necessity. At least in this— examining Angelica's space—I could regroup, regain my equilibrium, and reestablish my professionalism.

I was so consumed in my thoughts that I couldn't recall the path we'd taken. But Nicolas finally led me to a small room through an arched doorway. Light illuminating from the sconces in the hallway, I stepped into the space and scanned the quarters briefly.

With the strike of a match, I turned back toward Nicolas who was lighting a candle just inside the entry.

I realized quite suddenly, we were all alone.

Six

Nicolas stepped closer, following me to the center of the room. The door was still wide open but the combination of our solitude and the look on his face made me feel trapped. His stare was intent. He clearly wanted to look at me.

And look he did.

Stepping back quickly, I fought for balance and control. Gazing determinedly away, I vowed to appear calm and collected, not the emotional creature I constantly became in his presence. If I couldn't see Nicolas watching me then I could ignore it as if it wasn't happening.

Rather than drown in his attention, I took in the room. It was long and narrow, as if it had been a cupboard in another life. A small bed occupied the length of one wall. It was worn and the linens were unmade. A feather-stuffed pillow lay at one end with a wool blanket across the other for additional warmth. There was no fireplace in this room. A tattered and well-loved blue knitted blanket covered the majority of the pillow.

I reached over and fingered the soft wool threads, considering. It did not appear a new addition to Angelica's environment, but perhaps if it was a gift or newly acquired, the blue hand-knit could be the culprit for her episodes of unrest.

"It's her favorite thing in the world—that blanket. She's had it since she was a baby." Nicolas's words answered that question.

Frowning in concentration, I nodded and resumed my appraisal of the quarters. It was dark but the candle cast just enough light to see by. A small chest of drawers and a bookcase containing a few books were the only pieces of furniture to speak of. A collection of hand-carved horses resided on the lower shelf. Several were overturned or askew as if they'd recently been played with. A doll was propped against the wall. There was a coatrack in the corner, by the door, which housed an umbrella, a small brown jacket made for a child, and what looked like an adult-sized pelisse. It was patterned with minimal ornamentation around the collar. My stomach clenched with unease. I hadn't inquired after Angelica's mother. I didn't think I had the nerve nor the courage to do so just yet.

Continuing my examination of the room, I found a doorway on the far side but it was locked.

"It leads to another set of rooms," Nicolas offered helpfully.

There were no windows for noxious smells nor smoke to enter to cause Angelica's difficulty breathing. No cleaning agents or unidentifiable jars of anything I could ascertain that might cause a reaction in a curious child.

The top of the chest held three ribbons, and a handful of pins had been carefully arranged. There were no clothes or bonnets or shoes strewn about. Nothing at all to point me in the direction of the information I sought. It would be up to Nicolas and the other people in Angelica's daily life to track her condition for some sign as to the nature of her reactions.

Turning back, I found Nicolas observing me from his position by the open doorway, candleholder still in hand. "I'm afraid I don't see anything here that explains Angelica's episodes."

Nicolas nodded as if he expected that. The light from the candle flickered, casting half of his face in shadow. I could feel myself looking but remained helpless to stop. My eyes were desperate to fill in the darkness.

"I'm sorry I couldn't determine the cause by visiting, but thank you for showing me the space." My voice was shaky and nervous and I didn't know why.

"Of course. You have my gratitude for coming to check on her." Gone was the performer from the stage. Equally absent was the entertainer from the parlor. This Nicolas looked sincere and serious.

I couldn't stop thinking about how comfortable he'd been with the cast and crew of the play. They did seem like a family—constantly in each other's business and so knowledgeable about one another. It had been startling to witness. For so long, I'd imagined him suffering, adrift from his family and his home.

That flicker of resentment was reemerging. A combination of feeling left behind and left to wonder. Years of guilt and frustration, and here he was making new memories while I'd been paralyzed by mine.

Abruptly I asked, "Do you enjoy performing?"

If Nicolas was uneasy with the change of topic, it didn't show. "Yes, I do enjoy performing. I like the work I do. Being on stage is … an experience. I have plans for the future actually—"

"Was it worth it?" I cut him off, voice sharp and accusing. I didn't want to hear about his plans for the future. Too raw and bitter, I wanted to know how he could trade his fate for another. Nicolas's frown was filled with confusion. I clarified. "To live your life here in London, pursue a career, and abandon your family. Was it worth it?"

I watched the words drift in the space between us, following the progression of their path to their intended destination.

His eyes hardened. "I could ask you the same question."

Those words landed like a blow. He was right. I'd done the same thing, but the Morgan's didn't need me like they needed Nicolas. I was a reminder of their pain and the loss of two of their sons. I'd been a surrogate daughter, a duty acquired through honor and obligation to my dead mother. The Morgans could not have mourned me the way they'd grieved the absence of Nicolas.

The candlelight made his angry features that much more severe. "I know you left them. Cut ties with everything involving my family—*your* family. Thomas's townhouse sits empty in Mayfair, and yet his widow resides a half mile away."

I didn't know how Nicolas came by those details, but I was too weary to question it. We were being spiteful and lashing out, and I was so very tired. I never should have come to the theater tonight—any of the nights. As much as I wanted to regret it—at least now I knew. Nicolas was alive. He was whole and hearty and living a happy life. The damage to our past was done but the guilt I felt over the future I'd stolen, well that didn't need to consume me anymore, did it? I didn't have to punish myself on Nicolas's birthday nor on the anniversary of my marriage—the day that had ruined everything and caused the unrest between us all.

I let my hands cover my face as I murmured, "I don't want to do this with you. I should have said: Thank you for your time tonight. You are a talented actor and a joy to watch. The audience is always entranced, at every performance, morning and night, evening and matinee. You are captivating up there. And I am so happy you are well. So relieved you are alive and happy after all this time." I choked on a sob as I uttered the last. And then he was there, pulling my hands from my face and gathering me to him. I'd gone from slumped and achingly alone to surrounded by Nicolas and his warmth.

"Eliza," he crooned. "Come here."

I cried into his chest, fingers clawing and clutching him to me … in relief and hurt and penance. "I didn't know what had happened to you, Nicolas. You were gone. I didn't know." My voice was weak and broken.

"God, Eliza. I was here. I'm sorry. I was here all along. If I had known—" He cut himself off and held me tighter. His breath was all rough exhales beside my ear, stirring the fine hairs there. His touch grounded me in the moment. The strong hand smoothing gentle circles across my shoulder blades calmed the panic within.

I was in the comfort of Nicolas's arms—something I'd never even let myself consider. It was too painful a dream. Too unattainable a reality.

Moments passed and my emotions quieted. With slow, deep breaths I began to contemplate how exactly I would extricate myself from the awkwardness of this situation. I couldn't believe I'd been so overcome. But I suppose when you held so much within yourself, it was bound to come pouring out eventually. Likely from the slightest provocation and at the most inopportune time.

"I can hear you panicking." Nicolas's deep voice rumbled beneath my ear.

I huffed a quiet laugh at his ability to do that—know the very heart of me.

"We can stay this way for a while longer. It's easier to talk to you like this, when I can feel you in my arms." My heart stuttered a beat at that, but then resumed its pace as Nicolas went on and I fought my laughter. "And you can't get away. That will also aid in the painful awkwardness you're exuding. We'll just prolong the situation, shall we?"

My left hand which had slipped around his waist while I'd cried all over his shirt, maneuvered to his ribs to dig into a historically very ticklish spot.

Nicolas yelped and clamped his arm down to his side, trapping my hand and preventing me from seeking my revenge. Laughing, he finally said, "Is now a good time to mention that you complimented me earlier? I believe you called me captivating."

Feeling levity slowly spread throughout my chest, warm and thick as honey, I replied, "Did I? I don't recall."

I could feel Nicolas's chin resting atop my head. "Yes. You did actually. And you also told me how entranced the audience is by me …" I froze as I remembered my exact words. "Morning and night, evening and matinee. An odd distinction considering you'd just attended an evening performance." His tone was smug and teasing as he continued, "Which begs the question. Just how many of my shows have you seen, Eliza?"

My face was hot. I could feel my embarrassment at his insinuation. He could likely feel it warming through his shirt. "I'm sure I was merely estimating how the audience responds to you. You likely recite all your lines correctly in the daytime as well."

Nicolas laughed again, vibrating under me. "Oh, is that how it is? I've gone from captivating to merely reciting all my lines accurately." I was smiling, but he couldn't see it. "I'll have you know, I occasionally forget my lines but I can generally make something up on the spot with none the wiser." Of course he could, he was quick-witted and a natural showman.

I said nothing, hopeful he'd move beyond this mortifying subject—not to mention my initial and lingering discomfort of having cried all over him.

Finally, he said, "I can feel you smiling, you know."

"I know."

After a quiet, comfortable moment, Nicolas asked, "If I release your hand, do you promise not to resume torturing me?"

"I suppose. I'd hate for someone to hear the way you screeched. They might assume a small child was in danger."

"Ha. Ha. You are very funny," he deadpanned. But his lips were suddenly by my ear when he spoke, and I could feel his heat and his breath wash over me. The moment was startling. I never let myself think about this. How being close just made me ache to be closer. Warmth descended through my middle, my stomach giving an agonizing flip before heat pooled low and indecent.

I wanted to cling to Nicolas, breathe in his lemony scent and beg him to keep holding me. I wanted to feel his breath along my jaw, behind my ear, and down my neck. But I needed to remember myself and remember the uncertainty of the man before me. He had a daughter, but did he have a wife? Was there a woman who held a claim on Nicolas? The thought speared someplace deep within, and I made the conscious decision to pull away.

His arms tightened reflexively, but then he slowly released me as I stepped back. "We should return. I left Cassandra alone with a room full of strangers."

Nicolas's gaze was searching but he finally nodded. "Something tells me your friend can handle herself, but I shall escort you back."

He moved toward the doorway and blew out the candle he must have placed on the chest of drawers before taking me in his arms. I followed him out, and together we made our way to the parlor, bodies close but never touching.

Laughter and conversation spread beyond the entryway to meet us in the corridor. As we stepped inside, I suddenly recalled the whole reason for our passage through the hallway.

Just inside the threshold, I turned to Nicolas. "I know my efforts in Angelica's room were unsuccessful, but I hope you'll send word if she has another spell. It's important that you take note of her environment. If I can't be there when her episode begins, I'll need the most information you can gather to figure out the cause—"

Nicolas leaned in close and interrupted me. "It's quite loud, I'm sorry. What was that at the end?"

Frustrated, I scanned those gathered, taking in the scene. Drinks were in nearly every hand. A group of actors in the corner were singing a jaunty tune—which under different circumstances I would have quite enjoyed. But I needed to impress upon Nicolas the importance of these next steps for Angelica.

Raising my voice to be heard, I tried again, "You need to be aware of the initial signs of environmental contagions that could trigger Angelica's spells of labored breathing. Try to keep track of where she is, what she's wearing, what she's eaten, who she was with, if there were any animals nearby or strange smells. Just any information you can pass along, the more detailed the better. Or you can send word to me and I'll come to you here." Nicolas was frowning in what I hoped was concentration.

I scanned the room once more and found Cassandra laughing within a small circle of revelers. An indulgent smile tugged on the corners of my lips. But as my eyes continued across the space, I spotted the woman from before, the one with the emerald green gown. She was watching me and Nicolas, and her demeanor hadn't changed. I quickly looked away from her venomous stare to realize how close Nicolas and I were to one another. In trying to speak and be understood in this crush, we'd drifted very near. The length of my side was pressed firmly against his chest and his hand encircled my elbow, holding me close. Nicolas's face was tilted to mine, bringing his ear nearly to my lips.

Flustered by our proximity, I glanced back to the unfriendly actress but she was gone. Was she ... someone to him?

I felt suddenly very out of place and inappropriate in my actions tonight, especially in a room full of Nicolas's friends. More eyes were finding us, not hostile like the beautiful woman, but no less curious.

In an effort to end this discussion that had somehow become more intimate than I'd intended, I raised my voice once more and attempted to conclude the conversation. "Just send for me. I'll do what I can to help keep your daughter safe." My statement ended overly loud.

Nicolas pulled back and stared at me with wide eyes. Only then did I notice that the group singing in the far corner had stopped. With so many people curious about my presence, I'd drawn their attention as conversation seemed to stall all at once.

Well, if they weren't staring before, they were now.

Feeling mortified flames crawl across my cheeks, I searched the area desperately for Cassandra who seemed confused by the attention I'd drawn.

I made to move toward her so we could get out of this bloody room and abandon the embarrassment I was wading through. But a hand grasped my own desperately and Nicolas called a frantic, "Eliza."

His tone gave me pause. It helped push away my unease at being in this crowded space. Something in that one word spoke of necessity. The walls had been closing in on me, but Nicolas had given me time and space to think and breathe. He was suddenly pulling me back into the hallway, fingers laced through my own. His touch was warm and assured, no hesitancy as he led me away.

We didn't go far. We didn't need to.

Nicolas stopped walking and turned back to me, intent and focused. "Eliza … I thought you knew. Angelica. She's … not mine." I could feel my lips part in confusion. "She's not my daughter. She's the daughter of one of the performers here. I've known her since she was a baby. And I care for her a great deal, but she's not mine. I have no children, Eliza. Nor a wife." He spoke quickly as if in a rush to impart these facts.

My brain slowly turned over the meaning behind his quickly uttered words. "Oh," was all I could manage. I could feel myself staring but I couldn't seem to stop. I'd accepted the version of events in which Nicolas had an ailing child. I hadn't pressed for more about a wife or the child's mother because I honestly hadn't wanted to know. My willful ignorance on the subject was my own doing, but I'd made peace with the fact that this new semblance of Nicolas had a little girl. And to learn that wasn't the truth, well, I was feeling something that felt suspiciously like relief.

I released a long breath and fought for words to say in this moment. My mind was empty save for the knowledge that Nicolas had neither children nor a wife. And my idiotic brain found this to be good news. I wasn't even going to consider what the implications were doing to my heart.

Apparently I didn't need words because Nicolas seemed to know exactly what I was feeling by the expression on my face. His smile turned smug and knowing. I pulled my hands from his grasp.

Damn my inability to regulate the honesty of my facial expressions.

"You thought she was mine."

"Yes, obviously. I just called her your daughter in front of a large group of people who all know that she is not."

"Except for Cassandra," he added helpfully.

I gritted my teeth in irritation. "Except for Cassandra."

"You seem very surprised and very something … else." His absurd face was grinning at my expense.

Willing my embarrassed flush to recede was obviously not working, so I strove for indifference and moved to pluck nonexistent lint from my royal blue evening gown. "I'm sure I have no idea what you mean. Of course I was surprised. You gave every indication that Angelica was your child. I don't know why you're surprised that I am surprised."

"The fact that you are surprised is not the part that is surprising to me."

"You're making no sense whatsoever, Nicolas." I made my tone purposefully condescending. I knew what he was getting at, and I didn't like it one bit.

The smug smile hadn't gone anywhere. "I think you are relieved to hear that I have no children and no wife. And just in case you were curious, I have no sweetheart or mistress either."

I laughed at his egotism.

"What's so funny?" he asked.

"You. Your male superiority with a carriage load of arrogance."

It was his turn to laugh. "Tell me I'm wrong, Eliza. Tell me that beyond the shock of finding out the truth, that it wasn't relief coming fast on its heels. Can you be honest in this? Because I'll admit right now: if I'd thought you had a child and a husband somewhere—a family you belonged to—I'd be devastated. Finding you alone in that clinic lifted a weight pressing down on my chest that I hadn't even known was suffocating me."

His smile was gone, extinguished by the seriousness of his words. Nicolas was staring at me with intent. I realized he was waiting for me to answer him. To admit my shame and pettiness.

I couldn't give him that. My humiliation was my own. And somehow after hearing him admit that he felt that same relief—I couldn't find amusement the way he had. There was no smugness in my countenance. Just an impending sense of … something. It felt immense and unwieldy, like the sea. My wants and desires were waves crashing upon the shore, and I was the fool sinking in the sand around them.

"I want to go," I finally managed.

Nicolas stepped forward. "Wait." That urgency had returned to his tone. A desperate need to impart.

"I *need* to go." I hoped he could hear the distinction in my words.

Without waiting, I turned and hurried the short distance to the parlor once again.

Cassandra was just inside the door, as if she'd been waiting for me. "Oh, Eliza. There you are!" Yawning dramatically, she widened her eyes. "I'm afraid I'm just so exhausted from our exciting evening. We will have to do this again sometime."

I stiffened as Nicolas move to stand beside me. "It was lovely to meet you, Lady Cassandra. I do hope you'll return. In fact, you're both invited to return for midmorning rehearsals in the theater anytime." I could feel his attention on my profile but I couldn't meet his gaze nor those of the curious onlookers. "I promise to be on my best behavior."

Swallowing the emotion lodged in my throat, I finally managed, "Thank you again. We'll just be on our way."

And with those parting words, we made our escape.

Cassandra and I worked to navigate our way through a side exit and back to our carriage. The night air was cold and damp and I wanted nothing more than to put the events of the evening behind me.

"So," Cassandra began. "Did you get what you came here for tonight?"

As I considered how to answer my friend, I thought back to Nicolas's arms around me and the quiet desperate way he'd said my name.

I wouldn't be escaping this night any time soon.

Seven

After delivering Cassandra back to her home and thanking her for accompanying me to the theater, I made my way back to my father's residence. To torture myself, I asked the driver to go past Thomas's townhouse. It sat dark and abandoned on the street corner.

I'd never been inside. Wasn't even aware I'd inherited the space upon Thomas's death. He'd made it a stipulation upon our marriage and his eventual death. It felt ungrateful to ignore Thomas's wishes in this, but the guilt of accepting overwhelmed those thoughts.

We'd hardly been married and not at all in the traditional sense. I'd wed my friend to comfort his family, never considering the future of our relationship because deep down I'd known. There would be no future for Thomas. He'd needed a miracle that never arrived.

So, when the solicitor had found me in London several months following my husband's death and told me about the home I'd acquired, I'd thanked him and said nothing else. I hadn't hired servants nor aired out the house. I'd never stepped foot inside. I didn't deserve anything from Thomas nor the Morgans. I'd done enough.

Now, several hours later, I hummed quietly to myself while I inventoried our supplies in the treatment rooms. It was past ten o'clock and my father would likely be furious with me, but I needed the space and equilibrium I found here.

Rationally I knew it was late and no one was coming to seek a physician. But something drove me to stay and busy myself within. The clinic made me feel purposeful—necessary in a way I hadn't felt earlier in the evening. The theater employees hadn't required my services at all. Or perhaps they did, but they didn't trust me to provide them. Whatever it was, I felt wholly off balance by the entire experience.

Not to mention what the encounter with Nicolas had done to me.

No, I wouldn't think on that.

I hummed louder as I searched the cabinet and counted suturing needles.

"You always were slightly tone deaf."

I whirled around at the sudden insult and found Nicolas just inside the doorway. He was dressed in the same shirtsleeves and waistcoat from earlier at the Collins. His smile was warm and amused.

So distracted, I evidentially hadn't heard him enter.

I frowned in confusion. "What are you doing here?"

His smile evaporated suddenly. "I wasn't done talking. You can't just run away every time someone says something you do not wish to hear."

I refused to be baited, but Nicolas knew precisely how to provoke me. "I didn't run. There was no reason for me to remain. I examined Angelica's room. And your friends didn't want or need me, as I'd been led to believe."

It was his turn to frown. "They don't know you, Eliza. Just because they didn't turn their hearts out for you doesn't mean they don't need your help. Does every patient who walks in that door trust you simply for occupying the room?"

"Typically, yes," I admitted. "They are here to seek my services."

Nicolas rolled his eyes in disbelief. "Did you honestly expect Laurence to inquire about the boil on his arse while having drinks after a performance?"

"No, of course not," I acknowledged. "But I did not get the sense that any of them were terribly approving of my presence tonight." I thought about the woman in the emerald green dress in particular, but also the less hostile performers who were mostly just indifferent. Was Nicolas right? Could they have simply been cautious in my company, desiring to know me better before requesting my help?

Blowing out a breath, he finally said, "They're just curious about you, Eliza. Can you understand that? They're good people. Excitable at times. But hardworking. They enjoy the lifestyle of entertaining. But they—"

"They what?" I asked, actually interested to know.

"They were interested in you, but probably hesitant because you were with me." Eyes shifting away from me, he seemed reluctant to continue. "I haven't brought anyone there. Not in a long time. My friends weren't sure what to think, and probably a little standoffish with you as a result."

"Oh," I managed, considering what that meant. They'd seen me with Nicolas and had assumed we were involved in a romantic capacity? It was fairly obvious they all cared about him. Of course they'd be suspicious of me. They thought I wasn't good enough. And they were right.

"I'm sorry you felt uncomfortable. They'll warm up to you. I assure you, they don't mean any harm."

But could these people, friends and acquaintances of Nicolas, view me through the lens of a professional? If there were those who needed me, I had to try.

Coming closer, Nicolas finally stood before me. "Can we talk, Eliza? There's so much about you I'd like to know. So much has happened."

My chest felt tight with emotion. I didn't know if I could do this—play this game with Nicolas. Catching up and pretending we were just old friends reconnecting. I looked up to meet his solemn gaze. "What is there to say?"

"It's been six years. Where have you been? What has your life been like in the time we've been apart?" His green eyes searched my face, sincerity bled out of every pore.

I didn't know how to tell him that I'd been nowhere, making the choice to devote myself to study instead. This was my life—medicine, tending the sick, delivering babies. I'd fully committed myself to my profession and my father's practice. There wasn't much left over. I wouldn't even know where to begin. Nicolas had gone on to lead this exciting life of fame and distinction. He entertained the London masses. Undoubtedly travelled for performances to other cities. Everyone knew the name Silas Viso. I was a sad, fearful young woman who'd done her utmost to stop living when she'd been seventeen. My dedication to my craft was noble and required a tremendous amount of courage—as a woman— and drive. I wasn't belittling my accomplishments, merely contrasting the very different lives Nicolas and I led.

Without answering, I looked away from Nicolas and took in the clinic—my life's work.

"I wrote to you, you know," he announced abruptly.

I was so shocked, I forgot my stubborn pride and met his open gaze.

"A few months after I left. I wrote to you. Every week for … for a long time," Nicolas admitted.

Surprised by his confession, I answered without thought. "We left Wiltshire right after Thomas died. I couldn't be there anymore and Father knew that. He bought our home here in London. You recall that my Uncle Tobias actually owned our family home in Wiltshire, well, he decided to sell it after we'd gone because he was content to remain in France. We sent for the servants to join us in London and I've been here ever since. I … I never got your letters."

"I see." He smiled without humor. "I thought you must have hated me."

"No." The word was involuntary and so was the step I took toward him. Only a handful of inches separated us now. The sudden fragrance of citrus was striking in its intimacy. Being close enough to appreciate the scent of lemon on Nicolas's skin felt intoxicating.

"I guess that explains why you didn't know of my whereabouts."

His reference to my breakdown in Angelica's rooms made my cheeks heat, but I felt compelled to reassure him. "I wouldn't have ignored your letters, Nicolas. I haven't spoken to anyone in your family since Father and I left for London. I didn't know what had become of you until I saw your likeness in the newspaper advertising your show at the Collins. I was shocked, to say the least." Thinking back to that moment in Fiona's drawing room when I'd happened across the newsprint, and I'd nearly fainted.

Nicolas stepped forward, closing the remaining distance between us, and causing me to suck in an unsteady breath. "Well, we're both here now," he said quietly. "Our paths have crossed once more."

My heart was uneven and wild in my chest. The way he was looking at me …

My instincts told me to flee the danger before me, but I'd been accused of running away once already tonight. Standing tall, muscles tight with alarm, I watched as Nicolas invaded my space. His right hand slid around my waist. I could feel his warm breath on my face as he gently brought our foreheads together.

I stood tense and unmoving, arms at my side, fighting the urge to lean into him— to admit defeat in this. I longed to relax into his embrace and let someone else bear the burden for a time, to strip off these doubts and insecurities and just be a woman in the arms of a man she—

"Eliza," he whispered my name with that same quiet urgency. "You must know. You must see that we've been given a second chance. Finding each other once again." A pause. "I still love you." Nicolas leaned in and his lips nearly grazed mine before his words registered.

Practically stumbling back into the supply cabinet, I regained my footing and clutched the cupboard for support. "You what?"

Nicolas looked resolved. He'd come here wanting to rehash the past, I realized. This was his intent all along. "You heard me. I loved you then and I love you now. We have a chance to be—"

I cut him off. "How can you say that? You didn't love me before."

Eyes suddenly more angry than determined, Nicolas declared, "I did, Eliza. I loved you when we were children and I loved you as we grew older. There has never been a time in my life when I didn't seek your attention. I've always wanted your heart."

My brain was physically incapable of drawing the same conclusion from our shared history. "That's not possible. You flirted with everyone, Nicolas. Every girl, every young woman in the village, at house parties. You passed out your affections like candy. How was I to know? You never communicated your feelings to me. We shared two kisses and then you forbade me from marrying your brother."

"I was seventeen!" he declared, throwing his arms out wide. "I was young and an idiot, but I knew I wanted you to be mine. And I didn't want you to throw your life away to make my mother happy. I was a bastard to issue that ultimatum. But I wasn't so much of a bastard to admit that I loved you before you made the hardest decision of your life. If you thought you belonged with Thomas, I wasn't going to sit by and watch. I couldn't, Eliza. Don't you see that? I couldn't. I had to leave."

I was staring, shocked to my very core.

In my foolishness, I tried to conceive of how seventeen-year-old Eliza would have reacted to a declaration of love from Nicolas. Yet I was so far removed from that girl, even my imaginings wouldn't align.

He thought he'd loved me. He thought he loved me still. Even allowing the truth of his words to penetrate, I couldn't let him continue thinking we had a future here and now. It was wrong and it was cruel.

Shaking my head sadly, I admitted what Nicolas couldn't yet see. "I'm not the person I once was. You can't love me because I'm not her anymore." Denial was written all over his features, so I pressed on out of necessity and out of decency. "I'm no longer the shy, foolish girl who so eagerly snatched every scrap of your attention. I'm not that pathetic, starry-eyed adolescent."

Nicolas was frozen now, watching me. "Is that truly how you remember yourself?" His tone was confused and held deeper notes of pity.

I said nothing. I couldn't. I'd choke on shame and regret.

"I'll tell you about the girl I remember, the one I loved. She was shy, yes. And quiet. But observant and perceptive. When you were lucky enough to hold her attention, it was because you were worthy." He smiled then, one of nostalgia and wistfulness. "She was clever and quick-witted. So damn funny in her own sharp way." I felt the first tear slip off my cheek and land at the base of my throat. "She was kind and thoughtful. Someone responsible, who took care of everyone around her. She was someone I wanted a future with."

The determination to stand my ground was completely destroyed following his speech. Retreat was necessary. I was once again a woman who ran from her pain.

As I turned my back on Nicolas, another tear fell. With one final glance over my shoulder, I admitted the truth that Nicolas needed to hear. "I'm not her either."

THE FOLLOWING morning emerged gray and soggy. I knew because I'd spent the majority of the previous night tossing and turning to the sound of rain against my windows. I'd given up as light began illuminating the dense cloud cover and peeked through the sliver of thick curtains in my bedchamber.

Sleep had been elusive and my mind had run rampant, reliving the past and rewriting history. If self-flagellation could put one in a restful state rather than excruciatingly alert, I would have been abed for a fortnight. Instead, I'd stared at my canopy and considered Nicolas's confession of love. The sweeping, dark fabric had failed to yield any wisdom on the matter. My middle swooped violently whenever I reflected on his whispered admission. When the feeling became warmth just verging on helpless wonder, I'd think about his stony disappointment as he'd fled the clinic. Best to counteract any wistful notions. Nothing could come of what Nicolas had said. For as firm in his regard as he appeared, I'd been equally fixed in mine.

I was no longer the girl I once was. I'd been damaged by the past and remade as a result.

In what world did someone like Nicolas want someone like me? He was exuberant and outgoing—beloved by one and all. His charms and countenance would be wasted on a lonely widow who was frozen in place by the decisions of her past.

There was simply too much history between us for whatever future he was imagining. How could his family ever accept me after what I'd done?

There had been more than anger and disapproval on Nicolas's face before he'd left last night. I'd read determination and resolve as well. That had given me more pause than anything else. I feared whatever threads still connected us were not yet ready to loosen their grip.

Our story wasn't finished, and I didn't know if my heart would survive.

After reluctantly dressing in a serviceable blue day dress and completing my morning ablutions, I wandered down to the dining room for breakfast. Father was nowhere to be found which, while troubling, was not unusual. He'd been oddly absent for the past several months. It was always without rhyme or reason, no discernable pattern I could deduce. But I'd seen him less and less at mealtimes and on several occasions I'd been called on in place of my father to see patients in need. His behavior was odd and confusing, but I didn't know how to broach the subject. Father was a grown man. It wasn't my place to question his whereabouts.

With one last glance at his empty place setting, I prepared my tea and slathered jam on two pieces of toast.

Moments later, Botstein entered the dining room with a blandly disapproving expression and a letter clutched in his hand. "My lady," he greeted woodenly. "A young boy dropped off this correspondence at the servants' entrance."

I took the letter—a note, really, for it was unsealed and hastily scrawled. Recognizing the handwriting immediately, I straightened in my chair and willed my hands to steady. I quickly scanned the contents before turning to Botstein. He'd been nearly to the threshold of the dining room. "Botstein, have you seen Dr. Finley this morning?"

With a sigh, he faced me. "Yes, my lady. He's just arrived at the clinic." Well, that was good news. I could leave straight away.

"Please have the carriage brought around and let my father know I have a patient to attend to in Covent Garden. I should be able to join him in the treatment rooms this afternoon. Thank you, Botstein."

The surly butler took his leave and I took a final, hasty sip of tea before retrieving my medical bag from the front hall closet.

Soon enough I was trundling along the cobblestones on my way to the Collins. Fingering the paper in my lap, I did my best to prepare myself for what would await me there. Nicolas had written of Angelica's mild episode the previous night. He'd looked in on her after his late return from my home. She'd been awake and uncomfortable with red, watering eyes and persistently runny nose. There'd been no breathing difficulties nor a rash of any sort. He'd done a wonderful job of noting details and information as he'd been able. What he'd passed along was enough to paint a picture, but I still wanted to examine her for any underlying issues or lingering symptoms.

Using the carriage ride to gather my composure, I attempted to focus my energy on Angelica and what I could do to help her. It wouldn't do to be distracted by the thought of seeing Nicolas—the man who a mere handful of hours ago had confessed the secrets of his heart.

A SHORT WHILE LATER, I followed Nicolas's written directions to a nondescript door in the alleyway at the rear of the theater. After a few swift knocks, the heavy door opened to a simply dressed young woman and a little girl—the same one I'd seen accompanying Angelica last night.

I couldn't believe it had only been twelve hours since I'd been here. In the daylight and after the exchanges with Nicolas, it felt like a lifetime had passed.

"You're Eliza?" questioned the stranger. Her blue eyes were wide and curious and they matched those of the child by her side.

"Yes, I'm here to see Angelica."

Stepping aside, the woman ushered me in before letting the door clang shut behind me. "I'm Pippa Dotson and this is my daughter, Celia."

I smiled warmly at mother and child. "It's lovely to meet you both."

"The girls are quite close. They've grown up together here at the theater. I took Angelica to our rooms to rest after she woke in the night. She stays with us sometimes when her mother is away." We were moving down a dimly lit hallway in the direction of the performers' quarters. "I'll take you to her."

"Thank you."

We finally arrived at Pippa and Celia's quarters. Entering through a small sitting room, I noted a fire in the hearth and the room's cozy, inviting environment. Through an open doorway, I spied Angelica curled up on a small bed.

"I need to return to rehearsal. But you're most welcome here."

I thanked Pippa for her hospitality and watched as she and Celia made their way out of the apartment and down the corridor in the direction of the stage.

Approaching quietly, I observed Angelica. She was on her side, carefully tucked under the blanket. Her breathing was slow and even. I could see a handkerchief laying just out of reach beside her.

Placing my bag down on the rocking chair in the corner, Angelica began to stir. With a noisy sniffle, she sat up and pushed her hair from her face, eying me curiously.

I smiled in greeting. "Hello there."

"Hello," came her quiet reply.

"I'm Eliza."

"I remember." Her voice was so small and sweet. I noticed some lingering redness rimming her eyes. Her nose seemed mostly dry now.

"Nicolas sent for me this morning. I heard you had a hard time sleeping."

She nodded, but said nothing else.

Picking my bag up once more, I approached her bedside. "Would it be okay if I had a listen to your heart again?"

Again a small nod was my only answer. She seemed more curious than distraught, so I took that as a positive sign.

I sat down on the narrow bed by her feet and administered a short examination. I asked if she could explain what had happened, but Angelica offered no more information beyond what Nicolas had provided in his note.

"Do you mind if I step across the hall into your room and take a peek at your bed?" After receiving another tiny nod of agreement, I packed up my instruments and stepped into the little room that was Angelica's. Her covers were pushed to the bottom of the bed and that same tattered blue blanket was unfolded and spread across her pillow. It was unlikely that something so long in her possession could present a sudden reaction. I didn't find anything else unusual so I returned to Angelica.

"Are these the bedclothes you were wearing last night?" I inquired softly.

She looked down at herself before replying. "Yes."

"Did you eat anything before bed? Anything new that you'd never had before?"

Angelica shook her head in the negative.

At a loss, I couldn't understand why the episode was less severe this time with some symptoms absent entirely. For now, she was well, if a little tired. "Well, how about you find a dress to put on and show me this rehearsal I've heard so much about. I should very much like to have your company while I watch."

The girl's smile was wide as she scooted from Celia's bed and went across the hall to change clothes. I had a brief look about Pippa and Celia's space—nothing invasive. Beyond the child's bedroom, there was one other doorway attached to the main living space as well as a small kitchen with a table and chairs for four.

In no time at all, Angelica stepped into the hall and beckoned me forward. I closed the door to Pippa's apartment and joined her in the corridor. She'd changed into a pale pink frock and tied her hair back with one of her precious ribbons I remembered from atop her chest of drawers.

As we walked toward the backstage area, I asked curiously, "Do you stay with Celia often?"

"Yes," she replied skipping along. "When my mum is away or busy and I feel scared at night, Celia lets me stay with her. Sometimes she comes and stays in my room, too. I like having dinner with Celia and her mum. They always have pudding and pudding is my favorite."

I grinned. "I like pudding, too." Trying to piece together the mystery of Angelica's parentage, I inquired delicately, "And is your mum rehearsing today as well?"

"Oh, yes. She came back this morning in time for it," Angelica answered readily as she led me around a corner before bringing her finger to her lips in a request for quiet.

The reason was soon obvious as we approached the stage. Moving toward the wings, I heard Nicolas reciting his lines from the second act. Angelica smiled broadly at me as if thrilled to deliver me to my first rehearsal. We stood close to the curtain where it was retracted and simply watched the story unfold. The performers were in casual dress, not a full dress rehearsal.

Nicolas's eyes snagged on us briefly before he gave a quick wink and resumed the action. I became distracted as the performance progressed. Nicolas was magnetic as always and I found myself entranced whenever he spoke.

As the play reached the end of the scene, the director whom Cassandra and I had met the previous night called for attention. All the performers gathered round for a quick conversation. At the conclusion, the men and women disbanded moving toward the rear of the stage and the dressing area beyond.

"Angelica!" the sharp exclamation turned my head. It was the angry, glaring woman from the parlor. Her remembered fury had me swallowing nervously. Too distracted by Nicolas to note her small role in the rehearsal, I was very aware of her now. With a glare aimed in my direction she ordered Angelica to her side. The girl gave me a shy smile before darting off to join the woman—her mother, I realized all at once. They shared the same dark hair and delicate features. Angelica was a tiny version of the aggrieved woman before me. I couldn't recall her stage name. The woman finally turned her back to me but not before shooting a parting glower.

Feeling oddly vulnerable by the unfriendly nature of Angelica's mother, I was slightly startled when Nicolas approached. "You're here."

"Of course. Thank you for sending word." I paused in my nervous rambling, reminding myself to proceed cautiously. "Angelica seems to be doing well now. I'm afraid I'm no closer to understanding her condition however." Nicolas nodded in understanding.

He looked invigorated by the stage, eyes alight and expression open. "I'm happy to see you."

In my distracted state—caught up by the performance—I answered with words I hadn't intended to say. "I'm happy to see you as well."

His smile was radiant. The dejected and angry man who left the clinic in the early hours of the morning was nowhere to be found. I didn't wish for his return, if I was being honest.

"You were wonderful out there," I said, indicating the stage with a tilt of my head.

His grin turned sheepish. "Thank you, Eliza."

Silence descended when I didn't know what else to say, how to further this conversation without encouraging Nicolas's attentions. We were very clearly ignoring the emotionally charged argument we'd had just hours ago. Nicolas appeared content to keep smiling and staring at me. I cleared my throat, suddenly uncomfortable with the attention.

Nicolas offered quite suddenly, "Would you like to know how I came to be an actor?"

"I would," I answered honestly, realizing that this was a detail of his life I'd often wondered about. How had a young gentleman become such a darling of the stage?

Grinning and obviously delighted at the prospect of grand storytelling, Nicolas held out his arm with a flourish and led me to a small worn settee near a clothing rack in the corner of the dressing area. A few stagehands were still about moving set pieces but the majority of the people who'd been present at the rehearsal were now gone.

Sitting down beside me on the modest piece of furniture, I was doubly aware of Nicolas's body beside mine. The length of his thigh was a warm and solid weight against my own.

Once settled, Nicolas faced me and began his tale. "Well, you see, when I was newly arrived in London, I found a pub that I was frequently fond of. One night at John's, a man struck up a conversation with me. He was deep in his cups, but I'd always been a fine companion for that sort. I helped the poor man into a hack at the end of the night and he quite earnestly pressed his calling card into my hand and told me to pay him a visit the following day once he'd had time to sleep off his drink. So I went to see my new friend—Mr. Dierks—here at the Collins, as directed, and he offered me a job. Said he was the owner of the theater and could use a good lad he could trust."

I smiled as Nicolas relayed his story. Of course. Of course Nicolas would stumble upon someone who owned a bloody theater and charmed his way into service just by being himself. I watched him as he spoke, entertaining even as he recounted a story from his past.

"So I started out doing any odd sort of job. I built sets and made deliveries. I listened and I learned. I made myself invaluable to those around me. And then one night, an actor was too ill to go on stage. Well, I'd been at the theater for nearly every performance so I knew the lines. Mr. Dierks told them to put me on in place of the sick man. I panicked for about thirty seconds before instinct took over. That performance became the talk of the town. I gained attention and notoriety and was offered a part in the next play the Collins acquired. And then the next and the next." With his attention still firmly on me, Nicolas concluded his account. "That is how I became a performer on the Strand."

I smiled and shook my head. "That is quite the tale. I'm happy it worked out for you. I was shocked, to be sure, when I discovered your role here. But it makes so much sense. You're perfect up there."

It was his genuineness and innate charisma that made it nearly impossible to remain cross in Nicolas's presence. I didn't understand it, but it had always been thus. Despite the turmoil of our previous conversation and my intentions to remain distant, we were smiling together now.

And Nicolas's smile remained firmly in place. However, if I wasn't mistaken, a small blush painted the crest of his absurdly symmetrical cheekbones. Eyes twinkling, Nicolas leaned forward conspiratorially, "Do you want to know a secret?"

Did I?

The last thing Nicolas had confessed to me had left me a confused, emotional mess. But there was something in his expression just now. Beyond the amusement and the devil-may-care attitude. A vulnerability lurked in the depths of those beautiful green eyes. This secret was important to him. It meant something.

So, I gathered my courage and nodded solemnly. "Yes, I would like to know a secret."

With a bracing inhale, Nicolas quietly admitted, "I'm writing a play. Writing is just part of it though. As a new playwright, I need funding to stage a production. Mr. Dierks has agreed to let me use the Collins and will take a portion of ticket sales in exchange. But I'd still need money to pay wages for the actors and theater employees, fund the production of the set, and a thousand other things." His words were coming fast and nervous, as if this was the first time he'd said them out loud. This was a dream, I realized. And by the end of his admission, he'd realized it too.

My reaction would be crucial—the difference between nurturing a tiny seedling and denying it the sunlight it so desperately craved.

Making my features earnest and serious, I said, "You'll do it. I know you will."

Nicolas swallowed audibly and looked down at his hands where they hung loosely between his parted knees. "Thank you for saying that."

I took one of his hands, warm and strong in between both of my own and squeezed gently. I wanted him to hear me. I needed him to believe. "You are the most stubborn person I've ever met." The laugh burst out of him, unexpected and grateful, all at once. "That's how I know you won't let anything stand in your way. You'll write your play, find funding from some rich lord, star in said play and be worshipped by legions."

"I like your version of events." Somewhere along the way, he'd taken my hands and laced our fingers together. "I like you believing in me." We were pressed close together on the small settee, and Nicolas filled my vision. He consumed the space and narrowed my focus to the here and now. For once I wasn't struggling with reminders of our past. In sharing his plans for the future, I could see beyond the version of Nicolas who haunted me, to the flesh and blood man by my side. The one with feelings and vulnerability. The man slowly leaning closer, cupping my cheek.

Feeling his breath fall warm across my lips, I closed my eyes and let myself go.

Eight

Nicolas's mouth was soft and warm. Everything about this kiss was careful and slow, as if he was afraid I'd bolt at the slightest movement. But all of that changed when I parted my lips and darted my tongue out to taste his full lower lip. His fingers along my jaw moved to the back of my head to tighten and pull me closer. I felt his control slipping as we came together more fully.

My arms wrapped around his shoulders and his free hand met my lower back, anchoring me to him. Our tongues clashed in a battle of wills that perfectly echoed the people we were here and now. When I used my teeth to nip his bottom lip, a groan escaped Nicolas. His hand moved from my waist to my ribcage, thumb nestled just below my breast. One great gulping breath would have his body grazing my own in an indecent caress. Fortunately for propriety's sake, I didn't have the inhale to spare. I was busy discovering what it was to kiss Nicolas as a woman—one with adult wants and desires.

My fingers drifted into the hair at the nape of his neck. I sifted through the soft locks and another groan escaped the chest pressed so tightly to my own.

Without warning, a loud jarring sound jolted us apart. The unexpected slamming of a door backstage brought us abruptly back to the present. I stood on shaky legs and brought the pads of my fingers to my kiss-swollen lips.

What had I done?

Looking wildly around the space, I realized we were alone. No one from the earlier rehearsal remained. The sound of the door was likely someone exiting.

Nicolas looked wrecked. He was gazing at me with a resigned expression, whatever panic he was reading on my face likely eliciting his response. "Don't do this, Eliza."

My walls slammed down hard and fast. Allowing this misstep could ruin everything.

My breathlessness from our kiss had morphed into heart-stopping regret. I didn't want to be this person. Someone who hurt others—discounted their feelings and was careless with their hearts. Nicolas thought he loved me. How could I have allowed that kiss to happen? It would only give him hope, confuse his emotions, and destroy whatever peace we had been building between us.

I lived in London; I knew the damage that could be done to a reputation. Being odd, a woman, and a professional each brought their own sorts of struggles. The combination meant I wasn't welcome in certain circles. However, being caught with loose morals—widow or not—could damage not only my reputation, but my father's as well.

Thinking only of escape, I rushed to my medical bag next to the settee. But Nicolas stood smoothly and blocked my path. "Please don't leave. You don't need to run from me. We could be happy. I could make you happy, Eliza."

Voice shaking, I admitted, "I don't want to hurt you."

It would be wrong of me to encourage anything more between us. A romantic relationship would be too complicated and fraught by our past—doomed, more than likely. I'd made so many mistakes, all the wrong decisions. I couldn't be trusted with my own heart much less his.

Nicolas reached forward to pull me in, and I stepped back deliberately. With a frustrated sigh, he shoved a hand through his hair before demanding, "Why won't you let yourself be happy? You need to stop punishing yourself for the past and all that happened before. Be selfish in this and stop being a martyr. It's over and done."

That was as ridiculous as demanding I stop breathing air or cease having emotions.

When I spoke it was with quiet certainty. I didn't want to appear a hysterical woman. "I warned you that I didn't know how to let the past die. You can't just tell someone the right way to feel, Nicolas. It was the same back then. I couldn't be just one thing. I couldn't only be in love with you. I was still a daughter and a friend—a sister to a dying man. I couldn't even simply be a seventeen-year-old girl. My path was taken and molded for me, as was yours. You were a brother and a son and a friend. My decisions changed your course as well. I'm sorry that you were hurt, but I was too, you know. I was too," I repeated on a broken whisper. "It's not about you getting what you want—then or now. It's not about losing. There are no winners, don't you see that? How can I forget all that came before when it's made me who I am? You were gone," I choked out. "Your family was devastated and I was the cause. Thomas was dead and I was left behind. I need you to understand … it wasn't all about you."

His eyes were shining and my cheeks were wet, but he managed, "You loved me? Back then?"

Still, I thought to myself. *Always*.

I laughed, a hollow and reckless sound. "Everyone loved you, Nicolas. Every woman between the ages of eight and eighty. You charmed us all."

His face closed off. "Don't do that. Don't diminish something because you didn't have faith in it."

"We shared two kisses. I knew better than to get my hopes up. And then … then it didn't matter because everything changed."

Nicolas appeared struck whether by my callous dismissal or by the truth being laid bare so tidily—I didn't know.

He stepped forward again and seized my hands, holding them to his chest. I was too weary and drained to protest. He finally spoke, "I'm sorry for telling you not to marry Thomas. It was wrong of me to issue that demand and threaten to leave if denied. I singled you out for my blame and hurt when you were never the one I was angry with. I was young and stupid and so fucking selfish. I loved you and wanted you for myself." His hands tightened as if afraid the admission would have me suddenly pulling away. "I resented Thomas for befriending you, for claiming all of your attention, and then agreeing to marry you when it was so obvious you were being manipulated. But I must atone for my part. I am so very sorry for leaving and making you feel like it was your fault. It wasn't. I made a rash decision that you spent six years suffering for. I was wrong. Please. I beg your forgiveness."

Since Nicolas had reentered my orbit once more, I'd felt like he never truly understood what I went through in the intervening years. He hadn't taken the time to address our history and offer an apology for his role in it all. I realized, now that he'd acknowledged it, I *had* been resentful. I'd needed Nicolas to confront our uncomfortable past instead of asking me to brush it aside.

A very large part of me blamed myself, but apparently some other part of me had blamed him too. The guilt I've lived with, day in and day out, wasn't for Thomas's death. I couldn't save him. I knew that even then. Cassandra was right. If I hadn't agreed to marry Thomas, I would have regretted it for the rest of my days. I didn't have that decision to weigh on my conscience. But I lay awake at night in the knowledge that I didn't give Nicolas what he wanted and so he'd abandoned his family as a result. They'd grieved the absence of one son while facing the death of another. It was too much pain to bear. And my decision had been the root cause for both.

I'd needed to hear Nicolas admit he'd been wrong. It didn't absolve me—not completely. But it went a long way toward healing the flood of guilt that lived in my soul.

"I forgive you. I do." I gently extracted my hands before I continued. "But I need you to understand. I'm not that girl anymore. Not the one you remember nor the one I actually was. She made mistake after mistake, and the woman I am now is still paying for them. My grief over the destruction of your family and the guilt from that has shaped so much of who I am. I don't know how to be someone who forgets and moves on. Someone who starts over and leaves the past firmly behind them. I wouldn't even know where to begin." Could I find the courage to move on and move beyond all that had come before? I took in Nicolas before me and all he represented. My heart gave a hopeful thump behind my ribs.

"I don't want to forget the girl I loved."

My chin wobbled before I firmed my resolve. "I don't know how to find her again. And I don't want you to waste your time waiting."

"Then let me know you as you are now," Nicolas pleaded. "You don't deserve to punish yourself for the rest of your life, Eliza. It's not fair."

"Sometimes people have to change. I believe that. What happened to us—all of us—it altered me. I've dedicated my life now to helping others. I can't face doing any more harm."

Shaking my head, I admitted, "I refuse to hurt you. I refuse to let us hurt each other. And I refuse to let our actions hurt anyone else ever again." I'd been foolish and naïve to think that months ago I could simply go to the theater and watch Nicolas with no one the wiser. There could be no one-sided resolution.

Feeling one final rebellious tear escape, I said what I should have long ago. "You need to let me go."

IN THE ALLEYWAY behind the Collins, I pressed my forehead to the cool bricks and took in big mouthfuls of air.

Walking away from Nicolas had been more difficult than I'd imagined. I think I was panicking in a deserted lane because I knew this would be the last time I'd see him. I couldn't tell him to let me go while I held on with both fists. There could be no more trips to the theater just to be in his presence. I didn't think I could face the pain of seeing him and knowing there wasn't a place for me in his life—not in any healthy, meaningful way. Not anymore. Dragging things out would only hurt Nicolas.

I needed to forget that kiss had ever happened. And I needed to put some distance between us to put him out of my mind.

With my fingertips biting into the worn brick, I closed my eyes and fought to calm my racing heart. If I could only catch my breath, I could walk to my carriage and be gone from this place. When I felt stable enough to straighten, I was startled by the presence leaning against the wall.

Angelica's mother was just watching me, bearing witness to my misery without uttering a sound.

"Is Angelica all right?" My voice emerged rough and strained. I wasn't comfortable in her company, and I didn't like the fact that she was observing me, weakened and diminished as I was.

"You don't need to worry yourself with my daughter." Her tone was matter-of-fact but the glint in her eyes conveyed a warning. "We don't want you here, and we certainly don't need your pity or your charity."

"Angelica needs help. If you won't accept it from me, my father can see her." And if I was distancing myself from Nicolas, I would need to ask this favor of my father anyhow.

"We don't want anything to do with you. You're embarrassing yourself and Nicolas by continuing to turn up. Do you think you're special? That Nick doesn't bring other women to rehearsal and kiss them and more backstage?" Her laugh was dark and grating.

It had been her. The door slamming backstage. She'd seen me with Nicolas.

I suddenly wanted to be far, far away from this woman. This was not the kind of attention I sought. I never meant to force my presence on anyone. But Angelica needed me. Perhaps the others at the theater resented my being there, but Angelica was just a child. They relied on adults to make the right decision for them. However, this was her mother. How could I go against her wishes? Even if she was wrong and spiteful and slightly unhinged.

I knew she was trying to manipulate me, to drive me away by feeding me lies about Nicolas kissing other women. He'd told me he hadn't brought anyone to the theater in a long time, and I believed him. Our past was very complicated, but Nicolas Morgan had never been a liar.

But the venom this woman spewed played on very real fears. That I wasn't wanted or needed. That even in my role as a physician—the one part of my life that felt relevant and necessary—I wasn't good enough. That I had no business being here and no ability to help anyone.

"Run along now, and go back to where you belong. Because that certainly isn't here."

And with those words ringing in my ears, I made for my carriage and didn't look back.

Nine

The carriage ride home from the Collins was cold and gray and full of self-recriminations.

The confrontation with Angelica's mother had unsettled me. It served to confirm what I'd known about the performers and theater employees. They truly hadn't wanted me there. It clearly went beyond being cautious of my profession and my place in Nicolas's life—however misguided that notion had been.

Nicolas had been trying to do a good thing. His efforts to bring medical and preventative care to the theater was noble, and hadn't been well received. I only hoped my presence there hadn't damaged his reputation or his standing within the community.

Nicolas had plans and lofty goals. Being a playwright was something he desperately wanted. I'd heard it in his voice. I would never want to endanger that dream or prevent him from attaining those goals.

I wanted to apologize. But after today—things had gone so far off course—I feared I'd never be able to explain. And I didn't wish to cause Nicolas any more pain. I'd done enough damage as it were by dredging up our painful past, and then kissing him back as if we had any hope for a future together.

Why had I done that?

I mean, I knew why. Being with Nicolas was as natural as breathing. It was denying myself that was the challenge.

I'd fallen into those old patterns of being enchanted and captivated. It was a heady thing to be his sole focus. When he'd been talking about writing and his future—he'd been so passionate yet vulnerable. I'd needed to make him understand. As a person who had a dream, having my father there to support and cultivate my efforts had made all the difference. I didn't imagine my role was quite that crucial for Nicolas, but I still wanted him to know that I believed in him.

And then I'd gotten caught up in the moment, and let my guard down.

Bah.

Upon my arrival, I went straight to the clinic to assist my father with any afternoon appointments. I longed to feel in control and competent instead of the reckless, emotional thing I'd become.

I found Meg already in residence helping examine a gentleman with a gash along his brow.

What was she doing here? I'd said she could assist me in the evenings. It was not my intention that she abandon her household duties entirely to work alongside my father.

Not that I particularly valued her attempts at household duties. She was a terrible lady's maid. Thus far she'd proven a somewhat reliable—yet irritable—assistant in the clinic. Nevertheless, I didn't want to deal with her right now. Nor my father. My feelings were too raw. I mostly wanted to beg some raspberry tarts off of our cook and hide in my room for the remainder of the day. Possibly tomorrow as well.

Finally registering my presence, Meg discarded the used supplies before meeting me by the sink.

"What are you doing here?" I hissed.

She spared me an annoyed glance before resuming her handwashing. "I'm assisting Dr. Finley."

"Yes, but why? I offered to let you shadow me at night. It's early afternoon on a Saturday, Meg."

"Well, you were due in the clinic this morning. Botstein asked me to deliver your *urgent* message to your father." She said *urgent* with a verbal eye roll. As if I had been taking in a show at the Collins this morning to avoid my responsibilities.

"It was an emergency," I enunciated through gritted teeth. "I had a patient in need of attention—a child."

Meg appeared skeptical but held her tongue against further arguments. "There were several patients here when I arrived, so I offered to assist Dr. Finley. He's actually a wonderful teacher."

"Yes, well, I know that. Obviously." This woman brought out the absolute worst in me. And he was my mentor—of course I knew he was an excellent instructor.

Eyeing me suspiciously, Meg asked, "What is the matter? Did something happen with the child?"

Not wanting to argue or draw attention to myself or further antagonize Meg, I took a deep breath. "There's no change in her condition. I'm … I'm going to go. I'll leave you to it."

Meg looked shocked by my acquiescence but nodded once before returning to my father's side.

Seeing as my presence was no longer required in the clinic, I exited through the interior door and entered the foyer of our home. Botstein was waiting with a note from Ashleigh Winstead delivered shortly after I'd departed for the Collins this morning. My friend was apparently coming for tea this afternoon in just under an hour.

I didn't really feel like company, but perhaps being alone with my thoughts wasn't the best solution. Ashleigh was a historically excellent companion. She would take my mind off of Nicolas and the theater and all the riotous emotions currently plaguing me.

Forty minutes later, I greeted Ashleigh in the second-floor drawing room. It was cozy and informal, and my preferred locale for entertaining my friends. Plus, it had the most comfortable armchairs.

"Eliza, it's good to see ye. Hope ye doona mind that I invited myself for tea." Ashleigh settled herself across from me and straightened her green-patterned day dress. Lovely mahogany curls framed her heart-shaped face and a jaunty green cap sat atop her head. My Scottish friend appeared in fine spirits today.

"No, of course not. You're welcome to visit any time," I told her earnestly as I poured tea for us both. I quite enjoyed Ashleigh's company and getting to know her in recent years.

My friend retrieved a biscuit before turning a scrutinizing eye upon me. "Are ye well?"

Frowning in confusion, I opened my mouth to assure her that I was indeed quite well, but no sound emerged and to my abject horror, my eyes filled with tears. I feared after the morning's events, I was simply overwhelmed. After years of bottling emotions and avoiding the unpleasant affairs of my past, it had all come to call in that past week. I'd been woefully unprepared, and now my emotions were wreaking havoc.

Ashleigh nodded knowingly. "Oh, dear. Ye poor little lamb chop."

A watery laugh escaped, as I'm sure was her intent. "I don't know, Ash. Everything is a mess."

"Come." She patted the seat beside her. "We'll eat biscuits and ye can tell me all about it."

So I did. I unburdened myself. I told Ashleigh about Nicolas, past and present, my brief marriage to his brother, Nicolas's sudden presence in my life again, my attempts to treat Angelica, and Nicolas's ludicrous admission of love.

"And then this morning at the theater, we kissed in a moment of weakened distraction. I knew it was a mistake."

Incredulous, Ashleigh asked, "Why the devil would it be a mistake?"

"Because he thinks he loves me. I can't do that to him. It's cruel."

"So, ye do care about him still?"

"Of course, I care about him. I … don't want to hurt anyone."

With a thoughtful expression, my friend continued, "Have ye ever taken a lover? Since ye've been widowed."

I was surprised by her question and could feel my cheeks heating. "No, I haven't."

"Ye've been a widow for nearly six years, Eliza. It's rather acceptable. If yer discreet, of course. Why haven't ye?"

I balked. "If you have some romantic delusion that I've been in love with Nicolas this whole time and refused to indulge in an affair for that reason alone —well, I'm sorry to disappoint you."

"Well, what's stopping ye now? Ye admitted ye care about him. Be happy with Nicolas. Make him yer lover. Live yer life."

I was frustrated by Ashleigh's oversimplification and my inability to articulate the complexities of our situation. "I don't want to start something painful with Nicolas. He could be hurt in so many ways. He doesn't realize it yet, but I'm not the girl he remembers. He can't possibly love the real me. He wants an idea, a nostalgic impression from his past. I'm not the moony-eyed girl who followed him around. And—and—we make no sense together. I am serious and prickly and he's the most charming individual in existence. We've just hurt each other too much. It's not a good idea. What I did … marrying his brother … Nicolas fled the country, Ashleigh. It was so hurtful that he ran away—not just from me, but his whole family. How can he ever forgive me for that? How could he ever move past it?"

Ashleigh's blue eyes were wide and serious. "I think that is for Nicolas to decide."

A weary sigh was my only response.

"Let me ask ye this. Have ye forgiven Nicolas for his part? Running away when ye needed him, and causing ye guilt and torment for so very long?"

I considered her question and thought back to Nicolas's sincere apology. Had I forgiven him? "I … have forgiven him. But I can't make myself forget. Is that wrong? Am I a terrible person?"

Smiling sadly, Ashleigh said, "No, Eliza. I think that makes ye very human." After a protracted moment, she continued, "This is all pretty recent—Nicolas coming back into yer life. Ye've had a week of new memories to contend with six years of regrets. It would take anyone time to recover, to prioritize the new and good over the old and traumatic. Perhaps ye can give yerself time to get to know this new version of Nicolas—get used to the idea of him being forgiven. And mayhap he can forgive ye as well."

With a minute shake of my head, I looked toward my lap rather than Ashleigh's hopeful gaze. "I don't know. You didn't see his face today." The way he'd been so open and raw and hurting when I'd rejected him. I feared I'd made our kiss into a regret for both of us. And a future between us an impossibility.

For the first time since our odd exchange at the medical talk, I thought about Dr. Kenneth Miles. "And then there is the strange non-relationship I have with Dr. Miles."

Ashleigh made a rude sound before she took a sip of her tea. "He is boring. Ye don't care a wit for him. Ye've been keeping him on the fringes wasting his time and yer own. If ye'd wanted to take him as a lover, ye would have already done so. Ye can't stomach the idea of it because ye can barely stand the man."

I frowned as I considered my friend and her brutal honesty. She was right, of course. My emotions were not involved with Dr. Miles. With Nicolas, all my emotions were in a tangle with one another.

"I don't know what to do, Ashleigh."

"I can't tell ye what to do. But I will say this: ye claim Nicolas can't possibly love ye but ye won't engage in a relationship with the man because ye don't want to hurt him—because he loves ye. Ye can't have it both ways, Eliza. Yer acknowledging his feelings with yer actions and then refusing to believe the truth of them. Trust the man to know his own heart. And for the love of god, woman, trust your own."

FOUR DAYS LATER, I was awakened in the dark of the night, startled and confused. Meg shook my shoulder again. The candle she was holding illuminated her fearful expression.

Rising in alarm, I shielded my eyes from the light so close to my face. "What is it? Is it Father?"

"No," Meg whispered frantically, passing me a cotton robe. "A man came to the kitchen entrance with a child. He said to find you. I put them in the clinic and then came straight away. The girl, she's having trouble breathing."

I was moving before Meg finished speaking, tugging the wrapper on and shoving my feet into the slippers at the foot of my bed.

Meg handed me the lit candle and loitered awkwardly by my bedside as I opened the door to the hallway beyond. Looking back in confusion when she didn't immediately follow, I realized she meant to stay—unsure of her place. Unexpected shame clenched my already fretful stomach. In my poor mood some days prior, I'd questioned her place in the clinic. I'd diminished her presence in a fit of annoyance that had come from within but had unfortunately been directed outward. I hadn't been fair. If she and I were going to build any sort of working relationship, I needed to start seeing Meg for who she wanted to be—not the perpetual thorn in my side.

"Well, come on, then."

We raced down the corridor intent on our patient. I ran through possibilities and treatment methods, hoping Angelica's symptoms were not as desperate as I feared. I considered the steam spray inhaler, licorice root tea, and a steam bath to alleviate her labored breathing. Focusing my mind became second nature. Angelica needed my concentration and my skills as a physician.

I couldn't let myself be distracted by my emotions nor the man waiting at her side.

Ten

As Meg and I breached the interior doorway, Nicolas's head snapped up from his place near Angelica.

"She's improving." He moved to stand at our approach.

I took in the little girl who looked so small and fragile on the bed. Meg had settled her in the treatment room before fetching me. Angelica's dark hair was fanned out on the white bedlinens. Her tiny chest moved visibly with each inhale and exhale. While I would still categorize her breathing as labored, it was clear that however her symptoms had first presented, they'd been much more dire.

I approached and offered a smile to the girl. "Hello, Angelica. I'm going to listen to your heart and lungs again. You just keep breathing and lay still and rest."

Angelica merely watched me with wide eyes.

Meg shadowed me to the bedside and spoke quietly. "He's right. She was struggling for breath—nearly wheezing—when they first arrived." She checked the timepiece on the desk. "Almost ten minutes ago."

I nodded, pleased with her assessment. "Very good."

While Angelica's breathing calmed, I listened and couldn't detect any irregularities in her heartbeat nor any fluid in her chest. Her eyes and nose were indeed watering and reddened from the irritation.

I was resolved to do better by Meg. To offer guidance and training, and to stop questioning her presence in this clinic. She was obviously dedicated to the work being done here. I could do more than give her the benefit of the doubt. "Meg, why don't you retrieve some boiling water from the kitchens and we'll try some steam inhalation until Angelica's breathing has returned to normal."

"Yes, my lady," Meg replied before hurrying away.

With a deep breath, I fought to gather control of myself. I needed to be professional and unaffected by Nicolas. Moving to the chair on the side opposite, I sat and asked him to recount the evening's events and how he'd come to find Angelica.

"I awoke to the sound of her coughing, gasping, trying to catch her breath." With a glance in the girl's direction, he lowered his voice before continuing, "Her mother, Melinda, was away and not in her adjoining room. I tried to gather Angelica to bring her but she was panicked over her missing blanket."

Ah, so the blue blanket was absent and she'd still had an attack. There went that theory.

I nodded. "Tell me everything you can."

And he did. Nicolas recounted what she'd been doing before bedtime, the meal she'd consumed in the dining room with the performers, the area of the theater she'd occupied that afternoon. He was incredibly thorough upon my instructions, and I was impressed by the information he'd memorized.

"Something in her room is likely causing this. She's improving before our very eyes simply by being absent her bedchamber. Has she ever had an episode while staying with Pippa and Celia in their rooms?"

Nicolas frowned considering. "Not to my knowledge."

"If Pippa is amenable, perhaps Angelica can stay there for the time being. Or Angelica can stay in her mother's room."

"I will share your recommendation." Nicolas appeared vaguely uncomfortable. Perhaps he knew what a difficult sell my opinion would be to Angelica's mother.

Meg returned with the heated water and I motioned Nicolas over to the area beyond the curtain where we could sit and speak at my desk.

"Meg, can you—"

"Yes," she interrupted. "I've got her."

I smiled. "Thank you." Then I opened the curtain so I could keep my patient in view while I spoke to Nicolas.

After asking Angelica—who seemed much more comfortable now—to sit up with a few pillows supporting her back, Meg wondered aloud, "Perhaps if Miss Angelica starts feeling improved, I could even braid her hair."

Before I could make my way around the desk to my chair, Nicolas reached out and grabbed my hand, squeezing gently. "Thank you for coming. I know things between us are—just—thank you for seeing her."

With a slight press of my palm, I squeezed his hand in return. "Of course, Nicolas. I want to help Angelica."

As I loosened my hold and pulled away, I rounded the desk and indicated Nicolas should sit in the armchair before me. "We need to talk."

After a quick glance over to Angelica, he turned his attention to me and there it remained, resolute and ready for whatever I had to say.

"Angelica's day-to-day life is terribly inconsistent. It makes understanding her environment a challenge. What is going on with the girl's mother? Why is she never home?" I kept my voice low and out of earshot.

With a resigned sigh, Nicolas shoved a frustrated hand through his dark hair before answering. "Melinda is selfish. She had a hard time adjusting to the idea of a baby. And she still refuses to let Angelica's needs inconvenience her own desires."

That aligned with the bitter, resentful woman I'd met in the alleyway behind the Collins.

"She's not your child, Nicolas. Why are you here?" I knew he was a kind-hearted person. But I didn't understand why he'd absorbed the responsibility of this child unto himself.

Suddenly uncomfortable, Nicolas shifted in his seat. I noticed he was still wearing his greatcoat over his shirtsleeves and gray trousers. His hair was disheveled and stubble lined his angular jaw. I felt sympathy for this man who sprang from bed and managed an emergency for a child that wasn't his own.

"I care about Angelica. She deserves better than the life she has. Angelica needs someone to watch over her. I do what I can—the other performers as well. You met Pippa and Celia. There are a handful of others who make sure Angelica is fed and cared for. She is a wonderful child—sweet and thoughtful, funny and smart. All in spite of a mother who ignores her at best and routinely abandons her at worst. I want Angelica to know that someone cares for her, wants her healthy and safe." With another awkward shift, Nicolas's gaze slid away from me to the desk.

I didn't like where this was headed. "What aren't you telling me?"

After an awkward moment, Nicolas finally spoke. "I've known Melinda a long time. When I was first in London, she was part of another production, at another theater. We were … involved for a time." Ah, so he didn't want to admit they had been lovers. Despite never having any claim on Nicolas, a tiny jealous flame burned deep in my belly. "She wanted more, and I was not ready for that. So I ended things. And then a year later, she showed up at the Collins, landing a role with a newborn baby in tow. I think she blames me for her lot in life. After our liaison ended, she became a mistress to some lord but once she was with child, he cast her out. She believes if I hadn't broken her heart and instead married her, she wouldn't have accepted an arrangement she didn't truly want and then been saddled with a child as well."

Incredulous, I said, "Nicolas, you don't truly feel guilty, do you?"

He looked away again, and I had my answer.

"Look at me." Once I had his attention, I continued softly. "This woman and her failings are not on you. We all choose our own paths and it's up to us to answer for the decisions we make." Nicolas frowned. I wondered if he realized how much I was speaking about my own mistakes. "What you're trying to do for Angelica, it is admirable and noble and will likely make all the difference in her young life. But she is not your responsibility and neither is Melinda. You've done nothing wrong and have nothing to atone for."

Nicolas's gaze was resigned and sad.

I glanced once more over to Meg and Angelica. Nicolas followed the direction of my gaze, and we took in the amusement passing between the pair. Meg was smiling and appeared happy and approachable. And Angelica—finished with her breathing treatment—appeared delighted by the attention from the other woman. Meg was teasing her as she braided sections of hair around her crown. She was creating an elaborate coiffure the likes of which Angelica had probably never been privy to.

My eyes moved back to the man before me. He was still turned, an observant guardian for this tiny girl. In his distraction, I let my greedy eyes look their fill. His masculine profile and tousled hair were drawing me in and before I could catch myself, thoughts tumbled unguarded from my lips. "You're a good person, Nicolas."

He turned back to me then, neither acknowledging nor accepting the compliment I'd paid him. It had merely been a statement of fact, but I was still awash in the notion that Nicolas was trying to be a role model and a physical presence for this child. It was an unselfish, thankless undertaking.

And I wouldn't make it harder for him, nor would I further question his motives for remaining in Angelica's life. It wasn't my place. Just like the Collins wasn't where I belonged either.

I thought back then to the confrontation with Angelica's mother outside the theater. Her accusations and insinuations. "I'm sorry if my presence at the theater has caused you problems. I never intended to embarrass you or damage your reputation. I apologize if I've made things difficult for you in your home." A regretful smile touched my lips. "I will admit I'm quite stubborn and felt deter-mined to figure out the cause of Angelica's reactions. I should not have presumed so much and invaded your space the way I did."

Confused brows drew low over Nicolas's green eyes. "What are you talking about? You could never embarrass me. I understand if you don't like the atten-tion. You seem a rather solitary creature and my life is a little loud and full."

That was the most accurate comparison he could have ever made. His life was full—full of people and vigor and so much unabashed emotion and heart. Whereas I'd backed myself into a very small corner of a very large trunk in order to ensure I was protected on all sides. If you took my life and shook it all about, I'd be rattling around in a big empty vessel.

Lost to my thoughts, I was surprised when Nicolas continued, "I can understand if it's not worth it."

The vulnerability in those words triggered all my protective instincts and a fair amount of defensiveness where he was concerned. Nicolas and I had a complicated history, but I'd never allow anyone to discredit him—not even himself. I'm sure my tone was affronted. "Of course you're worth it. How could you think that?"

Nicolas suppressed a small smile. "It's not exactly fashionable for a lady to associate with and befriend an actor."

Snorting indelicately, I replied, "I'm a female doctor. I'm not all that acceptable myself."

Nicolas's smile was shy.

"Is that what we are then—friends?" I asked. My mind had snagged on that word, *befriend*. I guess there wasn't a better term to describe our complicated relationship.

That quiet smile of his firmed up significantly, getting louder and louder until it was all I could hear. "I'd like to be."

I kept my greedy eyes trained on him but didn't answer one way or another. I didn't know if I could just yet. I'd been trying to wrap my head around losing Nicolas because of a kiss just days ago. Entertaining the idea of keeping him felt selfish and too good to be true.

Expression sobering somewhat, Nicolas cleared his throat. "In the spirit of our unconfirmed friendship, I wanted to be honest about something. I think you're under the impression that my family and I are still estranged." My brows rose. "But we're not. I've seen and spoken with my family since I've been living in London."

My mind was reeling. Another piece of the guilt I'd lived with for the past six years chiseled away. I thought I'd robbed Nicolas of the relationship with his family. I'd assumed he'd been separated and alienated, pushed from their lives forever.

"How?" I breathed, stricken.

He must have been able to read my torment because he leaned forward, forearms resting atop my desk, reaching for me. "Nearly a year after I left, I received word of my father's passing. I wrote to my mother. I can never make up for abandoning them when both Thomas and Father died. I'll hate myself forever for being so stubborn and wrong. But after so much loss, I knew I needed to reach out to my family and be a presence in their lives again. I wanted to make amends. Be a good son and brother. I typically travel to the country twice a year to see them. When one of my siblings is in town, I visit for dinner or a short stay. They support me in my career. I'm lucky to have been forgiven."

"Oh," was all I could manage through the churning of my thoughts.

A small part of me felt relief that Nicolas had re-established contact with his family. I didn't want his guilt to consume him the way it had done me. But another small part of me felt confused. How could he seek out his mother and his siblings … and not me?

"Eliza, tell me what you're thinking?" he begged.

I pulled my embroidered wrapper tighter around myself as I focused my gaze anywhere but at him. The honesty of my thoughts would break me in half and any pity in his reaction might just finish me off. "Why did you reconnect with your family and not with me?"

His fists clenched on the desktop. "Eliza." His voice was strained and devastated. "I thought—I thought, please look at me." Helplessly, I did as he asked. His eyes begged me to see reason. "When you didn't return my letters, I assumed that you wanted to cut ties with everyone—myself included. And who could blame you after what you'd endured: what my mother had pressured you into, the pain of losing Thomas, what I'd done. The way I'd hurt and punished you. I'm so sorry. I thought I was honoring your wishes. I never wanted you to feel cornered by a Morgan. Not ever again."

He was right. I had run. Overcome by my pain and circumstance. But I hadn't fled because of what had been done to *me*, like he'd thought. I'd left because of the pain *I'd* inflicted and all the regret I'd accumulated. So much regret.

"They still miss you, you know."

I nodded as a rogue tear slipped off the edge of my jaw.

Realizing that Nicolas hadn't remained in exile, made the familiar guilt flair to life. He hadn't cut off his family after all. I'd been the one to do that. I'd fled my life in the country and ignored their letters and their calling cards. Had my father separate himself as well. If I attended a society event inadvertently with one of Nicolas's siblings, I immediately made my excuses and a quick exit. I shouldn't have abandoned them. We were all grieving. But I was so stubborn and thought a clean break would be best for everyone.

And I'd tried to do the same thing with Nicolas just days ago. Perhaps I'd learned nothing in my exile.

Warm rough hands extended across the desk and grasped mine where they'd be clutching the edge in a white-knuckled hold. "It's possible to come back from something, Eliza. I started over with my family. They love me and support me. Even in my chosen career and profession. They would rather have me in their lives as I am than not at all." I looked up as another tear tracked down my cheek. Raising our joined hands, Nicolas brushed the tear away with the backs of his knuckles. "I think we should start again, too, Eliza. I understand if you can't forget our past. I wouldn't ask you to, but perhaps we can make new memories. I want to see you and spend time with you—beyond emergency visits in the middle of the night." Somehow I managed a smile at that. "I want to go for walks, get lemon ices, go horseback riding, meet your other friends, even dance together at balls … but not more than two dances. I know the rules. We'll have to attend at least six balls a night just so I can get my fill of dancing while maintaining propriety."

I huffed a small laugh. His hands squeezed mine gently in response.

Reluctantly I admitted, "I never really dance."

Nicolas seemed incredulous. "Of course gentlemen ask you?"

"You mentioned how I seemed a solitary creature. I think that translates to unfriendly. I suppose, I don't encourage that sort of attention, so I don't dance with men."

"Eliza, you can dance with someone without the intent to marry. Even in high society, that's rather acceptable."

Gently pulling my hands away, I sat back in my chair. I didn't know if I liked talking about this. "You can perhaps. My dances mean something."

Nicolas smirked. "I simply appreciate it for the activity—something frivolous and fun."

I rolled my eyes. "Of course you do. You're likely a fantastic dancer."

With a dramatic hand upon his chest, Nicolas said, "I am a trained thespian. A man of the stage, Eliza. Of course I can frolic around a ballroom with a beautiful woman in my arms."

I laughed lightly before remembering myself. I'd forgotten what this was like—being charmed by Nicolas. I could feel him tugging the amusement out of me like a string. He was encountering several snarls and snags along the way, but he was nothing if not relentless. And my smiles were coming easier and this lightness was growing, replacing the guilt and the hurt and the darkness at the edges.

Perhaps this was what Ashleigh meant by giving it time, letting new memories grow. Could starting over with Nicolas and becoming something as innocuous as well-acquainted be a possibility?

Reading my mind, Nicolas sought to confirm. "What do you say? Can we start again? Get to know each other as we are now. No expectations. No history to cloud our judgement."

I kept my face passive as I considered. "Is that what you want? To be acquaintances?"

"No!" he exclaimed. "I want to be friends, you goose." I smiled at his exasperation, finding it rather rewarding to tease him. "You could use some friendship, I think."

Affronted, I declared, "I have friends, thank you very much. We do embroidery together every Tuesday."

Comical brows rose across the desk. "Every. Single. Tuesday. Well, that does sound rousing. I think I shall take up sewing."

I laughed at the image of Nicolas sitting in Fiona's drawing room—or Mary's or Cassandra's—and how much they would all adore him.

"It's good to see you smile." Nicolas regarded me warmly and seemed to catch himself before sitting up straighter and extending his hand. "Friends, then?"

I slid my hand into his warm, waiting one and let myself have this moment, this little piece of happiness—just for me. Beyond the guilt and the remorse and the pain of the past. With a gentle squeeze, I looked into Nicolas's brilliant eyes and agreed, "Friends."

Eleven

"In typical respiratory ailments, the inhalation of medicated vapor from aqueous solutions continues to be the standard method of treatment. The approaching spring blooms, growth, and seasonal hay fever may attribute to the increase in patients with episodic shortness of breath."

I discounted the seasonal implications surrounding Angelica's symptoms despite the knowledgeability of the speaker. My colleagues and I were again gathered for a medical lecture several days following my latest encounter with Nicolas and Angelica. This time we were meeting in our own spacious library and I'd assisted my father in hosting the event. I may have also put forth a recommendation for several presentation topics to gain further insight into Angelica's condition. Thus far, Dr. Allen's thoughtful analysis hadn't unearthed any scenarios nor root causes that I hadn't already considered. I'd been hoping to gain more knowledge in order to report back to Nicolas with a plan for Angelica's care moving forward. I'd need to be discreet in continuing to monitor the girl, considering the antagonism from her mother, Melinda.

It had been quite difficult to send Nicolas and Angelica on their way at nearly four in the morning following her episode. After Meg had finished her hair and we'd both observed her improved health, I'd called for our carriage to escort them back to the Collins. Nicolas was going to take Angelica to stay with her friend Celia, and promised to talk to Melinda as soon as possible about keeping the child out of her own bed at night. I prayed her mother would listen.

"There are several tea blends and tinctures used to reduce swelling of the nasal passages and airways following these episodes and are fairly useful in relieving lingering discomfort."

The monotone recitation wasn't telling me anything I didn't already know.

Eventually the talk concluded and those seated dispersed for refreshment and conversation. Perhaps I could approach the speaker with a few specific questions. I rarely spoke at these events—very aware of my place among the predominantly middle-aged men. But perhaps through consultation with my peers, I'd be able to help Angelica. It was worth the risk.

I'd spoken with my father earlier in the day from a hypothetical standpoint, and he hadn't been able to think of any alternate diagnoses beyond allergens from her environment causing sporadic distress.

My inability to provide appropriate and long-lasting treatment was extremely frustrating. Nicolas had entrusted me with her care and thus far I'd been a failure.

In my distracted contemplation, Dr. Miles's "Good evening, Eliza" caused me to nearly jump out of my skin.

I looked to where he'd joined me in the neighboring armchair. "Hello, Dr. Miles. How are you?"

The remembered awkwardness from our previous encounter was tangible. He had disapproved of my behavior and after-hours care, claimed I was needlessly reckless. So I wasn't sure why he'd bothered approaching me now. My greeting sounded wooden and detached to my own ears. I was surprised my tongue had even successfully formed the sounds.

"I'm well," he said, still smiling in greeting. It was actually a rather nice smile. Straight, even white teeth and lips that were surprisingly full and soft-looking. "I wanted to apologize for our earlier disagreement. You were right that it wasn't my place to question your activities. It's no excuse, but I was honestly concerned for your safety. I should not have mentioned your reputation. You are a well-regarded lady."

A well-regarded *lady*, not a physician.

"I see. While I do appreciate your concern, I value your apology even more." Offering a tight smile, I assumed our conversation was finished and further contemplated ways I could approach the speaker with my questions.

However, Dr. Miles remained. Turning my head slowly to look at him, I realized his cheeks were pink and he looked rather uncomfortable.

"Eliza, I wanted to see if you would be interested in a formal outing with me. We could attend the opera, if you like, or if you'd prefer, the theater—"

"No!" My response nearly exploded from my lips, drawing a few curious glances. "I mean, not the theater. I have no interest." My outburst had been instinctual and bordered on self-preservation. The mere thought of seeing Nicolas on stage while sitting placidly beside Dr. Miles made my stomach clench miserably.

Wearing a confused expression, Dr. Miles gamely pressed on. "Oh. Well. Your father mentioned his box at the Collins and seemed to think you enjoyed the performances there." I smiled awkwardly and shrugged in a *What do fathers know?* sort of gesture. I cringed inwardly. "No matter. We could go riding if the weather holds or to one of the tea houses. I don't actually care what we do. I would just like to spend more time together."

Swallowing audibly, I offered a weak, "I see," in response.

I noticed Dr. Miles's fingers were nervously rubbing his knuckles in his lap and I felt a sudden rush of sympathy. But before it could manifest fully, he met my gaze and announced, "I would really like it if we could pursue a courtship. We have a great deal in common, and, well, I think we could be content with one another."

Was that what I wanted? A content courtship with Dr. Kenneth Miles? My mind inadvertently strayed to Nicolas. His twinkling eyes and bright smile. His teasing and his desire to dance together. Something warm unfurled in my middle at the thought of folding myself into his embrace, moving in time to music, and being seen together in a ballroom—or six. But then I considered his warm hand closing around mine and the earnest way he'd asked if we could be friends. Our new beginning didn't include romance or courtship. How could it, with so much history between us? Even starting anew and making new memories—that didn't wash away the past.

A courtship that led to a betrothal was not something I wanted with Dr. Miles. I knew this. I just didn't see that future for us. But Ashleigh's encouragement to take a lover suddenly seemed like sound advice. If I behaved in the manner of widows in London, I could engage in a discreet affair if I so chose. Perhaps that would take my mind off Nicolas and the impossible connection I still felt for him. Then I could move on and dedicate myself to our burgeoning friendship— like he wanted.

Eyeing Dr. Miles, I considered. I would need to be upfront. I refused to hurt him if having me for a wife was his only aim. He mentioned contentment between us, so I didn't assume he had aspirations for a love match, but neither did I want to presume and be negligent with his feelings. I found him attractive. His golden hair was lovely and he was very fit sitting next to me in his brown suit.

Clearing my throat delicately, I said, "Dr. Miles, I enjoy your company." His smile was just this side of self-satisfied. "But I don't think I'm ready for a formal courtship." That smug smile dipped down to confused. "Perhaps a *less public* arrangement would be an option." He appeared wary. "I understand if that is not suitable to your needs. If your goals are betrothal and marriage, I'm afraid we don't share those objectives. You know I was once married. I'm afraid I'm not prepared to follow that path once more."

"Oh," was all he managed for a time. "But it's been years since you were widowed," he said without an ounce of tact.

"Yes, well. Time doesn't heal all wounds, I'm afraid. As a physician, I assumed you would know that."

If my flippant reply gave him pause, he didn't show it. He was likely stuck on the fact I'd propositioned him for an assignation while in my father's library. What had I been thinking? This was a horrible idea. I didn't even know if I wanted to take a—

"I see." Despite his words, Dr. Miles seemed confused. Rather by my unconventional suggestion or my attempt at humor, one could never tell with him.

"Do you truly? I don't want you to expect that anything further would come of this arrangement," I warned.

"You mean you only desire intimacies with me and won't change your mind and wish to court me or marry me?"

"Correct." I took a moment to glance around the room, making sure we hadn't garnered any attention. But all those assembled appeared deep in their own conversations and their whiskeys.

Dr. Miles appeared thoughtful for a moment before saying, "I did truly wish to court you properly, Eliza. I think we could have a promising future together. But I can understand if that is not your aim. Your suggestion is quite unexpected. Might I take some time to consider your offer?"

"Of course. Nothing need be settled. Take all the time you need," Was my cowardly response. I was honestly surprised he was even considering my mad proposal. There was a tiny voice screaming in my head that this was a mistake and I was an idiot.

Dr. Miles nodded. "I'll be in touch soon with a decision."

Mouth suddenly dry, I cast about for an appropriate response. Shockingly the curtains and the bookshelves supplied none. My attention snagged on Dr. Allen, tonight's presenter. He was alone by the darkened bay window. Now was my chance to speak to him about Angelica's symptoms and condition.

In my haste to reach my colleague, I'd stood and already turned away from Dr. Miles. Momentarily forgotten, he hissed, "Eliza," at my retreating back.

I whirled around, impatient and embarrassed. "Yes. Sorry! I'll … I'll look forward to hearing from you." I resumed my determined march toward the window before spinning back once more, wincing at my manners. "Good evening … Dr. Miles."

I noticed he returned my farewell with an odd expression. But then I put Dr. Kenneth Miles out of my mind and made my escape, intending to get some answers for my patient and for Nicolas as well.

THE FOLLOWING day I received a letter from Nicolas. Nothing dramatic or excessive—a friendly letter, he'd called it. He'd told me about his day and an amusing story about a recent rehearsal. It had made me smile. Nicolas was even entertaining by correspondence. He'd also informed me that Angelica was staying with Celia and Pippa for the time being. I felt relief at that.

After receiving Nicolas's letter, I hadn't known how to respond exactly. I didn't have anything humorous to discuss. No daily updates to relay. I couldn't imagine that anything I could share would be half as entertaining for Nicolas.

However, thinking about the medical lecture yesterday and my exchange with Dr. Allen following his presentation, gave me the motivation to retrieve some parchment and pick up my quill. And perhaps sharing a few moments of my day would be just as interesting for Nicolas as his had been for me.

It wasn't a love letter.

Just a friendly missive, like he'd said. I could do that.

After fretting and staring at the blank page for a quarter of an hour, I growled at myself for being a ninny and set to writing. I told him I had a few new ideas to discuss regarding Angelica's care. I also included several questions to ask Angelica the next time he saw her. And on a whim and before I could change my mind, I told him about the charming dockworker who'd visited the clinic last night with an infected wound and how he'd flirted mercilessly with Meg until she'd gotten so flustered and irritated that she'd returned to the main house. That had been wonderfully entertaining. I hoped Nicolas enjoyed it as well. And perhaps Meg would stop scowling at my good-natured teasing eventually.

It was now two days later and I hadn't yet heard back from Nicolas. I knew he was busy with rehearsals and performances. But I was hoping to visit The Collins soon to check on Angelica and I needed help orchestrating a visit without Melinda in residence. Therefore, for a variety of reasons I was eager for his response. And there was a slight chance that I may have missed him. I didn't want to think on that too closely.

I was also unresolved on whether I should bother mentioning my confrontation with Angelica's mother outside the theater last week. She didn't threaten me, per se, but she'd made it clear that I wasn't welcome. I wasn't sure how Nicolas would respond to the information, so I decided to keep it to myself for now. Currently, I was the odd man out, newly back in Nicolas's life. His relationship with Melinda was part of his life now—his present—and it was far more intimate than ours had ever been. Nevertheless, she hadn't harmed anything more than my pride. I resolved to stay quiet on the subject and just avoid her as much as possible.

It was Tuesday afternoon and I was preparing for embroidery with my ladies at Cassandra's home. Meg was happy to assist my father in the clinic in my stead.

The weather was cold and dreary. Clouds heavy and menacing, I feared I might wake tomorrow to a mid-March snow storm.

As soon as my fur-lined boots cleared the stairs, Botstein materialized with a letter. My heart leapt considering the source. Knowing I had a bit of a carriage ride ahead of me before reaching the Duke of Crait's estate, I carefully folded and placed the letter in my reticule to read en route. Clutching my cloak tighter around me, I thanked Botstein and made my way out to the carriage. The wind was biting and frozen rain pelted my face but I was too excited with the prospect of a note from Nicolas to care too overly much about the foul weather.

After settling in the carriage and throwing a blanket over my legs to ward off the chill, I pulled out the letter. The horses lurched and so did my stomach when I realized the parchment I held was not from Nicolas but from someone else.

It held no signature but it needn't one.

This is the last time I'll tell you to distance yourself from what is mine. No more questions. No more notes. You do not have consent to see my daughter ever again. I tore that silly braid out of her hair the moment I saw it. She doesn't need you or want you. And neither does Nicolas. He's happy in his life here. You're only hurting him by asking for more than he is capable of giving. If you can't stay away from the Collins perhaps I shall come to Mayfair to make my point.

The ride to Cassandra's home took no time at all while I panicked over the note I'd read repeatedly. I didn't know what to do.

It felt like a threat.

It was definitely a threat. But how serious of one, I didn't know. What could Melinda even do to me? Ruin my reputation? Physically attack me? Punish Nicolas for my interference?

Ashleigh was pulling off her cold weather garments and passing them to Cassandra's butler when I entered the foyer.

"Eliza! How are ye? Any new developments with—oh dear, what's happened?"

I couldn't tell if my hands were shaking from cold or alarm. I'd stuffed the letter in my reticule upon exiting the carriage, uncertain how to proceed. "I—I got a foul note from Angelica's mother."

Her eyebrows winged high on her forehead. "When? Just now? Ye look as if ye've seen a ghost."

I nodded and passed over my cloak to the butler.

"Let me see it. What did that harpy say to ye?"

Wordlessly I extracted the letter from my belongings and held it out.

A few moments later, Ashleigh passed it back. Putting her hand through my arm, she led me down the corridor. "Come. Let's get ye warmed up. Then we can figure out what to do."

I felt pressure behind my eyes, beyond grateful that my friend was here. Ashleigh was riding to my rescue. Sometimes having someone calmly take charge when you're paralyzed with emotion, can be the purest form of support.

Ashleigh and I were the last two ladies to arrive. We were greeted with enthusiasm as we entered the informal drawing room. That was, until they got a good look at our faces.

"What's the matter?" Fiona asked, worry coloring her tone.

Ash led me directly to the armchair closest to the fireplace before pouring me a cup of tea, dropping in two sugar cubes, and placing a slice of lemon on the saucer. "You English ladies could benefit from a little Scottish whiskey at your social gatherings. I think I'll host the next time Eliza has a trying week."

"Eliza had a trying week?" Mary's concerned question following Ashleigh's declaration had all eyes on me.

"Yes, she has," Cassandra answered helpfully. "While I don't know what has her shivering in front of the fire, I do know our outing to the theater recently had her all in a tizzy—rightfully so." So much had happened since then.

My eyes scanned the room at the curious and worried gazes directed my way. "I suppose I have had a busy week."

"Ye should tell them," Ashleigh said. "We can help, Eliza. Ye don't need to do this on yer own."

I did my best to set my worry aside for the time being. I told my friends about Nicolas—our complicated past and our equally complicated present—and how we'd come to be in contact once more. After explaining about Angelica and her condition I was attempting to treat, I also disclosed Melinda's hostility toward me. Cassandra helped fill in the gaps as I recited the events of our trip to the Collins. I left out the kiss and subsequent emotional unburdening however. But I did relay the plan to engage in friendship and start anew with one another. I told them about Nicolas's letter and how I'd been expecting another when the note from Angelica's mother had surprised me instead.

Rather than read the contents aloud, they'd simply passed the letter from one lady to the next until it had made a circuit of those assembled.

As quiet descended on our typically boisterous group, I made an effort to consider a rational course forward. Not underestimating Melinda was a top priority.

"What do you think this woman will do, Eliza? Is she dangerous?" Jane was the first to break the silence. I smiled inwardly, my best friend had voiced my own concerns aloud.

Answering honestly, I said, "I don't know quite what she is capable of beyond neglecting her child regularly and achieving minimal success in her chosen profession."

"Ohhh, quite cutting. I approve." Cassandra's brand of levity was well-timed. A reluctant smile tugged my lips.

Jane wasn't dissuaded however. "I think you need a guard. Especially at night. I realize Meg is training with you and assisting with your late-night patients, but she poses no deterrent if someone meant you harm. She'd merely be able to run for help. I'll discuss it with Q."

"Jane, that's unnecessary." I didn't particularly want to be a favor to someone.

"I agree with Jane," Fiona said. "If you're intent on continuing your work, it would be wise to take some precautions until you talk to Nicolas and figure out what Melinda is capable of.

I was stubborn but not idiotic enough to discount the level of improved safety I'd have with one of Quinton's hired men at my back. With a reluctant nod for both ladies, I conceded. "I'll talk to Father about it."

After a moment, I picked up a biscuit and nibbled nervously. "Do you really think I need to tell Nicolas about this? What if I'm merely overreacting?" Everything with Nicolas felt so new and fragile. And who was I compared to this woman?

A chorus rang out in the crowded room.

"Yes, of course!"

"You must tell Nicolas."

"Really, Eliza."

Wincing at their collective reaction, I admitted, "Alright, fine."

"Eliza," I looked toward the duchess's concerned frown. "This woman sounds unstable. You've done nothing but try to help her child. As a mother, I can honestly say that her reaction is unusual—and concerning. Nicolas needs to be aware of the danger Melinda presents to not only you, but to himself as well."

I could understand where Fiona was coming from. What if Angelica's mother blamed Nicolas for interfering or for simply bringing me into her sphere? I sighed, considering the trouble I'd wrought by my renewed presence in Nicolas's life. I didn't wish for more circumstances to hinder our fledgling friendship. We had enough challenges as it was.

"Do you think Melinda considers Nicolas hers as well?" Kathleen's quietly uttered question drew our eyes. No one spoke, whether in an effort to draw out more conversation from Kat or in an effort to soothe our shyest member, I didn't know. "In the letter she warns you to stay away from what is hers. I worry that she's attempting to claim more than just her daughter."

I frowned in confusion as I absorbed Kat's thoughtful observation. "I had only assumed Angelica in her meaning. But you're right. The wording is odd." After a reluctant moment I admitted, "Nicolas and Melinda used to be lovers."

Ashleigh's teacup clattered on her saucer. "Whoops, sorry. Ye surprised me."

Mary spoke what everyone else was undoubtedly thinking, "But Angelica—"

"Is not his," I interrupted. "Their attachment ended over a year before she landed a role at the Collins. She showed up with a baby and a poor outlook on life. Nicolas said she's bitter regarding the hand she's been dealt—unexpected daughter included. He feels misplaced guilt and has tried to be involved in Angelica's life—be a comfort and safe place for her when her mother is unreliable and neglectful. There are several individuals at the theater who have taken responsibility for the girl to ensure she's fed and cared for."

"That's quite admirable," Fiona said quietly.

"She might still be in love with him," Cassandra mused from behind her teacup. "Perhaps she thinks you're attempting to gain both Nicolas's and Angelica's affections, and she's lashing out as a result." Several heads nodded their agreement around the room.

"Either way," Ashleigh muttered around her biscuit. "Ye need to be careful. That one sounds unhinged, if ye ask me."

I needed time to think about this new development. It complicated everything— my attempts to treat Angelica, the new relationship with Nicolas, and potentially the safety of all involved.

Twelve

There was a man in my bedchamber.

It was late, half past eleven and I'd been down in the kitchens retrieving warm milk and shortbread. After the events of the afternoon I had, unsurprisingly, been unable to sleep. Reading hadn't held my interest, and my fingers had been too nervous for embroidery. The prospect and comfort of food seemed like the appropriate answer to my internal fretting.

However, I had not expected to find Nicolas sitting on my bed when I'd returned.

I startled, nearly sloshing milk over the rim of the cup. "What are you doing here?" I demanded in a rough whisper.

His smiling face didn't dim one bit as I quickly shut the door behind me with my foot and then proceeded to my dressing table to deposit my smuggled goods from the kitchen.

"You said in your letter that you had some things to discuss regarding Angelica's care." He waved his hands in a "ta-da" gesture as if that explained his presence in my private quarters in the middle of the night.

Incredulous, I stood staring for a moment longer. "I meant a discussion via letter, Nicolas. Or a socially acceptable visit during daylight hours."

As I spoke, Nicolas's gaze wandered, smile slipping from his lips. His eyes skimmed my body slowly and seemed to stick on the return trip somewhere near my chest.

Abruptly my eyes widened and I spun toward my wardrobe to retrieve my wrapper. How could I have forgotten I was only wearing my thin cotton nightgown? It hadn't seemed notable when I'd been moving about a quiet household with everyone abed. I could only imagine the indecent view he'd witnessed.

Hastening my movements only made me clumsy but I finally managed to don my cover-up. Taking a deep breath, I pulled my long blond braid from beneath the lapels and turned to face Nicolas once more. He was still seated at the foot of my bed. His cheekbones were dusted pink and the heat in his unwavering gaze was unmistakable. Perhaps I could do more than imagine what he'd seen through my thin cotton nightgown. The blush on his cheeks conveyed Nicolas's embarrassment at witnessing my state of dishabille, but the look in his eyes told me he wasn't sorry. Not at all.

I endeavored to ignore the awkwardness now swimming in the room. Seeing the attraction written all over Nicolas's face made a small part of me very pleased indeed. But I needed to remember that he and I were starting over. Our friendship would only get muddled from eager and knowing glances. Despite Nicolas's admitted feelings, I knew his offer of friendship was sincere.

With a deep breath and heated cheeks, I finally cleared my throat. "How did you even get in here?"

After a long look, Nicolas finally answered. "I came to the clinic but the door was locked and no light came from within."

"I've reduced my hours in the clinic for after-hours care. Meg and I are only available certain nights per week, and tonight was an off-night."

Nicolas's brows rose, considering. "It wasn't actually that hard to find you here, with only you and your father on this floor. My regards to your gardener. Your trellises are well constructed."

His cheeky grin and blatant disregard for his own safety made my eyes bulge. "You could have fallen and died!"

"No," he countered, all levity. "This is only the second floor. A fall from this height would have likely only maimed me."

"Fine. You could have fallen and been maimed," I said through gritted teeth.

"Lucky for me I know a brilliant physician."

"You are …" Unable to finish the thought, I simply shook my head in exasperation.

"I am … what? What am I, Eliza?" He leaned forward, forearms balanced across his spread thighs. His coat had been removed. I could see it draped across my bed. His sleeves had been pushed up to his elbows and for some reason I found my attention drawn to his exposed arms. The strength there. The dark hair contrasting with smooth tanned skin. Nicolas looked comfortable in my room in his shirtsleeves and patterned waistcoat.

An indulgent smile tugged the corner of my lips. "A menace. That's what you are."

He smiled as if I called him something complimentary. Almost as if he could hear the things I didn't say. *Charming. Entertaining. Dangerous.*

A thought suddenly struck. "How did you know the light from this room was not my father's?"

Nicolas crossed his legs in front of him before replying. "Actually, if you must know, I tried his room first. The fire was banked but he wasn't about."

I frowned. "He wasn't in his rooms?"

Whether detecting something in my tone, I couldn't be sure but Nicolas fidgeted before reluctantly admitting. "There was no one in the bedchamber."

That was odd. Father had bid me goodnight after our dinner together. He'd made a habit recently of being mysteriously unavailable at times during the work day and even evenings occasionally, but I hadn't realized he'd been away at night.

I answered in an effort to divert my thoughts. "Perhaps he's working late in his study or reading in the library." In truth, I knew his habits well enough to know this wasn't the case, but I didn't want to consider the implications of his absence any longer, and definitely not with Nicolas sitting on my bed.

"Actually." Nicolas looked down at his hand before continuing. "I believe I take back my kind words for your trellis. I think I have a splinter."

I moved forward without thought. "Why weren't you wearing gloves?"

Nicolas gazed up at me sheepishly. "I couldn't grip the trellis quite as well, so I removed them."

I tightened my wrapper and sat down beside him on the bed. Holding out my own bare hand, I ordered, "Let me see."

"I don't want to."

My eyes flew to his. "Whyever not?"

His gaze fairly sparkled with amusement. "You'll likely scold me." I snorted. "And I doubt your bedside manner will be as accommodating to me."

I reached over and yanked his hand into my lap.

"Ow," he protested. "See? I was correct."

I gave him an aggrieved eye roll before turning to examine his hand. He did indeed have a tiny sliver wedged into the fleshy part of his palm. It was miniscule, barely even noticeable.

Sighing, I looked over to Nicolas. "Is this where you are injured?"

Nicolas nodded solemnly. "Yes. It's quite painful and I fear it may become infected." I bit my lip to contain my mirth. There would be no containing him if I smiled right now. Nicolas hardly needed encouragement. If he thought he'd accomplished amusing me despite myself, he would be unmanageable.

Huge green eyes pleaded. "Please, Eliza. Save my hand."

My huff of laughter escaped against my will.

He continued, "You know I have that scene in the play where I hold a bottle. This is the hand I prefer for that. Please, I beg of you. I don't want my career to be restricted to pirate roles."

"Stop," I laughed. "Just stop. I will remove this infinitesimal sliver from your dominant acting hand."

He clutched my hand in his. "Thank you, doctor. I can't tell you how much I appreciate—"

"You're squeezing me with your injured hand." I pointed out.

He nodded and released his grip. "Right. I'm losing feeling already. You better work fast."

Shaking my head at his ridiculous antics, I moved away to retrieve some tweezers I kept in my dressing table. Nicolas had always been this way. Seeking amused parties to entertain. His greatest efforts had always been to make others laugh. Perhaps he consistently tried so hard with me because of my quiet and serious nature as a child. I guess some things weren't going to change despite our agreement to begin again. Nicolas would always be Nicolas—playful, flirtatious, and, as I'd said, a menace. A charming menace.

After washing my hands in the water basin, I then took a linen cloth and wetted half of it with cool, clean water. I turned the lamps up a bit higher for improved light. I'd need it for the sad excuse of a splinter I had to remove. It had probably already fallen out on its own by a small exhalation from the injured party.

Returning to Nicolas's side, he turned to angle his body toward me. The position had me facing him and situated between his spread thighs. Our bodies weren't touching but it was a near thing. I glanced quickly at his face and then away, attempting to keep my greedy eyes to myself.

Taking his warm hand in the palm of my own, I inspected his wound and got to work with the tweezers. Nicolas didn't speak and neither did I. Despite my focus on his hand, I was painfully aware of him. I could feel his attention on me—beyond how I was manipulating his body. The heat of his form so near my own was a distraction. And the feel of his strong, rough hand was humbling. I knew his injury was mostly imagined, but it took a level of trust in this situation, some vulnerability. Not to mention I was wielding a metal instrument in his general area. Some men refused treatment from a woman. Nicolas had practically begged me for it.

I settled into the quiet and focused my mind on the task before me. When I felt the tweezers catch the very edge of that tiny little sliver, I held my breath and gave a slight tug.

"Will I survive?" Nicolas interrupted, startling me and making me lose the splinter all together.

"You did that on purpose," I accused without glancing up from his hand.

His voice was surprisingly soft when he replied. "I wasn't ready to let go."

I froze like a frightened animal sensing danger but unknowing the origin. I couldn't meet Nicolas's eyes after that quietly uttered statement. So I refocused my attention and redoubled my efforts to get the piece of wood out of his hand. I needed to get him out of my bedchamber. It was the middle of the night. What the bloody hell was I doing?

With a final tug, the sliver was removed. I used the wet linen to clean the area. He hadn't even bled. There was nothing to bandage. The idea of his injury seemed less humorous and indulgent now. It felt dangerous. My heart was pounding suddenly, and I couldn't seem to look at Nicolas's face. Standing abruptly, I attempted to dispel the nervous energy pumping through my veins.

"Thank you," he murmured as I bustled about the room—washing my hands and returning my supplies.

I remained near the dressing table before I turned to face him. It seemed safer to put some distance between us. "You're welcome." After a moment, I attempted to lighten whatever odd moment had passed. "I'll be sure to pass along your regards to our gardener and ask him to see about removing all the remaining splinters from the trellis."

Nicolas's eyes lit and I knew I'd misstepped. "See that you do. I don't want to damage my hand the next time I visit."

I closed my eyes and groaned inwardly. I didn't want to consider more late-night calls to my bedchamber. Abruptly I remembered the reason Nicolas had actually made the journey to Mayfair.

I returned to my wardrobe and reached in the bottom to retrieve a thick cotton blanket. I'd had it for years and it was actually one of my first large-scale embroidery projects. The fabric was layered and would be warm. It had daisies along the edge. The pattern was a bit uneven and I could see now how my amateur hand had improved over the years, but for its next iteration, it would do quite nicely.

I approached Nicolas determinedly. "This is for Angelica. It was one of the ideas I wanted to discuss with you. I spoke with a colleague about certain materials and fabrics that can be irritants to some individuals. I noticed Angelica's scratchy wool blanket at the foot of her bed. I don't know how often she uses it or if that coincides with her episodes, but perhaps replacing it with this cotton one would help eliminate a factor moving forward."

Nicolas nodded and stood, accepting the blanket from my hands. He didn't move away, and with him so close, I needed to tilt my head back to meet his gaze.

Before I lost my nerve, I opened my mouth once more. "I received a letter from Angelica's mother."

Nicolas's brows lowered. "What? When?"

"Today actually."

"What did it say?"

Rather than repeat the words aloud, I simply moved to my narrow secretary desk and retrieved the letter from Melinda. I wordlessly handed it over.

Nicolas scanned the page, his frown deepening. "'The last time' she'll tell you? What does that mean? Are there other letters?"

I licked my lips nervously. "No. No letters. She caught me as I was leaving the Collins after your rehearsal." Nicolas's eyes flared. I didn't know if he was remembering the timing of our kiss or he was simply startled by Melinda's persistence. "She told me to stay away. That no one there wanted me or needed me and—and—I was just embarrassing you."

The letter abruptly crumpled in Nicolas's fist. "She had no right to approach you."

"I'm treating her daughter, Nicolas. She had every right to approach me."

"Not like that," he said, irritation plain across his features. "Not with lies and hostility. I wish you'd told me. I'll speak to her. Tell her she can't make demands of you or of me."

"No," I rushed out. "Don't confront her. I fear it will only make things worse." I didn't admit I'd reached this conclusion after determining that Melinda was incapable of reacting rationally either due to some form of malaise or diminished mental capacity. I didn't want to draw more attention to myself by appearing as anyone other than a theater patron. And I was honestly a little worried for Nicolas. I didn't know what Angelica's mother was capable of.

Nicolas appeared poised to argue, but before he could, I spoke again. "I still want to try to help Angelica, but we need to be discreet. I don't want to draw Melinda's attention with my presence at rehearsals or at your residence. I need to figure this out."

"I don't like this. You're … my friend. You're in my life. And you are welcome at the Collins and in my home. Just because she is unhappy about it, doesn't mean it changes anything."

Taking the letter back from Nicolas and smoothing out the wrinkles, I asked quietly, "Is Melinda dangerous? Do you think there is any real threat behind this letter?" It seemed best to keep my voice low. It was irrational, but I didn't want to give my fears any real weight by voicing them overly loud.

Nicolas stepped forward into my space. He took the letter from my hands and cast it onto my dressing table. "No. I won't let her hurt you or intimidate you. I'm so sorry, Eliza. For bringing this madness to your doorstep."

"No. It's not your fault. You have nothing to apologize for. Don't be silly. You've done nothing but help Angelica and her mother. Hopefully these episodes will be resolved and my presence will no longer be an affront to Melinda."

Nicolas's stare was troubled. "Who is assisting you in the clinic at night? Is it that girl who braided Angelica's hair?"

"Yes," I admitted. "Meg is training with me now. But after speaking to my friends today, I'm considering a hired guard for the late-night shifts in the clinic. It's something I probably should have already done."

"That's a good idea. You have someone you trust?"

"Yes. My friend's new husband is the Earl Sullivan."

Nicolas's brows rose high on his forehead and he interrupted before I could explain further. "The owner of Piker House?"

"That's Quinton. He employs a handful of men to secure his establishment. Jane said he could spare one a few nights a week to keep watch in the clinic. I'll speak to her soon about arranging it."

"Good. I worry about you," Nicolas said and looked at me for a moment before reaching forward and pulling me into his arms.

The embrace surprised me. It reminded me of the last time I was this close, sharing the same space, breathing the same air as our mouths met in a heated exchange. But while this moment was reminiscent, Nicolas's hold felt different. Comforting. Whether for me or himself, I didn't know. But after the worry plaguing me about the letter and the implications, I let myself indulge in the consolation he offered. I melted into Nicolas, feeling the warmth of his body and the surety of his embrace.

I felt safe and protected. Unburdened in a way I seldom allowed.

As I clutched Nicolas, the weight I'd been carrying lessened as his hands cupped the back of my head. He stroked the length of my braid and rested his chin on top of my head. As I absorbed his warmth and his citrus scent, a tiny voice whispered that this embrace didn't feel very friendly at all.

THE FOLLOWING morning found me alone and unexpectedly busy in the clinic. My father had indeed been missing at breakfast which, in turn, had me mulling over his absence the night before. I had neither the time nor the inclination to delve into where he could have spent his evening and—more troubling—with whom.

When I'd first noticed my father's odd behavior and frequent disappearances several months past, my friend Jane had still been our house guest. She'd noted his absences and wondered if he perhaps had a paramour. At the time, I'd vehemently disagreed for a variety of reasons but the most pressing one had been my late mother. My parents were a rare love match and had been happy before my mother passed away during my early childhood. I couldn't imagine my staid and loyal father taking a lover.

But now, well, I didn't know what was going on. I wasn't ready to confront him, however. I'd wait and gather more information.

Rather than work alone in the treatment rooms, I'd sent for Meg to assist me with patients. I'd talked her through several small procedures. It was nice to see her confidence grow and expand with every interaction in the clinic. We'd worked steadily until midmorning when my father arrived. He'd greeted us but provided no explanation for his whereabouts.

Meg shot me a curious glance, but I remained silent.

Our work progressed to early afternoon, until Father encouraged me to take a substantial break before I returned to the clinic for my late shift. Meg went on ahead to the kitchens for her midday meal while I happened upon Botstein and Jane in the foyer.

"Eliza!" Jane greeted me warmly. "I'm sorry to drop in unannounced, but I wanted to see if you'd like to have tea. I thought we could catch up."

Taking my friend's hand and giving it a gentle squeeze, I said, "Of course. I'm so happy you're here. Why don't we head out to the gardens? The day is fair and I could use some fresh air."

After requesting tea from Botstein, we made our way outside. The sun was shining and while there was a chill in the air; it wasn't uncomfortable but quite energizing. I couldn't remember the last time Jane and I had shared tea or a meal together, just the two of us. I was elated to spend this time with my newly married friend.

"So, how is training going with Meg?" Jane smoothed the skirt of her floral-patterned day dress as she settled herself on the stone bench. We'd selected a small seating area in the sun and donned out bonnets. There was little greenery in the flowerbeds but the surrounding hedges provided a sense of seclusion.

"Very well," I answered honestly. "I think she's more content with her work now than when she merely attended me. I wouldn't say we're friendly, but we're … something. She's intelligent and willing to learn, and I find I enjoy instructing her. We work surprisingly well together." I didn't share the outburst Meg had had about wanting more in her life than being my lady's maid. It felt wrong to share something so personal. Especially to someone who'd only ever known Meg as a servant in my household, albeit a reluctant one. Jane hadn't witnessed Meg's transformation from averse maid to engaged medical assistant.

Jane smiled in response. "I'm pleased to hear it. I imagine you'll both be happier in the long run with the change in her circumstances."

Botstein arrived with the tea tray and placed it on the bench between us. I poured before passing a lemon tart to Jane. She thanked me but eyed me warily. "I wanted to tell you that I spoke to Quinton, who said that Daniel or Mr. Stanley could be spared to be of service to you at the clinic in the late evenings."

I felt so conflicted. It simply wasn't in my nature to accept help—even from my friends. Hence Jane's hesitancy. I envied individuals who were able to identify weaknesses within themselves and just … allow outside assistance. It was difficult enough to admit that I wasn't safe in my place of business, but to also swallow the hard truth that I wasn't capable of defending myself, if necessary. I didn't relish feeling weak.

"And before you object," I opened my mouth to argue, but Jane went on quickly. "Please know that I want to help. I have these connections now that could benefit you, and you should utilize them. It's the very least I can do. You were so very kind to welcome me into your home when my father all but sentenced me to the country. I didn't have the means nor the standing in society to live independently. Your selflessness and friendship made all the difference at a very tumultuous time in my life."

I frowned at her commendation. Of course I had offered Jane a place in our household. She was my friend. She could have remained as long as she liked.

Again, I attempted to interject but she pressed on, "I think it's important to consider your safety. We live in a time when women who are strong and capable are seen as something other. You have a target upon your back simply for achieving your goals. I hope there comes a time when women are valued for standing out in a world, where now they are made to feel small and contained. But for the time being—especially with the threats from Angelica's mother— being wise about your welfare seems a necessary precaution."

"I agree," I said matter-of-factly. The painful truth was this: I was a woman who rejected the mandates of my sex. I preferred a career in medicine over an estate to manage or a household to run. Marriage and family were edicts of society, but I'd effectively turned my nose up at following the prescribed course. Some of my peers would disassociate themselves from me and my father, as a result. There were aristocrats who would speak ill of me and others who wished me harm. While my father was likely concerned with the ruffian types who required medical treatment late at night, I was far more troubled by the gentlemen who sought to put me in my place. Either way, the risks I was taking by opening the clinic needed to be addressed. The simplest response was to allow a hired guard to sit in my waiting room for four hours a night, three nights a week while I did my job undisturbed. I was intelligent enough to see the solution and seize it.

Jane blinked at my easy acquiesce but didn't comment, merely picked up her lemon tart and took a bite.

I sipped my tea and listened to the birds chirping while she finished her chewing.

"You know, after all the turmoil and upheaval yesterday at our embroidery meeting, I really just wanted to check on you. How are things with Nicolas?"

I took a deep breath, considering. "I don't know. I've been … conflicted."

"How so?" my friend asked.

"Nicolas has always been this larger-than-life presence. We've agreed to become friends and get to know each other—as the people we are now. But I don't know. The way I feel when I see him … it doesn't feel innocent. It feels complicated. I fear I'm doomed to always harbor feelings for him."

I didn't admit this to Jane, but fear was a very real concern. Nicolas had always made me feel too much, whether as a child or an adolescent or in the here and now as a woman. I felt alarmingly *awake*. Nicolas took my muted gray world and made it lively with brilliant color once more. It was easy to recognize the *before* and *after* with the catalyst staring you in the face. I was present in a way I hadn't been in years. Smiles and laughter came easier now.

Jane nodded slowly before saying, "Can I give you a direct assessment?"

"Of course," I answered readily. "I value your opinion."

"Thank you." She smiled before placing her teacup and saucer on the bench. "Eliza, I've known you for years now. I realize we weren't acquainted before you were widowed, so I lack that knowledge base. However, I can just imagine that you're a shadow of the person you once were. So many times I've seen grief and pain distract you and pull you from the present. You're held prisoner by your past. I know that pain doesn't just go away. But I think you deserve happiness. You should allow yourself to have more. And who's to say that *more* can't be with Nicolas … if you want it."

I considered Jane. I knew she meant well and I'd welcomed her thoughts. But I didn't know how to cut the threads tying me to the Morgans and our painful past. They were so snarled and tangled, it felt impossible to simply snip the ends and fly away like a kite, leaving it all behind.

"I don't trust myself, Jane. I'm scared I'm going to make the wrong decision. It feels easier to make no decision than risk hurting Nicolas again."

"How could allowing yourself to be with Nicolas hurt him?" she asked, genuinely curious.

I searched the garden rather than meet her eyes. My throat felt tight with unspent emotion. "I don't know. There's too much history, too much hurt between us."

"It sounds like he's willing to let the past go and begin again."

I nodded.

Then Jane gentled her voice. "Is it you, then? You don't think *you* can move past everything that happened?"

I didn't know how to answer her quietly uttered question. I'd let my past control so much of my life, never looking forward or moving on. Dwelling in my hurt and heartache seemed easier than confronting what I'd lost. Living a happy, fulfilled life seemed more than I deserved. "I've been living with this guilt for so long—letting it define my life, letting it define *me*."

Jane frowned. "What is it you think you've done to deserve to suffer this way?"

"I destroyed the Morgans. Hurt the very family who'd essentially taken me in. I chose Thomas and drove Nicolas away. I … let him go." My eyes were burning. It was so hard to confront these truths even to a friend who loved and supported me.

"So choose him now. Pick Nicolas over your guilt. Allow his happiness as well as your own. You loved him once. You could love him again."

Loving Nicolas was never the problem. I didn't know if I could accept his love in return.

Swallowing down my emotion, I didn't get a chance to respond.

"Just think about it," Jane encouraged. "Go slow. Give him a chance. Give yourself a chance."

My friend was right. Real change—intrinsic and fundamental change—took time. I wanted Nicolas in my life. That was true. If I wanted to enact the change required to confront my past and long-held regrets, then I needed to be patient.

Nodding my agreement, I took a slow sip of tea. It was starting to grow cold.

"He's really an actor at the Collins? He's truly *the* Silas Viso?" Her tone was approaching starry-eyed wonder.

"Yes. He performs several times per week. He's the lead in the current play."

Jane watched me carefully. "And he's very talented as a performer, you think?"

"Oh, yes. He's magnificent." I smiled. "So energetic and engaging. And wildly funny. And he told me recently he has further aspirations to become a playwright. He's writing something for the stage and is seeking funding for his project."

Jane nodded thoughtfully while I spoke. I realized belatedly that I'd likely given too much away as I'd spoken of Nicolas and his many talents. My ringing endorsement seemed to echo loudly in the gardens. Or perhaps it was only myself who could hear the affection in my tone.

Smiling suspiciously in return, my friend finally said, "I want to meet him."

Thirteen

Three days later I was seated in my father's box at the Collins feeling paranoid and jumpy.

"This is quite exciting," Jane said from beside me.

I glanced at my friend before replying. "You've been here before."

"Yes, well, not when I knew one of the stage performers."

A reluctant smile tugged my lips.

Quinton leaned around the other side of Jane. "You still don't know one of the performers."

Jane frowned. "Are you both *trying* to ruin this for me? I am excited for Eliza. She knows Silas Viso. Therefore I also know Silas Viso. In a way."

"You're correct. I will not utter another word to dim this experience for you." Q's lips quirked indulgently at his wife before he leaned back in his seat.

"Thank you," she replied smartly.

Following our afternoon tea on Wednesday, Jane had insisted on meeting Nicolas. I was reluctant to attend the theater with Melinda as an unknown quantity in my life. But Jane vowed to bring Quinton with us and the plan was hatched. Our schedules aligned for this Saturday evening showing.

I wasn't entirely sure how to avoid Melinda's notice following the play. I was hopeful that she would return to the residence and I could simply send word to Nicolas to meet us in the box after the performance.

I needn't have worried because Melinda wasn't performing this evening. An understudy had taken her place.

In Nicolas's opening monologue, he must have caught sight of us in our seats because he gave me a long look while reciting his lines. And then the same boy who'd retrieved Cassandra and myself at the previous show, arrived during the intermission with a message from Nicolas saying he'd come to us following the final act.

Once my worries over communicating with Nicolas and evading Melinda had been resolved, I still couldn't settle my nerves.

Jane was bright-eyed and watchful throughout the play. Quinton was his quiet, stoic self.

Meanwhile, I sat next to them with my stomach in knots and my fingers clenched in the skirt of my dark blue velvet gown. The thought of seeing Nicolas again after that night in my bedchamber made me anxious. Nothing had happened. Not really. Nicolas had been silly about his splinter, and then serious and concerned over my safety. After that embrace, he'd slowly pulled away and said goodnight. I'd threatened him with bodily harm if he tried to climb down the trellis while holding a large blanket, so he'd cheerfully allowed me to smuggle him through the kitchens and out of the house.

There hadn't been anything of consequence to happen, but this new beginning between us felt very fragile. We were making new memories together, a future. And my heart didn't know how to feel about that.

I'd received a new letter from Nicolas yesterday. Another *friendly* letter simply telling me about his day and that he hoped we could dance together soon. I wanted that, I'd realized. Desperately.

I didn't know how to resolve those conflicting ideas. I wanted Nicolas's friendship and the fresh start we'd promised one another. But I ached for his touch, vacillating between remembering his comforting embrace and the passionate kiss we'd shared. My mind was at war with my body.

And now my friend and her husband were about to meet Nicolas. It felt intimate. My worlds were colliding, and I felt on edge. Nicolas had always been part of my past. Something I'd locked away. And now he was emerging into the light, establishing a place in my present tense. Perhaps I simply needed time to adjust to this new reality.

As the show ended, the theater slowly emptied of guests. We remained in our seats, Jane and I chatting with Q quiet and watchful.

Eventually our curtain was pulled back and Nicolas entered. His dark hair was pushed haphazardly away from his face. He'd donned a waistcoat and jacket and looked ridiculously handsome.

Jane hopped to her feet, smile enormous on her lovely face. Quinton rolled his eyes at me before standing to join his wife. I stifled a laugh.

"Hello, I am Jane. Eliza's friend. You were magnificent onstage. Thank you for inviting us. I am so thrilled to meet you."

She couldn't stop speaking or smiling. My amusement grew as she continued talking. And Nicolas seemed charmed by her enthusiasm.

"Good evening, Lady Sullivan. It's lovely to meet you. And you as well, Lord Sullivan." He offered a short bow.

Jane laughed. "Oh, no. Call me Jane. And he's Quinton or Q, if you prefer."

Q, if you prefer, was staring at his wife as if she'd lost her mind but he offered Nicolas a nod of greeting and a stiff handshake.

"Alright, then. Jane and Quinton." Nicolas turned and faced me finally. "Good evening, Eliza. I'm glad you came. And brought your friends with you."

"Yes. Um. Thank you," I fairly stammered. Jane watched our exchange with maniacal glee. Quinton looked at me as if I, too, had misplaced my good sense. Attempting to recover, I said, "Excellent performance tonight."

Nicolas's smile was quiet and knowing, as if he could sense my nervous energy and pitied me not one bit. "Thank you, Eliza. I'm so happy you enjoyed it. Although you must be growing bored after having seen this show several times now."

"Oh, she's been attending for months," Jane chimed in helpfully. I shot her a pained look. Quinton's eyebrows were high on his forehead.

Reluctantly turning back to Nicolas, I ignored his smug amusement. "Well, this has been delightful. But we should probably retire."

Jane frowned immediately and opened her mouth to object. Quinton shot me a glance before drawing his wife's attention with a hand around her waist. I was grateful for the well-timed distraction.

Jade eyes sparkling, Nicolas argued, "Actually, Eliza, I thought you might want to check on Angelica while you're here. Her mother is away. I'm not sure when you'll have another chance."

"Oh. Yes, of course."

"Eliza, are you sure you should stay?" Jane's concern had evidentially finally penetrated the fog of Nicolas's charms.

"I'll be fine." I smiled at my friend. I'd attended in my own carriage in case I'd have the chance to visit with Angelica.

Once we all exchanged our goodbyes, Nicolas placed my hand on his arm and led me backstage.

Before we reached the performers' apartments, I asked quietly, "Where is Angelica's mother? I noticed she didn't perform tonight."

Nicolas sighed. "She didn't show up for rehearsals this morning and her replacement went on. Occasionally Melinda will disappear and miss performances, usually when she gets involved with a lord or is taken as a mistress once more."

"And she just abandons her daughter?" I couldn't fathom leaving a young child of four and expecting others to care for her.

As we turned down the corridor and made for Angelica's quarters, Nicolas lowered his voice and slowed our progress. "She knows that there are those of us who will ensure Angelica's safety and well-being. She has been spoiled by our concern for the girl and lives her life as she will."

I shook my head. Trying not to judge Melinda for her choices was difficult. Our lives were worlds apart and mine was marked unequivocally by my privilege.

But I couldn't fathom such neglect and disinterest for one's own child. It was disturbing and heartbreaking.

Nicolas led us just across the way to Celia and Pippa's door. After a quiet knock, Angelica and her friend stood before us grinning.

"I've been feeling so well, Lady Eliza. Thank you for the lovely blanket," the little girl said.

I smiled down. "You're very welcome. I'm happy you're feeling better. I brought my things. Would you mind if we stepped across the hall to your room so I can give you a little checkup before bed?"

Angelica nodded. "Just let me grab my blanket first." Moments later, little footsteps sounded and she returned. With quiet surety, the girl slipped her tiny hand in mine and led me to her room across the corridor.

Nicolas lit several candles for us, before stepping back into the hallway. "I'll leave you to it. Good night, Angelica." She returned his farewell and he retreated another step before speaking again. "Find me afterwards, Eliza. I'm just next door."

"Alright," I said before turning back to my patient. "I'm going to listen to your heart again. Does that sound okay?"

A small nod from Angelica as I listened to her chest and lungs.

"Have you been spending your time with Celia lately?" I asked, curious if her new environment was the cause for her renewed health or if simply switching her blankets initiated the change.

"Yes, we've had lots of tea parties and I even brought my ponies to Celia's room to stay." Angelica pointed to the lower shelf on her bookcase. The aforementioned carved horses were nowhere in sight.

"I see," I said, smiling.

"Nick said I needed to sleep in Celia's room while Mama was away, but today is Saturday. Mama said she would return Saturday to see me. Can I please stay in my own bed tonight?"

I frowned, unsure of what to do. Melinda was away and I didn't want Angelica to be alone.

"I want to see my mama." My heart broke for this child. "I promise to use my good new blanket, Lady Eliza. I won't use the scratchy one anymore that made me sick."

"I don't know, Angelica. I'll worry if you're in here all alone. Wouldn't you rather stay with Celia and your ponies? I don't even see your precious blue blanket in here."

Angelica appeared on the verge of tears. "But it's Saturday and Mama said she would come home. If I'm with Celia, I won't see her. I don't need my ponies or my blue blanket. I'm not a baby."

"I know, darling." Perhaps she could fall asleep here and I could move her back to Celia and her mother's rooms. I needed to talk to Nicolas. If Melinda was coming back tonight and expected her daughter in her bed, I didn't want to be here and risk mother endangering her daughter due to my presence.

"Will you braid my hair and tell me a story?" Angelica asked sweetly, sensing she'd won the battle.

I sighed inwardly, unsure if I was making the right choice. But as I plaited her hair and told her a bedtime tale about a girl with dark hair and her flying pony, I couldn't help but feel my heart squeeze at Angelica's sweet little voice and happy laughter. So different than the sick child I'd met weeks ago.

I tucked in my sleepy patient, finding no wool blanket anywhere in the room. While layering the cotton bedding and the daisy blanket on her small body, I continued my story until Angelica finally closed her eyes, breathing deeply.

I don't know how long I sat there watching her, wondering what her life might be like if she had parents who put her health, safety, and well-being first. It made me think of all the children in London who needed homes and love, too. Feeling overwhelmed by my sudden emotions and cynicism, I placed the candle on the dresser and blew it out before leaving the room. I pulled the door behind me but left it slightly ajar while I spoke with Nicolas and worked out whether we needed to move her across the hall. I wanted to be able to hear her if she needed something in the meantime. Nicolas's quarters were not far.

I approached his open doorway slowly, suddenly nervous to enter his personal space. When I peeked around the doorframe I saw Nicolas immediately, leaning against a small dining table. He was watching the door, lying in wait perhaps, and eating a shiny red apple. He'd since removed his jacket and waistcoat. This was a man comfortable in his own space. The short foyer opened into the kitchen and dining area with a corridor and several closed doors beyond, likely at least one bedroom, perhaps a drawing room. Nicolas's space seemed larger and more well-appointed than either of the other living quarters I'd visited. Apparently being the star of the show came with improved accommodations.

Nicolas's eyes stayed locked on mine as curiosity got the better of me and I surveyed his rooms. It was warm with a fire burning and gas lamps lighting the space. The area was tidy and welcoming, surprisingly cozy. It felt more like a home than even Celia and Pippa's apartment. That thought made me sad for some reason. Not that Nicolas had managed to make a home for himself here—I didn't begrudge him that, of course—but that he'd even needed to. So far from his family in Wiltshire.

Nicolas didn't speak, just allowed me to look. Then he took a large bite of apple. The crunch was loud in the space, but it could hardly compete with the racing of my heart. I could feel it in my blood, a drumbeat in my ears.

Nicolas's throat worked indecently as he swallowed the bite of apple. Watching him lick his full lower lip to taste the remaining juice made temptation pound painfully through my veins. Suddenly the events of the Garden of Eden made complete sense.

Striving to control my runaway heart and my inappropriate thoughts, I took a deep breath before speaking. "Angelica's asleep. She begged to stay in her bed after I examined her. She said her mother was returning tonight and was desperate to see her. Do you think she'll be alright? Should we try to move her to Celia's bed?"

Frowning, Nicolas set the apple on the table and straightened. "I didn't realize Melinda was planning on returning this evening. But Angelica should be fine in her own bed. If you think that's wise for her health?"

I paused, considering. "If the wool blanket was the culprit all along, it has since been removed from her environment. I'm hopeful that solves the mystery of her reactions. I suppose we shall see if returning to her room has any effect on her." I hated the thought of testing the theory but I also didn't want to force the girl out of her space. She'd been so intent on seeing her mother. Once more I was overcome by a wave of sympathy.

"Would you like some tea? I'm afraid I've eaten the last apple, if that was your preference. My apologies."

Blinking out of my thoughts, I turned to face Nicolas and his lovely smile and polite, reasonable question. "I don't know. If Melinda is due back tonight … perhaps I should take my leave."

Nicolas's gaze was thoughtful. "Do you want to leave, Eliza?"

Did I want to leave?

No, of course not. I wanted to cross this room and taste the fruit on his lips for myself. I wanted to eradicate every barrier and erase every bit of progress we'd made. But I couldn't *say* any of that, and I decidedly could not *do* any of that either.

Instead I opened my mouth and replied as simply as I could, "Tea would be lovely. Thank you."

Nicolas watched me for a beat before gathering the items for tea. He worked quietly, and I eventually made my way to his dining table, wading through my nervous energy and discomfort. I appreciated the space he was giving me. I didn't know if Nicolas could sense my nerves but giving me this moment to simply adjust to my surroundings felt necessary.

Tracing the wood grained pattern of the oak surface with my finger, I jolted slightly when a tea cup was placed before me.

Sliding into the chair across the way, Nicolas raised speculative brows. "Why are you so tense around me?"

"I'm not tense," I said defensively.

Rich male laughter met my ears.

I could feel my cheeks heating. "I'm not … tense." I glared at him. "It's just odd to be here, in your space. And see the life you've made. It's like staring the consequences of my actions right in the face."

"Ah, ah, ah. We're not doing that. We've agreed to a fresh start. A new beginning. You are my new friend who has been invited to take tea in my home. You have no prior knowledge of my previous homes."

It was my turn to laugh. And then sigh. "That is easier commanded than actually done, Nicolas."

"I know." His voice gentled. "But let us try."

I nodded and took a sip of my tea. It was warm and comforting and prepared just how I liked.

"You know, it was nice to meet your friends this evening." Nicolas's eyes fairly sparkled. He was clearly amused. I didn't want to consider why.

"Yes, well. Jane was rather enthusiastic. Sullivan is a bit of a grump, but there's not much to be done about that. He's devoted to Jane and her happiness, so I shall endure." I didn't want to talk about Jane and her new marriage. I liked Quinton—I really did. We actually were very similar in temperament. He and I were both serious, if a bit sardonic. But we had Jane in common. And for his commitment to loving my friend, I could tolerate our maddening similarities.

"You met Jane when you first arrived in London?" Nicolas inquired.

"Not right away. After a time, Father requested that I engage with my peers and attend society events for a portion of the season before he allowed me to commit myself to medicine and his tutelage. Jane and I met while attempting to avoid notice in ballrooms across Mayfair."

I noticed Nicolas's tea remained untouched before him. "And you didn't want to be out in society?"

It was odd to try to explain this part of my life—the part where Nicolas was gone and I'd attempted to move on from everything that had taken place with his family. But I would try, as I'd agreed. "No, I didn't. I was resolved to studying and becoming a physician. I knew finding a husband was not going to happen for me, but I indulged my father and did as requested until just after the holidays. My friendship with Jane—and others—had solidified by then. And here we are nearly three years later."

"Ah, yes. Embroidering together every Tuesday."

I smiled at that, growing easier in our conversation. "That is correct. Although Jane is rubbish at embroidery. She mostly comes for the conversation and the biscuits. Just like the rest of us."

Nicolas leaned forward, forearms on the table as he fidgeted with his teacup. He was looking down at his own movements but glanced up at me through absurdly long eyelashes. "I was serious about learning to sew so I can join your ladies' club."

"Oh, but if you joined, it would be a ladies' club no longer," I retorted, enjoying teasing him.

The smile slid off my face abruptly as a sound reached me from the hallway and through the open door. I froze, listening a moment longer for confirmation.

Pushing away from the table, I jumped to my feet and rushed toward the sound of coughing and wheezing breaths. Nicolas following me into Angelica's room as I moved to her bedside. Her little face was buried in her pillow as she coughed.

"Let's take her back to your quarters."

I gathered Angelica carefully in my arms. As I stepped into the passage, the door across the way opened revealing Pippa in her nightgown and robe. "I heard the commotion. You can bring her in here."

We moved our party into Pippa and Celia's small drawing room. I laid Angelica on the settee and asked Pippa to bring me a basin and ewer with water.

"I'll retrieve your bag," Nicolas said before disappearing down the hall to where I'd left my things in his foyer.

"Angelica," I said. "Try to breathe with me." I took exaggerated breaths to see if she could match them. She was able to do so but every deep inhale rattled in her chest.

With supplies from both Nicolas and Pippa, I took a cloth and wiped Angelica's face, neck, and hands. I hoped removing her from her bed would lessen the effects of her reaction quickly. And after some time, it did.

Eventually her breathing slowed and became less labored. I took a handkerchief from my bag and gently wiped her watering eyes and leaky nose. Poor little duck. Angelica was tired and close to falling asleep on Pippa's sofa.

Nicolas entered with the daisy blanket and laid it gently over the sleepy child. I met his concerned gaze as Pippa approached once more. "I'll keep her here with us for the time being. I'll watch over her."

I nodded. "Thank you."

Nicolas gave Pippa's arm a gentle squeeze before promising to check on Angelica in the morning.

Frustration and guilt threatened to overwhelm. I should have trusted my instincts and kept Angelica out of her room. Something from within affected the child as she slept. Thankfully her neighbors were kind and concerned for her well-being. But what would happen when Melinda reappeared? Would she allow the girl to share her quarters? Angelica couldn't return to her own bed. This evening's events made it obvious. Would her mother even see reason were I to intervene?

I knew the answer to that.

With one last look at Angelica's sleeping face, I stood and let Nicolas escort me out.

As the door closed behind us, I took my bag from him. "I should go. It's late."

"Don't do that."

Looking sharply at Nicolas, I replied, "Do what?"

He took my arm and moved us away from his neighbor's doorway. "Do not blame yourself. She has been having these attacks for months. There is no rhyme or reason. The episode tonight was not your fault."

I winced at how easily Nicolas had interpreted my dark mood. "I knew better, Nicolas. I should have insisted she return to Celia's bed. She had been sleeping comfortably there all week."

"Yes, but we assumed that was because of the new blanket. Now we know that is not the case."

I heaved a frustrated sigh. "Right. Now we're right back to the beginning and none the wiser."

Nicolas pulled us to a stop. "That's not true. We know that she needs to stay away from her own bed while we investigate further."

"You know as well as I that her mother will not allow my interference," I countered. "If I tell Melinda to keep her daughter out of her own room, she'll refuse my advice out of spite."

Nicolas's expression turned stony. "Then I'll make her understand. She might be unreliable and selfish, but she doesn't want Angelica to suffer. I don't understand why she's taken an instant dislike to you, but she will heed my warning."

I feared Melinda's aversion to me was directly related to my presence in Nicolas's life. The less I interfered, the more likely she was to take her daughter's situation seriously.

I didn't want to hide, but I wanted Angelica to be well. If that meant my involvement necessitated secrecy or to distance myself from Nicolas, then I would abide.

He searched my face, green eyes troubled. "You cannot blame yourself for everything, Eliza."

I knew that. Rather, I was learning to accept that. The desire was strong to chastise myself and consider my failings. But in order to care for Angelica—and all my patients—I needed to trust my instincts and know that, fundamentally, I wanted the best for them.

I would do everything in my power to ensure Angelica's safety and well-being, no matter the cost.

Fourteen

"And then, as I turned toward the footman, I knocked over the entire tray of champagne flutes." Several of us gasped as Cassandra's story reached the pinnacle. "On to Lord Grant," she finished amidst our shocked cries.

"He was positively drenched. I even managed to cover my hem and slippers. I felt terrible for the poor man," she groaned. "And nearly everyone in attendance at Lady Helm's soiree paused to watch Lord Grant's soggy exit from the ballroom. I'm quite sure the musicians even stopped."

"Oh, Cassandra!" Mary exclaimed. "I'm so sorry. That's horrid."

Cassandra nodded sagely, red curls bobbing in her wake. "I don't suppose Grant has any intention of proposing now. He was so embarrassed he could hardly meet my eye. He left straight away and I haven't heard from him since."

I marveled at my friend's misfortune. Lady Cassandra Fields was the unluckiest woman in all of London. She'd had numerous proposals and courtships, and nearly every time some unforeseen calamity had thwarted her attempts to wed.

"You can all laugh now, you know," Cassandra said. No one did. "It really was quite humorous. Now that several days have past, I can see the comedy and absurdity of the situation. Come now, ladies. Just imagine it. Me in a golden gown overlaid with ornate bronze beading positively mortified, smelling like a

French brothel, slippers squelching with every step I took in the oppressive silence."

I bit my lip to contain my mirth as Cassandra continued describing the event with her flair for dramatics and exaggeration. A small chuckle came unbidden from Jane to my left. Fiona's eyes were bright but she shook her head, resolved to resist Cassandra's hilarious storytelling.

"I'm surprised Lady Helm didn't instruct the maids to squeeze the liquid from my hem in an attempt to continue service."

Kathleen's snort from across the room set everyone else in motion. Laughter filled the room and Cassandra looked exceedingly pleased with herself. She stood and dropped into a deep curtsy. "There, that's better. You are my friends and are therefore allowed to laugh at my absurd misfortune. Although, I will say, the footman who served the drinks didn't look apologetic in the least. Now that I consider it, he looked oddly familiar."

"Cassandra, bless ye. I needed a bit of cheering up," Ashleigh said, after gathering her composure.

"What's the matter?" Fiona asked, motherly concern lacing her tone.

Ashleigh waved off her worry. "Oh, just a letter from home. My father is being a blighter, as usual, and my poor mother is too embarrassed to show her face in the village. I'm grateful to be here in London away from my horrible father and troublemaking brothers, but I feel awful for abandoning my mother. I wish she could be here with me."

Ashleigh had escaped her life in Scotland a few years ago in order to find a husband in London. She'd had several courtships but no serious offers of marriage. Her family's standing was in a state of mild disrepute and without a sizeable dowry to entice suitors, Ashleigh was still on the hunt. She didn't seem to mind however. Life in London had been happy for her thus far. And we all enjoyed her presence within our circle. We'd be devastated should she return to Scotland.

"Couldn't she join you here?" Mary inquired softly.

Ashleigh shook her head bitterly. "She won't leave my brothers and our business there. I've tried, but she won't hear of it."

"I'm sorry, Ashleigh." Fiona's warm gaze conveyed the helplessness we all felt at our friend's hardship.

Cassandra reached over and squeezed Ashleigh's hand. "If my sodden disaster gave you a reason to smile, then it was worth it." The two friends shared a grin before Cassandra continued, "In fact, ladies. Feel free to toss the contents of your teacups my way. I shall bear it if it improves everyone's mood."

Ashleigh shook her head at Cassandra but released a reluctant laugh that joined with the rest of ours.

"Speaking of enhancing the mood." Cassandra winked at me. "How are things with your actor?"

"Oh—um—we," I stammered as I took in the curious faces of my friends. "Well, we are getting to know each other again. Becoming friendly acquaintances."

"And how do you feel about that, Eliza?" Fiona's voice drew my attention.

"I suppose, I feel cautious yet optimistic. We both apologized to one another and said things that needed to be said—for both our sakes." I fidgeted with the saucer in my hands, slightly uncomfortable with the attention.

"That's good," Jane surmised from my left. "Do you think things will change in your relationship?"

"It's not that simple, Jane. We haven't—we're trying to simply be friends. Attempting to get to know one another as we are now. You know how complicated things are because of our history." I could hear the defensiveness rising in my tone against my will, so I took a deep breath and beat it back. Jane was my friend. I knew that. She was only curious and she wanted the best for me. Everyone in this room did.

"Would it be so bad if things did change? If he courted you or," Cassandra lowered her voice, "you became lovers? You deserve to be happy, Eliza."

"I am—happy." The word, forced from my mouth, landed like a painful denial.

The quiet in the room descended in a rush. Cassandra stared at me and opened her mouth to respond, but paused.

I loved these women. But this agonizing examination of my life was difficult to bear. They didn't understand. How could they? I'd been private, bordering on secretive. My history with the Morgans was as deep as the ocean and just as shadowed. My friends couldn't fathom that part of my life and how I'd lost part of myself as a result.

Did I want to move forward with Nicolas? Of course. He was … everything. Beautiful and kind. So incredibly smart and funny. He understood me in a way no one else ever had. But did I trust myself with Nicolas's heart when I'd made so many mistakes? No, I didn't. Not at present. I needed time. Honoring his request for friendship felt like the right decision.

Instead of Cassandra's voice, Fiona's rang out suddenly in the drawing room. "Mary, how are preparations coming for your mother's upcoming celebration?"

With an inward sigh of relief at the duchess's intercession, I pulled a biscuit off the serving tray before me. I listened to the ladies talk and nodded when appropriate, but my thoughts were a tangle. When the meeting concluded, I packed up my embroidery and said my goodbyes. And if it felt like I was running away, then I'd have to live with that.

I AVOIDED MY FRIENDS. I knew they were concerned but I wasn't ready to discuss my feelings or further analyze my relationship with Nicolas. Therefore I declined a dinner invitation with Fiona and her husband, the Duke of Compton, and a request from Jane to join her for tea the following day.

It was unfortunate timing combined with my odd mood that found me in the kitchen when my father sneaked in late that night.

"Eliza," my father said, startled by my appearance.

"Good evening, Father."

"I—um—what are you doing here this time of night?" he stammered.

I took in his disheveled state and the embarrassed flush creeping up his bearded cheeks. "Having trouble sleeping. I thought some warm milk might help." As well as the biscuits I planned on retrieving.

"Ah, I see." His nervous energy and inability to meet my eyes further irritated me.

"Where have you been?" I finally asked, weary of the secrecy. Even more tiresome was my willful ignorance. "You've been indisposed randomly and without warning for months now. What is going on?"

With a resigned sigh, my father met my eyes. "Let's sit down."

Feeling unsettled and aware that only bad news required chairs, I reluctantly moved to the kitchen worktable and sat adjacent my father.

"Eliza—I've been courting someone."

I'd had my suspicions, but to hear the words aloud didn't give me any satisfaction over being right. I felt grief rise up.

When I didn't react verbally, Father continued, "Her name is Mrs. Baker, Jean Baker. She's a widow I met during an appointment in the clinic. I … enjoy her company very much."

I pressed my fingertips into the wood surface of the table. "I didn't know courting took place in secret."

Another sigh, this one tinged with sadness. "I didn't know how to tell you, Eliza. You're so constant—immoveable. I knew you weren't ready to hear that I'd found someone to share my time with."

I frowned. He'd kept this from me because he'd feared my reaction. Beyond the hurt was a growing shame beneath my breastbone. "I didn't realize you were ready to move on from Mother. I don't mean to be … so … shocked."

"Shocked? Eliza, your mother has been gone for nearly fifteen years. I loved her. She was an amazing woman. And she gave me you. I'll always love her. I didn't plan on loving Jean as well. I didn't set out to find a wife. It just happened. And I'm happy. I hope you can be happy for us as well."

"Do you plan to marry?" I asked hesitantly.

"We do," he replied. And then as if remembering he was speaking to his child and not his peer, he concluded with more conviction. "This summer."

My mother died when I was a small child, but I still had memories of her. Of her and my father. Happy memories. I knew it was more than what some children had. I supposed I just never envisioned a future for my father that surpassed the cherished happiness of his past. How did he manage to let go of his love for my mother? How did anyone *choose* to forsake their past?

I certainly didn't know.

The pads of my fingers were pressed white against the tabletop. I consciously flexed my hand and removed it to my lap. "Of course. I am happy for you, Father. I want that for you." The admission felt odd. It wasn't a lie, but it didn't feel like I was the one speaking.

He cleared his throat. "Good. I should like to invite Mrs. Baker for dinner so you two can get acquainted. She has been quite eager to meet you."

"Alright," I agreed. My mind was in a selfish spiral, considering all the ways our lives would change. There would be a lady of the house. Would Father want me to leave? I didn't think I could take up residence in Thomas's townhouse. In fact, I wanted to speak with Nicolas about transferring ownership of that property.

"This is a good thing, Eliza. I'm relieved to finally tell you."

I nodded despite feeling unmoored.

With great effort and through an onslaught of emotions, I managed a wobbly smile as I stood. "Just inform me of our upcoming dinner plans with Mrs. Baker. I look forward to making her acquaintance."

Then I grabbed my cup of warm milk and made for the stairs, leaving my father, my childish expectations, and the blasted biscuit tin behind.

"ME MAM ALWAYS SAID TO SLEEP WITH our feet out from under the blankets when me or me brother had a fever."

I bit my lip to contain the smile that threatened. "Is that so?"

"Aye," Daniel O'Connor replied matter-of-factly from his seated position next to me the following evening.

MY GUARD this evening was Lord Sullivan's good friend and second in command at Piker House, one of the most popular gaming hells in London.

My current patient was a dockworker who'd required sutures for a nasty cut on his leg. I'd been explaining the importance of cleaning the wound and changing the dressings regularly to prevent sepsis or infection, noted by the presence of a fever. Daniel had offered his—and his mother's—opinions at various points during the exam.

Meg sneered from her place opposite me as she delivered a week's worth of bandages and supplies. I'd gotten our patient's permission for Daniel to observe. She was just feeling especially ornery by our guard's presence and surprising interest in our work. I was exceedingly amused by his curiosity and running commentary. His company had definitely enhanced the dreadful mood that had been present since my conversation last night with my father.

After finishing my discussion with the patient, Daniel kindly escorted the man out to the gardens.

Meg approached in his absence. "If you have no need of me, I shall retire for the evening."

I checked my timepiece, noting that Meg was retreating an hour earlier than usual. We had no other patients currently. I found it hard to believe she was so annoyed with Mr. O'Connor that she would withdraw.

I raised a questioning brow. "Why does his observation bother you so?"

"It doesn't bother me," she snapped, belying her protest. "I just find it unprofessional. You wouldn't have him in here with the lords and ladies during daylight hours. I don't see why his presence is tolerated now."

"Because he doesn't mean any harm and he's taking an interest in our work, Meg. Yours and mine. He's not telling us how to do our jobs or belittling us for being women. There is no grudging respect from that man. He admires us and what we do here. If there were more like him out there, I'd let them come and support me whenever they bloody well felt like it. Just because you're feeling encroached upon doesn't give you the right to demean his efforts. If I recall, that was rather a sticking point for you."

Her nostrils flared at my sudden outburst. It wasn't my intent to reprimand or shame her when I'd started speaking. But I hated her accusation. To imply that Daniel would be unwelcome among my peers made me react to the injustice and unfairness of it all. And perhaps Meg's objections were slightly reflective of her position in society.

I opened my mouth to apologize, but she dropped her eyes and gritted out a "yes, my lady" before bobbing a shallow curtsy and exiting the interior door.

Meg and I were destined to occupy separate shores with a frustrating lack of communication forevermore.

Sighing, I returned to my desk and updated the patient logs.

Moments later, Mr. O'Connor reentered the clinic with a figure trailing behind. I rose to my feet, prepared for another patient, but stopped in my tracks when I noticed the newcomer was Nicolas in his black greatcoat.

"I believe you have a visitor, Dr. Finley," Daniel remarked, brown eyes twinkling mischievously.

"Hello, Nicolas." Butterflies erupted behind my sternum as I took in his warm gaze.

Both men came to a stop before me. "Good evening, Eliza," Nicolas greeted.

His jaw was lined with dark stubble, and he looked so happy to see me that I knew my answering gaze was equally pleased.

After a moment, I heard a subtle throat clearing. I realized I'd been smiling at Nicolas for far too long. My eyes snapped to Daniel who still remained. Belatedly, I realized I should have made introductions. Why was I so bad at that?

"Nicolas, this is Mr. Daniel O'Connor. He's assisting me this evening and also acting as a night guard for the clinic." Daniel's smile was wide and pleased; whether because I'd introduced him as my assistant or he was just a jovial person, I couldn't be sure. "And Mr. O'Connor, this is Nicolas Morgan—my friend," Nicolas nodded approvingly, "and the actor Sil—"

"Silas Viso, I know," Daniel interrupted. "A fine pleasure to meet ye, Mr. Viso."

My eyes widened comically as the two men exchanged hearty handshakes.

"Mr. O'Connor, the pleasure is all mine. Are you a fan of the theater?" Nicolas inquired genuinely.

"Call me Danny," Mr. O'Connor insisted. "And yes, I am a patron of the arts. I've enjoyed yer performances at the Collins very much over the years."

Nicolas gifted this effusive praise with a beaming smile. "I appreciate that, Danny."

Daniel appeared on the verge of swooning, so I interrupted. "What brings you by, Nicolas?"

With a final smile for his new friend, Nicolas turned back to me before saying, "I wanted to see you." It was a simple statement delivered honestly. I couldn't imagine being so free with my own wants and desires. I feared if I uttered the same statement it would be a fairly shouted declaration. But Nicolas owned his sentiment and met my questioning gaze with an open expression of his own.

"Well, I'll give ye both some time to visit," Daniel said with visible reluctance.

"Actually, Mr. O'Connor, I think I'll lock up for the night. It's late and you were an incredible help this evening. Thank you."

After heartfelt farewells, I saw Daniel out and locked the door to the clinic before returning to find Nicolas with his coat removed, seated in the same leather armchair before my desk.

"And here I thought *you* were my biggest fan."

I laughed, feeling the balm of his presence loosen something in me that had been wound tight for days. After the tense conversation with the ladies at our embroidery meeting followed by the revelations about my father, I'd been lost and off-balance. Seeing Nicolas lightened the pressure I'd been drowning in.

"Perhaps you and Danny should compare notes. See who has attended the most shows." Nicolas looked quite proud of himself.

I was still embarrassed by how many performances I'd witnessed when I'd been finding excuses to see Nicolas without his knowing. I had yet to respond, uneasy with the topic.

Nicolas eyed me knowingly. "You know, I do believe if you should attend another play at the Collins, you should critique my performance. Provide honest feedback. Help me grow as an artist."

I smirked. "I fear if I help your ego grow any larger, you may not fit upon the stage."

He laughed. "Perhaps you are right. At least bring your bodyguard with you next time. He can praise my performance even if you refuse to do so."

A standing invitation from Nicolas would give me the excuse my subconscious so desperately clung to. Seeing him without purpose or friendly intent wasn't something I allowed myself. I knew it was wrong and muddled. We were starting again in friendship. There was no place for my outward attraction or the connection I felt for him. But as long as I could keep my glances innocent and my affection pure, I could be the friend Nicolas wanted. The last thing he needed was my confusing feelings to hurt him or allow him to envision more between us. Despite the progress we'd made with one another, anything beyond the parameters we'd established felt fraught and tenuous.

My smile lingered as I changed the subject. "And how is Angelica doing?"

"She is well. No further attacks. She's still staying with Celia and Pippa. Her mother has been mostly absent. I'm told through theater gossip that she's under the protection of a marquess."

"I see," I said, feeling both conflicted and relieved by Melinda's continued absence.

"And how have you been, Eliza?" Nicolas's gentle question made my throat tighten unexpectedly.

As he had been the subject, I couldn't exactly share the discussion I'd had with my friends recently. But perhaps I could share the struggle I was experiencing with my father's news. "Oh, there have been some noteworthy developments since I last saw you. My father admitted he has a paramour. Well, he didn't so much as admit it as I caught him sneaking in late one evening."

Nicolas winced. "So, he has a mistress?"

"No," I admitted. "He says they're courting. That he cares about her deeply and plans to marry her."

"But you haven't been introduced?" Confusion was evident in his tone.

I sighed. "No, she and I are not acquainted. Father said he was reluctant to tell me knowing how immoveable I am and averse to change."

Nicolas simply watched me without responding.

"So you agree with his assessment?" I accused.

Hands raised in supplication, Nicolas finally said, "I didn't say that. Tell me this … are you happy for your father and his intended?"

I fidgeted somewhat in my seat. "I am." And that was the honest truth. "If this Mrs. Baker makes him happy, then I am in support of their union. It was just unexpected."

"I suppose discovering your father returning from a tryst would be mildly traumatizing."

"Ugh, no. Not that. I mean, that part was surprising in and of itself. I just meant … I never expected him to marry again. He loved my mother and I thought that was enough."

Nicolas's features seemed to freeze. His eyes locked with mine before he said, "Do you think that this new relationship dishonors your mother? Does it mean he loved her any less?"

His words felt like an accusation, as if my interpretation of my parents' marriage was somehow misguided. "I —don't know."

Something shifted across Nicolas's face, slow comprehension—a key turning in a lock. The path before him cleared, much like the expression on his solemn face. "Remember when you told me—rightfully so—that you couldn't be just one thing? You were both a daughter and a friend and a woman in your own right. It was wrong to assign you just one role." I nodded cautiously. "Well, I believe our hearts are much the same. They can't be expected to carry our love for only one person. Imagine the burden. I think they are big enough to hold more than one love. It works for family, does it not? I loved my father. That doesn't negate the love I have for my mother. I don't have to choose a favorite sibling to receive the limits of my love—although, I will admit to having a favorite and it is definitely not Francesca." My smile was watery as he continued. "Perhaps it's possible to love more than one person in your life. Even at the same time. I don't know. Your father's heart can carry his love for your mother alongside his love for you and his new Mrs. Baker. Don't underestimate the capacity to love, Eliza. Maybe there are chambers in our heart, and some doors stay locked up tight while others stand ajar for new loves to come and go."

"I don't know if my heart works that way," I admitted to the desktop rather than meet his eyes. Nicolas's speech had resonated and for some reason I felt shamed.

"You think your heart has reached maximum capacity then? No room for anyone else? Ah, that must be why you consider everyone merely *acquaintances*." He said the word with exaggerated distaste.

"No—I don't know. I think mine might be in disrepair," I admitted.

"You have a broken heart, dear Eliza?"

I finally lifted my gaze. I hadn't meant it quite that way, but the truth of Nicolas's softly spoken question struck a chord somewhere deep. My poor heart had been battered and bruised, lost and left along the way. But my capacity for love hadn't changed. I knew that. I had my friends in London, my father, my long-buried affection for the Morgans. And the proof of the remaining pieces of my heart sat in the chair before me.

"Possibly," I said quietly, unwilling to disrupt the tender way Nicolas was watching me. "But perhaps as an experienced physician, I could treat it with care."

Fifteen

D*earest Eliza,*

I shall be adding a new character to the play I'm writing. She will be a physician, I've decided. Therefore I will be required to conduct abundant research to properly convey the role of ... Eloise. I fear I will need to call on you often in order to seek your professional counsel. It's imperative that my comedy be both accurate and humorous. One of those more than the other, but I won't say which. Perhaps we can have tea this week? Or an apple if you prefer.

Yours,

Nicolas

I read the friendly letter once more before tucking it into the hidden pocket of my dress. Botstein had delivered Nicolas's note during breakfast while I sat— alone once again—in the family dining room. Father was away, and now I knew where.

I'd thought a great deal about what Nicolas had said regarding my father and his betrothed. He'd been right, of course. I'd been immature and selfish in my reaction to the existence of Mrs. Baker. I would make every effort to know this woman that my father loved.

I couldn't help the smile lingering as a result of Nicolas's correspondence. It was the second letter in as many days since his last visit to the clinic.

I would write back in a similarly friendly fashion and invite Nicolas to tea. Perhaps I'd even request apple cakes from our cook. The thought had me smiling again.

But before I could allow some fanciful notion to run amok in my imaginings, I needed to focus on the day before me. I'd likely be in the clinic with Meg this morning as we awaited Father's arrival. I needed to make several house calls this afternoon to check on ladies in their confinement. And then tonight, Mr. Stanley would be arriving for his first night on guard duty as Meg and I worked after-hours seeing anyone in the community in need of medical attention.

Some nights were busy with a steady stream of patients while other nights none came at all. It was hard to predict—unless it was a full moon. On those nights, the strange cases never failed to materialize.

I greeted Meg in the empty treatment rooms a short while later. I passed a quick hand to straighten my skirts and felt Nicolas's letter in my pocket, remembering the warmth and joy it brought me. Those new memories were building now, like snowflakes falling. One after another until the entire countryside was blanketed in white. It was growing easier to focus on the present without being so consumed by the past.

Before my thoughts of Nicolas could run away with themselves, I bustled to the clinic doors and turned the lock, ready to begin the day.

ALMOST TWELVE HOURS LATER, I was exhausted. Despite the length and breadth of this day, it had been a pleasant one. No fevers or infections. No unexplained illnesses. No grievous injuries and no deaths. My patients in their confinement had all been healthy and well. It was not often that days in the clinic ended so fortunately.

"Meg, you're welcome to retire for the night. I know you were busy this afternoon helping Father while I was out."

My assistant eyed me warily. Always suspicious of my motives, that one. "I'll stay on for the next half hour in case anyone comes."

There had been no after-hours patients thus far tonight. Mr. Stanley was seated comfortably in the waiting room reading the paper by candlelight. He was a quiet man. Mr. Stanley and Mr. O'Connor were both excellent guards, and I didn't fear for my safety in the slightest while in their company. I felt foolish for having waited so long to have proper security precautions in place.

Nearing half past ten, Meg made her way toward her room in the servants' quarters.

After another hour of straightening supplies and writing patient notes, I decided to send Mr. Stanley on his way and thanked him for his service.

"Good night, Dr. Finley. Danny will be joining you next while I'm away at Piker House. Just so you know."

I smiled in response, happy for Mr. O'Connor's return.

Escorting Mr. Stanley to the exit, I intended to lock up and retire to bed. But before I could reach for the door, it opened and Nicolas was standing before me in a black greatcoat.

Mr. Stanley moved to stand next to me but didn't make any demands. I appreciated that. His support provided a sense of security but it was not overbearing.

"Good evening, Eliza." Nicolas glanced to my companion with a frown.

"Hello, Nicolas. I was just about to lock up. Come in."

Stanley looked to me and raised a brow but remained silent. "Mr. Stanley, it's alright. We're acquaintances."

"Friends," corrected Nicolas from where he'd shrugged off his coat and placed it on a chair in the waiting area.

Rolling my eyes, I turned back to my guard before opening the door. "I assure you. I am fine. Thank you for your assistance this evening. I'll see you soon."

After glancing at Nicolas and tipping his hat, Mr. Stanley bid me goodnight and finally exited the clinic.

With my hand pressed against the door, I took a deep breath before turning. I felt it necessary to center myself before facing the reality of being alone with Nicolas.

We were well acquainted. *Friends*, like he'd said. I could do this.

Nicolas was perched on the edge of my desk in his fine lawn shirt, expertly tied cravat, and patterned maroon waistcoat. His hair was haphazardly brushed away from his face, and there was dark stubble lining his jaw. He looked so handsome. My eyes felt like greedy little shut-ins getting a fresh gust of spring air.

I finally stopped staring and began walking toward him. "What are you doing here?"

His smile was small and secret. "Just visiting my friend." And then after a moment, "How was your day?"

Walking around Nicolas, I circled the desk and took a seat in my chair. He shifted and eased into the armchair facing me.

A smile came unbidden. "It was actually quite good. A long, busy day. But everyone remained moderately healthy and well. For that I am grateful." Nicolas studied my face closely. "How was your day? Did you have a performance?"

"No show tonight. Rehearsal this morning and then I had a few meetings with potential investors."

"That's wonderful, Nicolas. How is your writing coming along?"

Nicolas relaxed into his seat, propping his ankle across his other knee. "It's going well. I do have a new character to contend with, but I'm hoping you can help me with that."

I frowned. "You were serious about including a female physician in your play?"

"Yes," he drew out the word as if I were dim for having questioned it. "I told you. I felt inspired by you. Why wouldn't I want such an intelligent, lovely, and gifted character in my show?"

Warmth flooded my cheeks at his praise. The urge to drop my gaze was instinctual. "Well, I don't know about all that."

I could hear the smile in his voice when he spoke. "You have always been one of those people unable to accept a compliment. Why is that?" I raised my eyes at his question but didn't answer. How could I admit that hearing his admiration caused a visceral response in my body? That I wanted to feel his compliments whispered against the skin of my throat and pressed lovingly to my lips.

Nicolas held my gaze as he continued. "Now, take me, for example. I have no problem with praise and accolades. Feel free to tell me how lovely I am, Eliza."

Grinning at his cheekiness, I shook my head.

He cupped a hand to his ear as if to hear me better. "No applause then? Alright, I shall do my best to recover." I laughed. "But back to the subject of my new character. Additionally, I'll be able to authenticate the role with you and your knowledge base at my disposal."

"Oh, I'm at your disposal, am I?" The quip just slipped out without conscious thought, and Nicolas's responding smile was devious.

"Friends help one another, do they not?"

Eyeing him speculatively, I conceded. "I suppose."

He brought his hands together in a *there, you have it* gesture. "While I plan to pick your brain and gather your medical insights at a later date, I actually came here tonight with ulterior motives."

Cassandra's words from weeks ago come back to me then. *You deserve some ulterior motives.* She'd said it like it was something wicked or indulgent, visiting the theater under the pretense that I wasn't there to see Nicolas. And I suppose it had been. Those cravings were entirely selfish, but in the beginning I'd just wanted to content myself with seeing him, witnessing him alive and well on the stage. Knowing my definition of an ulterior motive, I wondered what Nicolas could possibly be indulging.

I didn't want to claim that I knew this version of Nicolas as well as I had when we were younger, but he gave the appearance of being a bit nervous. Now I was very curious.

When he was finally able to raise his eyes to mine, Nicolas admitted, "My mother is in town for the next month. I told her that you and I were back in each other's lives and she was quite desperate to see you." Now that, I was not expecting. I could feel the blood leaving my face at the implications. Nicolas, perhaps sensing the rise of my panic, hurried out, "I understand if attending a dinner at my sister's home would be overwhelming, but would you consent to having tea with Mother and myself? We could even come here if that would make you more comfortable to be in your own home, in your own space."

I didn't know how to answer. Fear and something edging toward anger gripped me. Did I want to see Rosemary Morgan again? The woman who'd begged me to marry her dying son. The consequences of which had plagued me for over six years. I didn't blame her, per se, but I didn't know how to separate Rosemary's involvement with my painful past. Similar to my initial reaction to seeing Nicolas, my heart and my mind had sealed away all of that hurt and those aching memories in a chest. And I'd never wanted to open it ever again.

Now I had this new relationship with Nicolas. We were trying. Could I do the same with his mother?

After much too long a time, I finally replied. "You told her we were reacquainted?"

"No, I told her we were friends," Nicolas said simply. His preference for that word was becoming annoying.

"Was she upset?" In truth, I had no idea how Rosemary would feel about my renewed presence in her son's life. Mothers could be tremendously protective. I had firsthand knowledge that this mother in particular, would do anything for her children.

Nicolas's brows lowered immediately. Dropping his foot to the ground, he leaned forward, placing his forearms on the desk. "No, Eliza. She's not angry or upset or any other thing you're fearing. Mother was relieved and so happy to hear you are well. She was thrilled to know we're no longer living separate lives here in London. I assure you, she wants the same. She wants to know you again."

I nibbled thoughtfully on my lower lip. Nicolas wouldn't lie to me about her reaction. He wouldn't exaggerate it either. Rosemary must truly wish to meet with me. Guilt was trying valiantly to overwhelm, but I pushed it down.

"Please, Eliza. I'll be there, I promise. She—just has so much she wants to say to you. And … I think you need to hear it." Nicolas's green eyes were pleading.

I swallowed painfully. "All right. I think I can manage tea."

Logically I knew that Rosemary would not come into my home with ill intent. She wasn't going to accuse me of ruining her family or failing in my marriage to Thomas. I knew this.

But fear wasn't rational. It built and fed off our innermost anxiety. It hardly mattered what she wanted to discuss. Nothing from my past felt like a safe topic. In an effort to avoid all the awful events from our shared history, I'd barred the pleasant memories as well. I didn't let myself think about the happier times from my childhood. How could I? When so much pain came after, eclipsing all the good.

I just hoped whatever Nicolas's mother had to say wasn't more than I could bear.

THE FOLLOWING afternoon was apparently as good a time as any for tea with my former mother-in-law.

Father and Meg were working in the clinic, and I was praying for an emergency to call me away. I was nervous and fretting over Rosemary's upcoming visit.

Checking the timepiece on the mantle of the drawing room proved I had forty minutes until Nicolas and his mother were due.

The majority of my fears stemmed from the unknown. I didn't know how Rosemary would receive me. Nicolas had said she wished me well and wanted to be a part of my life once more. But who could say whether her intentions would change when faced with the reality of me, here in this drawing room.

I knew Nicolas would protect me. I didn't necessarily like that idea nor would I wish to pit mother against son … once again. But I had to admit, the thought of facing Rosemary without Nicolas by my side felt terrifying.

Therefore, I was immediately gripped with panic when Botstein entered the room with Rosemary in tow a full thirty-eight minutes ahead of the appointed time. Alone. No Nicolas in sight.

There was a time when I would have been as comfortable with Rosemary as I was with my own father. She was my mother's closest friend prior to her death, and she'd accepted me into her family without reservation. We'd been as close as mother and daughter from childhood to early adulthood. The viscountess had never made me feel like an outsider, and for that I would be forever grateful. I'd been a lonely girl with no mother and a busy father. Rosemary had given me a loud and rambunctious family—a sense of belonging. Leaving Wiltshire had been difficult for so many reasons.

One of them was currently staring at me with tears welling in her beautiful green eyes.

"Eliza, my dear. Look at you." Her smile was wide but her voice broke on the final word.

I found myself suddenly choked with emotion and unable to speak. But it didn't matter. Rosemary rushed forward and enveloped me in her arms. Her tight embrace further robbed me of speech, but I squeezed her back just as tightly.

She pulled away enough to take me in, hands still clasping my shoulders. Her eyes moved between my own and seemed to alight everywhere: the blond curls spilling forth, my royal blue day dress, and the myriad of emotions flashing across my face.

Finally, Rosemary's hands moved down to clutch my own. "You're so beautiful. So grown up. I can hardly believe it." Her smile was still watery yet determined.

"Hello, Rosemary," I eventually managed. "Come. Let's sit."

With a final squeeze of my hands, she released me and proceeded to the settee near the fireplace. I took the paisley armchair across from her.

"Where is Nicolas?" I asked, still feeling off balance.

"He's meeting me here. Rehearsal this morning apparently. I'm staying with Roberta and her family for the duration of my visit and their home isn't very far at all." There was no accusation in her tone, but I couldn't help but consider the implications. There were Morgans in London and we lived in essentially the same neighborhood. My avoidance was noticeable but had it been noted? I couldn't tell from Rosemary's words.

"I see. And how is Roberta?"

She smiled. "Oh, she's wonderful. She and Victor have five children now. They keep their grandmother very busy." She continued with family updates, and I was grateful that I didn't need to ask. It was a reminder that I'd left them all behind and didn't know them anymore—no longer part of their lives or their family. "Francesca and Matthew are actually in Dover for the next fortnight with their three children. And Miller is making a fine viscount."

"That's wonderful. I'm so glad they are healthy and well." I took a bracing breath, knowing what I needed to say but unwilling to dim the happiness I saw in

Rosemary's eyes. "I wanted to say how very sorry I was to hear about Robert. I should have—"

"Thank you, Eliza." She cut me off. "It's alright."

It really wasn't. The reminder of her husband's death just a year after Thomas's was still painful. I didn't want to rehash the past but something told me this visit wouldn't be just pleasantries. We obviously had things to discuss. The very least I could do was pass along my condolences for the viscount. Lord Fritterton had been a wonderful husband and father. And he'd been welcoming and friendly to a young girl who'd been lost and lonely.

"It's not alright, Rose. I want to apologize for not returning your letters and for everything that came after. I was eager for a fresh start and overwhelmed. I am so very sorry for the pain I caused your family. I—"

"Eliza, stop this. You have nothing to apologize for." I opened my mouth to argue but she sent me a sharp maternal look that had me holding my tongue. It reminded me so much of how she scolded her children that my throat constricted, preventing further interruption. "I came here to seek *your* forgiveness. I've known for a long time now that I was wrong. What I asked of you. I should never have manipulated you in such a way. I knew how close you and Thomas were. Your friendship was special and I was selfish to push you toward him in marriage. Wrong to beg you for it. It's no excuse but I was a mother living in denial about his condition and his future. I thought I could will a marriage and family and normalcy into being. Can you forgive a mother's failing, Eliza? I was weak. I should have been brave for not only Thomas but for you as well."

"I don't blame you. I don't." I shook my head.

"You should, darling." Two tears rolled down her cheeks at her admission. "You were a child. And I put you in the middle of an impossible situation. Nicolas told me you blamed yourself for his departure, and knowing that you've lived with that pain for so very long is unconscionable, Eliza." She used a handkerchief to wipe her eyes. "I will understand if too much time has passed and if my presence in your life is too painful. I won't persist in seeking your company if you do not wish it. But I wanted to come here today to tell you how very sorry I am."

"Of course, Rose. Of course, I forgive you."

Her face crumpled at my words. I rose from my chair and joined her on the settee. Taking her in my arms, I felt emotion, thick and heavy.

Blame was a ruin. We'd likely been punishing ourselves for years. I'd buried myself under grief and guilt while Rosemary sought to atone for the damage long since wrought. I suddenly felt like a coward for allowing myself to be so consumed that I refused all contact with the Morgans and left Thomas's town-house to rot.

Voice rough with regret, I murmured, "I never should have cut you off. You were my family, too."

Rosemary's grip tightened in response before she pulled back to meet my gaze. "You did what you needed to do in order to protect yourself. I don't begrudge you that. And I don't blame you for it either."

I nodded, unsure how to proceed from here. Thankfully I was given a brief reprieve as Botstein entered with our tea service. I poured for both of us and we sipped in near comfortable silence for a few moments.

"There's no pressure, you know," Rosemary began. "I know you've reconnected with Nicolas and you both deserve a second chance together after I was so willfully ignorant in your youth." I frowned at that. "But there are no expectations from me or the rest of the family. Obviously we would love to be in your life, but if you aren't ready, I promise we will not push."

My mind was still lodged firmly behind her assumption that Nicolas and I were somehow involved and resuming the initial attraction from our youth. "I'm happy to become reacquainted with you and everyone else. I'd love to meet Roberta's and Francesca's children and see Miller again after so long—all of it. But I don't want you to think that Nicolas and I—we're not—we're hardly acquaintances. We're attempting to be friends."

Rosemary smiled sadly at my unconvincing rebuttal. "It would be okay if you were happy, my dear. I want that for you. And if you found that happiness with Nicolas. Well, I would be doubly happy."

My heart rate increased at the implication behind her words. I couldn't fathom she actually meant that she supported a romantic entanglement with Nicolas. "We're starting over. Trying to know each other as we are now."

She nodded and took a sip of her tea before replying. "I know." She either found my words unconvincing or seemed unbothered by their innocent nature. I didn't want her to get the wrong idea. Similarly, I didn't wish to hurt Nicolas. If both mother and son had visions of a future for us—I didn't want to disappoint anyone.

I shook my head and looked away. "I don't know how to resolve this, Rosemary. After so many years, how could your family—Nicolas's family—accept me as anything beyond a mistake, a sad footnote in our shared history."

She made a disbelieving noise. "Never think that way. *You* are our family. Just as much as Nicolas is. You're a daughter of my heart. And a mother wants happiness for all her children. Thomas is gone. But if he were here, he would want you to be happy. And Nicolas as well."

I took a moment to focus my attention, simply breathing through the revelations of the last half hour. While I was grateful for the opportunity to finally say what needed to be said, I couldn't ignore the overwhelming emotions and intensity of this meeting. I was simply unable to process the idea of having Rosemary's blessing to … be with Nicolas. In all my considerations, the Morgans were one aspect I didn't know how to circumvent. And here was their matriarch wishing me well in my relationship with her son.

I considered Jane's advice on the subject. As if love were simply a choice, and choosing Nicolas was as easy as that. Could I forego the guilt I'd clung to and allow Rosemary's visit to heal some of the pain I lived with?

Could Nicolas and I possibly be together without hurting each other? Would it be worth the risk?

Moments later, Botstein arrived with Nicolas whose steps slowed as he moved to join us. He immediately took in the nearly empty teacups and the intensity enveloping the room. His gaze moved to the clock on the mantle. "Am I late?"

His mother held out her hand. "No, come sit. The fault was my own. I fear I'm growing old and confused. I must have noted the time incorrectly. Elizabeth and I have been reacquainting ourselves." I laughed inwardly at Rosemary's assertion that she was anything but sharp and calculating.

Nicolas's eyes shot to me in concern.

I smiled to reassure him. "Come join us, Nicolas. I'll send for a fresh pot of tea."

He approached slowly and finally sat next to his mother on the settee, scrutinizing my face, looking for damage from the conversation from which he'd been excluded. He could likely see the tears I'd shed, view the wreckage of my discussion with his mother.

"No need to send for tea," he admitted. "I tend to drink coffee nowadays."

He was still uneasy, concerned with whatever had happened before his arrival. I knew why. Nicolas had promised to be here for me—to face this difficult conversation together. I'd made the mistake of relying on his presence and been blindsided instead. But none of it was his fault. He'd been handled by Rosemary as much as I had. I didn't blame him. Seeking to assure him of my well-being felt necessary in this moment. My protector was floundering and likely blaming himself for something he had no control over.

"I see." I smiled. "I'll be sure to have some on hand next time."

My words felt like an offering—a promise of a future that I hadn't entirely accepted. But I could give Nicolas this, friendship or something else. He'd be welcome in my drawing room with coffee instead of tea and the knowledge firmly ingrained that he'd be available for the difficult conversations I'd have to face.

Nicolas smiled gently. *Invitation accepted.*

"Well," Rosemary said suddenly, snapping Nicolas and I out of our shared moment. Her smile was satisfied. "I'm feeling rather tired. Nicolas, take your mother to rest."

Nicolas frowned. "But I've just arrived."

Sudden disappointment at his aborted visit had me frowning as well.

Placing her teacup on the table and rising from the sofa, Rosemary said, "Yes, but I've been here occupying Eliza's time. Now I am ready to retire, and I'm sure she is required by her patients."

Still pouting, Nicolas stood and offered his arm. He escorted his mother to me where I'd risen as well. She clasped my hands once more. "When you're ready, I would love to see you for dinner. We all would," she assured me.

Nicolas watched our exchange with such unveiled hope and yearning that I felt paralyzed. Swallowing against the emotion clogging my throat, I nodded and finally said, "I'd like that."

Sixteen

The early spring weather was quite fair today. The sun was shining and hints of green were transforming gardens throughout Mayfair.

Father and Meg were seeing patients while I worked on notes and bookkeeping. I had a quarter of an hour remaining before I needed to leave for Tuesday embroidery at Fiona's home and had no plans to discuss the latest developments with Nicolas with my circle. Everything was growing muddled. I was already waging a battle within. There was absolutely no need to add six additional perspectives. This felt like a decision I needed to make on my own terms.

I put away the patient files I'd reviewed, and after a quick goodbye for Father and Meg, I went to retrieve my embroidery and asked Botstein to have the carriage brought around.

The ride had cheered me somewhat. I was determined to be attentive and engaging with my friends. I'd never been comfortable being the sole focus of anyone's attention. But I refused to allow my lingering awkwardness to impact my visit today.

When I entered the Duchess of Compton's home, I realized I was probably the last lady to arrive. I heard loud laughter and conversation as I made my way down the corridor to the drawing room we occupied regularly.

When I heard the low tones of a man's voice mixed in with those of my friends, my feet slowed. And when I placed that voice, they stopped altogether.

What was going on?

I approached the open doorway slowly. My mouth dropped open as I took in the scene. Nicolas—my Nicolas—was here, in the Duchess of Compton's drawing room sandwiched between Cassandra and Jane on the large tufted sofa. He held an embroidery hoop—of all things—and presented his progress to Ashleigh and Fiona who were seated in the settee directly across from him. Mary and Kathleen occupied the adjacent armchairs in front of the fireplace.

"Eliza, you're liable to catch flies with your mouth hanging open like that." Cassandra's words drew every eye in the room to my position hovering by the entrance. A chorus of "Eliza!" went up from nearly everyone else.

My feet were still uncooperative as I stared at Nicolas, who appeared at home and quite comfortable at *my* ladies' salon. "What—what is happening here?"

"Mr. Viso—apologies—Mr. Morgan wished to learn embroidery," Jane replied. "Isn't that lovely?"

"He—what?" Stunned confusion overwhelmed. How was he even here?

"I told you I should like to learn to sew, Eliza," Nicolas added helpfully.

"Yes, but how did you find yourself learning the feminine art of needlework in the Duchess of Compton's home?

Nicolas's features conveyed exaggerated disapproval. "Really, Eliza. Feminine art? I'm fairly certain men can learn to sew. It's not a skill exclusive to your sex. You should really be more open-minded," he tsked.

Mary and Cassandra nodded encouragingly while I blinked slowly.

"Do join us, Eliza dear. Stop lurking in the doorway," Ashleigh called out.

With a concentrated effort I moved to the closest chair and deposited my bag on the floor. Mary shoved a teacup in my hands while Ashleigh forced a biscuit onto the ledge of my saucer. "Here, it looks like ye could use this," she whispered, eyes alight.

"I invited him," Jane admitted, belatedly answering my question. "Nicolas had a meeting at Fairbanks House with Q." My brows furrowed in confusion. Why would Nicolas consult with the Earl Sullivan? They'd only just met at the theater. Undeterred by my obvious confusion, Jane said, "I informed him that I was leaving for our Tuesday embroidery meeting and he said he'd heard of it. So I asked Mr. Morgan if he wanted to join us."

Incredulous, I met Jane's unaffected gaze. "So he just accompanied you here?" Why was I being difficult about this?

It was my friend's turn to look confounded. "Q escorted us, Eliza. He's here somewhere with Compton. Lord knows what they're up to."

"I believe Gregory had a horse to show him," Fiona smoothly cut in. Her expression was hesitant. She was evaluating my reaction and had likely anticipated the absolute upheaval Nicolas's presence here had wrought.

I looked to Nicolas. "Wouldn't you feel more comfortable with Sullivan and Compton … looking at a horse?"

I couldn't explain it, but I felt betrayed. My worlds were colliding once more. It was that same nervousness I'd experienced at the theater when Nicolas had met Jane and Sullivan.

I'd come here today with the intention of having a normal afternoon with my ladies. I hadn't wanted to discuss my friendship with Nicolas. They were opinionated and invested in our romantic future, and I didn't yet know how to rectify that.

"Why would I?" He appeared genuinely confused as to why I was questioning his presence in this particular drawing room. "I'm here to learn to embroider." I had no words. *Of course*. Of course Nicolas was being his charming self and my friends were fawning all over him. "Well, not from Jane," he amended with a wink. "No offense intended."

"None taken!" Jane beamed.

"This is highly inappropriate." I sounded prim and insufferable to my own ears.

His eyebrows lifted high on his forehead before he glanced pointedly at the occupants of the room. "There are rather a lot of women in this room, Eliza. While I appreciate the vote of confidence for my prowess, it's rather unnecessary."

Ashleigh snorted a laugh. I ignored it. I similarly disregarded Cassandra covering her mouth with her hand.

Nicolas had always been very much mine—my past and my … person. Why was I feeling proprietary over his time and choice of companions? Especially these women. I loved all of them. I was being ridiculous.

"It's not a dare, Nicolas," I admonished. I could not stop myself from speaking and making a fool of myself. His presence here had thrown me completely off balance. I'd just resigned myself to avoiding the topic of him, thinking it was best for all involved. But here he was, further insinuating himself in my life. Meeting and charming my friends, burrowing deeper. Was I ready for that?

"Challenge accepted," Nicolas retorted with a grin.

I stood abruptly, relinquishing the tea and biscuit I'd left untouched. "Alright. That's enough."

I marched over to Nicolas and grabbed his arm and essentially dragged him from the room. He still looked amused, either unaware of the seriousness in my tone or ignoring it in favor of his audience.

"No need to manhandle me. I'll accompany you anywhere you like." This earned him copious amounts of laughter in the wake of our exit.

Eyeing the far end of the corridor, I continued hauling Nicolas until we had a relative amount of privacy.

"I don't know why you're so upset. We were having a lovely time," Nicolas said as we faced each other beside a window and potted fern.

"Until I got there, is that it?" I accused, hands on hips.

He pursed his lips as he considered this. "Well, actually, yes."

"This isn't a performance, Nicolas. It's not some role in which you seek to entertain my friends and insinuate yourself. This is my life." Confrontation rarely sat well with me. My palms were damp and my heart was racing out of control—much like my words.

He frowned before saying quietly, "And you don't want me involved in your real life?"

"That's not what I—"

"You're embarrassed of me because I'm not a titled lord. I'm not part of your world, is that it?" He crossed his arms defensively.

"No, of course not," I argued.

"But I can't meet your friends." It wasn't a question. It was an accusation. "I thought I was your friend. Your friends can't meet your other friends?"

Why was he forcing my hand? Like an animal backed into a corner, I lashed out.

I thought of his letters and his heated gaze. Remembering my conversation with Rosemary and her open encouragement to find happiness with her son.

"Is that truly what you want, Nicolas? To be my friend?" My words were low, barely audible. I needed this answer, and yet I didn't know if I was ready for it. I'd been pushing aside these thoughts for so long that my willful ignorance waited with bated breath.

Nicolas's gaze was steady. Honesty had never been a problem for him. "No, Eliza. I do not want to be merely your friend. I want to be in your life, in all aspects. I want to share a home with you. I long for your comfort and warmth at the end of the day. I cherish your thoughts and ideas and do not wish to be relegated to correspondence on your desk."

Nicolas huffed a humorless laugh and rocked back on his heels. His eyes were determined, expression unapologetic. "It's not a secret, Eliza. I told you I loved you." Gaze locked on mine, Nicolas advanced. He moved into my space and backed me into the corridor wall. "*You* are the one who refuses to believe it." Another step. "The only one who doesn't see it." And then a press of his body, hot and hard along the length of mine. "It shouldn't come as such a surprise. We're inevitable, Eliza."

His face dipped down to mine and halted a breath away from my lips. "You want me, too. I know it." His words ghosted between us. I breathed them in and felt my eyes close of their own volition.

To be this close felt like a threat. Nicolas was angry and resolute. He was proving a point, and I lacked the wherewithal to refute him. It was simple. I wanted him. I wanted this. I craved the heat between us and the proximity of his lips to mine.

I swayed forward and our lips touched. Nicolas froze, clearly surprised. Perhaps the point he was trying to impress upon me wasn't supposed to go quite so far. I felt his resolve slipping and the moment he decided to pull away. Even knowing this was wrong and that I couldn't be trusted with Nicolas's heart, I didn't want this moment to end. So with lips still pressed to his, I placed my hands on his chest before sliding them up and around his neck, bringing us flush together. My mouth opened and I tugged on his lower lip gently—and then less gently.

My actions seemed to finally elicit a response because Nicolas's arms came around me, cushioning my back against the wall. He pulled us close and kissed me back. It felt like I'd been waiting for this moment for a very long time. His lips were warm and firm, and I was too full of sensation to worry about the consequences.

As quick as it started, he was the one to end it. Nicolas broke our kiss and pulled back. Eyes closed in refusal, I clutched the lapels of his coat and followed.

"At least you can admit you want me," he whispered. "Now why don't you admit that you're afraid."

My eyes snapped open. Releasing his jacket, I exploded, "Of bloody course I am! I've ruined your life once already. Isn't that enough, Nicolas? How could you possibly want anything to do with me ever again?"

Meeting my righteous indignation with a helping of his own, he demanded, "Because it's my life and my choice. You didn't ruin my life, Eliza. Everything that happened led me to this place, my career, and back to my family. I blame you for nothing. And we're not children anymore. We belong together. We always have. And now we're finally able to do something about it." Nicolas reached down and clasped my hands, bringing them to his chest. After a deep breath in and out, his voice calmed. "Be brave, Eliza. Be brave with me," he begged.

My brain and my heart warred with one another. One relishing in certainty while the other swam in regret. My poor heart filled dangerously at the thought of being Nicolas's foregone conclusion. But my mind knew the consequence of loving someone. I could simply reference the memories from my last attempt. Ruin and destruction ready in their wake.

I'd started crying at some point, angry, frustrated tears. Nicolas blurred before me as I did my best to stand tall. Removing my hands from his grasp, I stepped back. It was as good as a rejection and he saw it.

I could see the future, floating before me, hazy and hopeful. Afternoons at the theater. Nights at the clinic. This man in my bed. I wanted it with a desperation that caused my throat to constrict. But fear and a lifetime of regret kept the admission firmly locked away.

With a wretched and pitying look, Nicolas stepped back putting more space between us. "This isn't finished, and you know it."

I stayed alone in the hallway for some time, alternately crying and attempting to put myself together.

It wasn't long before Jane found me. She'd come alone undoubtedly knowing how horribly I'd respond to a hallway filled with my well-meaning friends. She didn't say anything at first, for which I was extremely grateful. She simply gathered her long mahogany skirts and joined me on the floor. The warm press of her shoulder against mine brought with it a kind of grounding. I was here, in this hallway—not spiraling through the past or lost to my guilt. I had a place and people who cared for me, many of whom were down the hall drinking tea and eating biscuits.

"We probably should have sent Fiona," Jane said finally, breaking our easy silence.

I smiled at the thought of my friends voting on a representative to send to check on me. My face strained uncomfortably as a result, tears having dried on my cheeks. "Why do you say that?"

She sighed. "Because I am not the best equipped to provide comfort or advice. These are not my strengths."

"I don't know that I agree with your self-assessment," I argued. "I also don't know that I require those services."

Jane turned to regard my profile. "Of course you do, Eliza. You need comfort for whatever just transpired with Nicolas. And you need advice to deal with the aftermath." When I neither agreed nor disagreed, she continued. "Do you want to talk about what happened?"

I felt tears gathering behind my eyes once more so I shook my head in the negative.

After a few moments, Jane said simply, "Would it be so bad if Nicolas was in your life as something more?"

I bit my lip and stared pleadingly at my friend instead of responding to a question I had far too many answers for.

I didn't know how to explain the terror I felt at the thought of loving Nicolas and being loved in return. How years of punishment and self-flagellation didn't just go away. Could the Morgans truly accept me as a daughter again? Would I be forcing Nicolas to abandon his family once more? And the ramifications to his burgeoning career as a playwright could very well be impacted by an association with me—a scandalous lady doctor from Mayfair. Our situation seemed complicated and destined for heartache. It already was—I was torturing us both with my indecision.

"I'm scared, Jane."

"Alright. Let's talk through it. Reason it out. What's one thing you're afraid of?" Jane, my logical and pragmatic friend. I almost smiled.

Grasping for something on the surface, I blurted, "I'm worried about his family. About being accepted or resented or … simply remembered as Thomas's wife."

Jane nodded. "What evidence do you possess that they might resent you? Have you spoken to the Morgans?"

I swallowed before admitting, "I actually took tea with Nicolas's mother recently, at his encouragement."

My friend's brows arched high on her forehead. "And? How did it go? Was she angry? Did she hurt you?"

"No. Not at all. We apologized to one another. I think we both said things we'd desperately needed to express. She was contrite and seemed to want to build a relationship with me herself. And—and—I felt relief after our meeting."

"Considering your experience with Nicolas's mother, I think you can lay this particular fear to rest, Eliza. Clearing the air with Nicolas's family and building a relationship with them again will support your future. Typically relationships experience less strain when one receives blessings and support from their respective families. This will be good should you and Nicolas move forward in your … acquaintance," Jane said easily.

I didn't know if she was considering her attempts to reconcile Quinton and his family, but her assessment of my situation had me glancing her way.

Could it be that simple? Did Rosemary's approval and affection reflect the feelings of Nicolas's family as a whole?

"She doesn't have a reason to lie to you, Eliza. His family was a concern and now they're not. They want you in their lives … for you. It's one less hurdle from your past to overcome. You said that Nicolas encouraged you to meet with his mother, to reconcile?"

I nodded.

"Do you think Nicolas wanted you to meet with his mother to bury the past, so you and he could move forward and be happy?"

Turning to Jane, I took in her hopeful and encouraging expression. I felt like a horse being led to water. My friend was corralling my thoughts toward an end goal—one I was frightened to accept despite everything.

And after the fight I'd had with Nicolas, I knew the outcome he'd been hoping for. Perhaps his urging to speak with Rosemary had been as much about healing myself as it was about initiating our future.

"I think you're right, Jane. But I also think he knew I needed to forgive and be forgiven for my own well-being." My heart squeezed as I considered Nicolas's guiding hand in reconciliation. And then I winced when I thought about his anger and my hesitation in this very hallway.

Jane turned to me again. "Can I ask you something different?" At my nod, she continued, "Why did you encourage Q in his attentions for me last autumn?"

I frowned. I hadn't expected that. "I suppose, I supported his suit because I felt like he was worthy of you in a way John would never be. You are my dearest friend and you deserve all the happiness in the world. I wanted you to find love and be with someone you felt passionate about. Not the lukewarm feelings Sir Soggy Britches inspired. The way Quinton looked at you … he was completely enamored. And I found I could support the man for loving you the way you deserved."

Jane nodded as if that was the answer she'd expected. "And that, Eliza, is how I feel now. I'm fairly confident that Nicolas loves you. Even I am not oblivious to the signs. He talks about you with such wonder and awe. As someone else who loves you dearly, I feel a connection to him—as if we both share the same secret. It felt natural to include him in our weekly gathering. For everyone in that room cares for you. Nicolas is just the newest inductee." My smile was water-logged. "I'm sorry if extending the invitation to him was the wrong decision. You were clearly surprised and it did not go the way I'd hoped."

"I don't know what to do," I admitted.

"That's alright. You're human. You need time to process and consider your options."

I nodded at Jane's encouragement.

Like most of humanity, I was about to do something incredibly stupid.

Seventeen

The home of Lady Mary Harris, daughter of the Earl Huffleton, must have been lit with one thousand candles. The ballroom was an absolute crush. Couples vied for the dance floor, and nearly everyone in attendance looked thrilled in their discomfort. Mary likely had *the* society event of the spring on her hands.

I cast a sly glance her way. She looked miserable. Her unfortunate fiancé, Lord David Shephard, was perhaps the only person absent from this soiree. I felt terrible for Mary. Luckily she was flanked on either side by Ashleigh and Cassandra, each holding two champagne flutes.

I wouldn't mind an extra champagne flute myself. It had been three days since my confrontation with Nicolas. After sitting in the hallway working through possible solutions to my problem, I'd had Jane pass along my apologies to the ladies and I'd quietly taken my leave and returned home. But I'd known that tonight was important for Mary and would be difficult with Lord David away on the continent. I wanted to show my support. So here I was, with my friends as they stood with Mary and discouraged outside attention. With Cassandra so well sought-after by eligible bachelors, avoiding notice was always a challenge.

Finally succumbing to the heat of the ballroom, I flipped open my fan.

"Oh, that's an excellent idea," Jane said from my side.

With fans fluttering, I caught a flash of blond hair moving through the crowd in my direction. My pulse jumped and I straightened, craning my neck to follow the path of Dr. Kenneth Miles.

"What is it?" Jane asked, having noticed the way my attention had strayed.

"I thought I saw someone," I replied absently from behind my fan, ducking discreetly behind her. God, was he coming to talk to me about the arrangement we'd discussed some time ago? I'd never received word from him in agreement or denial, and therefore, put him completely out of my mind. If I was being honest, it had not been difficult to ignore thoughts of Dr. Miles.

"Who did you see?"

Ah, yes. There. I lost track of him in the crowd until I spotted him again. He'd stopped his progress toward me and was speaking to Earl Huffleton. "Dr. Kenneth Miles."

Jane coughed suddenly into her champagne glass. Ignoring the subject of my attentions momentarily, I looked questioningly at her.

Her voice was slightly strangled. "Dr. Miles is Kenneth? He's Dr. K. Miles?"

My gaze narrowed. "Yes. We're acquainted due to the nature of our profession and, you may recall, he has expressed some interest in courting me." That was an understatement. But I was not prepared to admit to my dearest friend that I'd propositioned Dr. Miles and then completely forgotten about him.

"Oh." She remained thoughtful.

After a protracted silence in which I turned my attention back to the man in question and ignored her conflicted nature, Jane asked quietly from behind her fan, "Isn't it odd? For him to be here?"

"I suppose, a bit. But he is the earl's physician. And they attend the same club. I believe they are quite friendly."

"Oh," Jane repeated, frown still firmly in place. "Why are you so interested in his presence here?"

I didn't particularly wish to answer that. So I delayed my response.

Thoughts and scenarios played out in my mind. Options and routes simultaneously considered and then discarded, before something settled with uncomfortable resolution.

Dr. Miles concluded his conversation with the earl and was moving my way once more. Our eyes met, and his answering smile was wide and telling.

An option had unexpectedly presented itself and it was staring me in the face, quite by chance. I could resume my flirtation with Dr. Miles—if he was indeed willing—and endeavor to pursue happiness from an arrangement with the good doctor and allow Nicolas the freedom to find someone else to love—someone deserving, someone who didn't let fear dictate their every decision.

Dr. Miles's presence here and now seemed like a sign. Spontaneous and conveniently-timed. I should move on and allow Nicolas the same courtesy. He needed a partner who was worthy of him. Not his brother's widow who was trapped by their shared history.

Perhaps I was being rash. I was. I knew it. But after wallowing in self-pity and doubt for the last three days, I realized I needed to stop hurting Nicolas. I didn't know if I'd ever be ready to put the ghosts of our past firmly behind us. My fears and inability to give Nicolas what he wanted was tearing us apart.

"Eliza?" Jane's question pulled me from the fog of stubborn decision making.

"I'm so sorry. I'm distracted."

Approaching, Dr. Miles cut a rather dashing figure in his formal attire, I noticed absently. With a respectful bow, he stood before us. After an awkward moment, I realized I should introduce him to Jane and blurted, "Dr. Miles, this is my friend Lady Sullivan. Jane, this … my colleague, Dr. Miles."

Jane's eyes widened, and Kenneth, undoubtedly, frowned at my introduction, but he greeted my friend politely.

Turning to me, Dr. Miles took my hand and I fought to not jerk away. Not a promising start. But I ignored my instincts.

"Apologies for being out of touch. I've been frightfully busy," he admitted. "I'm so grateful that we are both in attendance this evening. It will give us time," he paused with a quick glance at Jane who watched us unabashedly. And in a lowered voice continued, "Time to resume our prior conversation for a happy solution."

Oh, god. He was going to agree to the assignation. Why did my stomach twist violently at the thought?

Kenneth was still speaking, "Perhaps we could take the next dance and then discuss?"

I fluttered my fan to dispel the oppressive warmth of the ballroom and fought to reach a decision. I could dance with him. I *should* dance with him. Dr. Miles could be the answer I'd been looking for, a way to let Nicolas go.

Jane's reaction was immediate despite the question not being directed at her. "But you never dance."

That was categorically accurate. And I'd told Nicolas the same. I typically didn't share my affections so openly. Dancing with Dr. Miles would be momentous in and of itself, and would hopefully lead to the outcome I sought: future happiness for all parties.

My heart attempted to intercede, reminding me of Nicolas's own request to dance—at six balls, if need be. I did my best to shake off the disquiet and the doubts.

With a deep breath for courage, I replied, "Well, perhaps it's time I start."

Dr. Miles seemed pleased and offered Jane another polite nod before attempting to lead me through the throng and to the dancefloor.

I felt an urgent tug on my sleeve. Turning back, Jane appeared alarmed.

"Just one moment, Dr. Miles," I said with false brightness before letting Jane drag me some distance away for a private word.

"This isn't you, Eliza," she hissed. "You are being rash and reactionary. What about Nicolas?"

I swallowed painfully before managing, "Nicolas deserves to be happy … with the right person. I think—I think this is what I need to do."

She said nothing, expression worried. Her hand slid off my arm as I turned.

Determination and resolve fueled my progress as I muttered apologies and forced my way through the crowd of revelers. I reached Dr. Miles, and after slipping my hand into his, we slowly made our way to the edge of the dancefloor as couples shuffled to either exit the previous dance or join the next waltz, the strains of which had just begun. Everything seemed to slow as my vision tunneled. I could feel my hand damp with perspiration as Dr. Miles held it loosely.

What was I doing?

I cast a quick, panicked glance to my friends across the ballroom. They watched as Dr. Miles and I moved in time to the music.

This was the right thing. Dr. Miles was the safer choice. He was staid and practical. We had much in common with our careers in medicine. Our pasts and families were not connected in any complicated way. There were no riotous emotions nor overwhelming passion between us. Therefore, it was extremely unlikely that I could ever hurt Dr. Miles. But for some reason my breath was coming too fast. Much faster than the dance warranted.

With Nicolas, there was always the risk of feeling too much. Just considering the confrontation we'd had in Fiona's hallway made me mentally pause. I couldn't fathom having an explosive row consisting of shouting and crying with Dr. Miles. Those kinds of arguments could only happen with someone essential—someone you loved. Or else you'd never recover. Even shouted demands and a deluge of tears wouldn't drive them away. Someone like family. Someone so deep in your heart you'd never extract them. Not through time or distance, nor force of will.

Nicolas had said it wasn't finished—whatever *this* was between us. And that was how he knew, I realized. He believed we were tied together and there was nothing that could drive us apart. Not surface emotions. Not drugging kisses. And not even the past.

We're inevitable.

Both body and mind rebelling, I swallowed against the painful lump in my throat as Dr. Miles moved us into the final turn. My body felt too tight. His touch on my skin unbearable.

Was Nicolas right? Were we destined to pull one another in an agonizing orbit for the rest of our lives? Was this how he felt when he thought of me? Like destiny—inescapable and certain.

We're inevitable.

With the wreckage of my thoughts and the final notes of the waltz ringing in my ears, I received Kenneth's bow with a curtsey of my own.

This was all wrong. I never should have …

Dr. Miles straightened with a hand smoothing his blond hair back into place. But the bright smile lifting his flushed cheeks died on his face when our eyes met. "Eliza, whyever are you crying?"

I couldn't do this. I was making a horrible mistake.

Searching and confused, I raised my gloved fingertips, surprised to find moisture on my face. I opened my mouth to speak but movement beyond Dr. Miles caught my eye. My lungs seized as my chest constricted. "Nicolas," I breathed.

And there he was. His stricken gaze moved between me and my dance partner and I knew exactly what he was thinking. The implications were written all over his face. With a visible tightening of his jaw, Nicolas met my eyes one final time before giving a hard, decisive nod. He spun abruptly and began winding his way through the crush.

My face crumpled and my feet moved without conscious thought. I had to fix this. I had to talk to him. I had been so very wrong.

Inexplicably, a hand tightened smartly around my wrist, garnering my attention and pulling me back. "Eliza?" came Dr. Miles's incredulous question, gaze trained on Nicolas's retreating back.

I'd forgotten our dance. He'd been so easy to abandon in the face of my pursuit. In that, I had my answer. I'd never feel more than a passing fondness for Dr. Kenneth Miles as evidenced by how quickly he'd fled my thoughts entirely in favor of another.

"I'm sorry, Dr. Miles. I never should have—I'm sorry. I have to go." I didn't have time to make him understand. There was no tactful way to end an aimless flirtation that had only existed in convenience for us both. Not here and certainly not now. How did you admit that your heart was already occupied? It was locked up tight and only one man held the key. He'd earned it years ago and would possess it as long as I lived.

I ripped free of his severe grip and made to follow Nicolas out the front entrance. My progress was excruciatingly slow. There were bodies everywhere. I could only hope that Nicolas was hindered similarly.

Finally emerging on the front drive, I bustled quickly toward the street, determined to spot any sign of his whereabouts. And then I saw him—on the next block climbing into a hackney. I'd never make it. I simply had to hope he'd return to his home.

Retreating to the front drive of the estate, I was surprised to see my driver and carriage trundling my way.

"Lady Mary sent word. Said you'd be ready to depart," said my driver, Harold.

"Yes! Thank you. Right away. To the Strand. The Joc Collins Theater." And without waiting to be helped, I pulled myself into the carriage and slammed the door behind me.

As we trundled away from the Huffleton residence, I shifted on the red velvet bench seat and finally noticed the hem of my gown trapped in the closed carriage door. With a frustrated jerk, I ripped the bottom edge of my dress, lace and beading spilling loose. It didn't matter. If I could just get there—to the theater residence—I could explain everything to Nicolas. I'd make it right. I just prayed he'd be willing to listen.

I BURST into Nicolas's rooms without knocking.

He must have arrived only moments ahead of me because he was just shrugging out of his jacket as I entered.

With a sigh, he finished removing the coat and began unbuttoning his cuffs. "What are you doing here, Eliza?"

His voice was resigned and wooden, so far from the demonstrative and engaging creature that was my Nicolas. Fear—bright and wild—slithered into my veins. I opened my mouth, ready to unleash the explanation I'd planned the entire carriage ride over. But nothing came out. Panic and alarm had stolen my voice. Had he decided to well and truly write me off?

"Well?" he questioned listlessly.

My purpose reengaged and anxiety slammed the words forcefully from my lips. "You don't understand." It rang like an accusation, angry and raw. And I couldn't call it back.

"On the contrary, I think I understand quite well."

"No." I shook my head, the denial sounding desperate to my own ears. "You don't. I—I—thought I was doing what was best. I was trying to protect you."

Nicolas frowned. "I saw you dancing with him, Eliza. You clearly made a decision. You told me before. You don't dance with anyone. That it has to *mean* something. And don't say it was to protect me. The only person I need protection from is you."

I blanched at his words, throat tightening with emotion. "No," I whispered.

"So, he's who you want then? Some fair-haired dandy in Mayfair?" Emotion had crept into his tone, but it wasn't an improvement. It was mocking and scornful.

I found my voice and answered honestly, "No."

"But he's who you've chosen?"

Before giving me a chance to answer, Nicolas snorted derisively. "You tried to warn me and I didn't listen. I thought I could convince you. Be present—be a part of your life. Make you see me and all the possibilities for us." He shook his head and looked away. "That was shortsighted and unfair. I thought it didn't matter how I won, as long as I did. But I was so very wrong. I *want* you to want me, after all. I'm desperate for it. And I want you to be as desperate as I am. Not through trickery or mind games. I want to be essential for you. Inevitable."

"You are," I interjected, eyes filling. "You are. I thought I could fight my feelings for you. I thought I could make a choice—change my fate—when all my heart wanted was to surrender. Our problems seemed too big. Our past too prevalent. But I'm tired of fighting myself when the only person I want to fight with is you."

Nicolas was watching me, gaze scrutinizing. There was something else too—a spark of hope. I needed to tread carefully or that tiny flicker might extinguish. But I still needed to be honest.

"What you saw—it was a mistake. A desperate attempt to convince myself that it would be better to let you go and to move on with someone else. But the whole time we were dancing, I wanted it to be you—across six different ballrooms. I knew it would never be anyone else." Frustrated, I wiped at the tears along my cheeks. "I'd already decided I couldn't do it. I couldn't be with him in any capacity. I wouldn't survive it. And then you were there ... at the worst possible moment. When all my truths had finally risen to the surface."

Stepping hesitantly closer to me, Nicolas asked, "What truths?"

I matched his tentative step and closed the distance between us. "Just one, really."

"Say it," he demanded, eyes intent.

"I love you. I never stopped."

And in the next moment, I was crushed in his embrace. Nicolas's arms banded tight around my body, drawing me in. I could feel his face in my neck, breath warm along my collarbone as he dropped kisses wherever his lips could reach. I returned the devastating intensity of his hold. We clung to each other as if escape threatened at any moment. I suppose when something intangible and elusive finally came to fruition, you never wanted to let it go.

Nicolas straightened suddenly lifting me from the ground. My shorter stature meant my feet dangled near his shins, ankles exposed where I'd ripped the fabric away. I kicked my slippered heels off to the side.

"I'm going to make love to you. Do you want that, Eliza? Will you be mine?"

"Yes," I said, nodding quickly for good measure.

Nicolas started moving then—toward the bedchamber, I presumed—and in a sudden moment of panicked honesty, I blurted, "I—I've never done this before. And, I mean, I'm a doctor. I know what to expect. I'm just somewhat anxious."

After pulling back slowly and placing me carefully on my feet, Nicolas's confused frown met my nervous one. "What do you mean, Eliza? You were— you were married."

It was my turn to be confused. "You knew it wasn't like that for Thomas and for me. We weren't lovers. He was like a brother. My best friend and companion. We had no plans to consummate the marriage." Nicolas appeared shocked, absolutely stricken. I felt exposed suddenly, having this unfathomable conversation following my declaration. "Tell me you knew that, Nicolas. Thomas and I did not marry for love."

He looked lost to his memories, replaying and considering. "I didn't know. I thought—I thought I was leaving so you could be happy with Thomas. And I couldn't remain in Wiltshire pining after my brother's wife."

I lunged forward and hugged him tightly around the middle. His arms came up automatically, his embrace desperate. "Oh, Nicolas. I'm so—"

"No more apologies," he cut me off before taking a shaky breath. "Not about the past. Not now and not ever again. This is our second chance, and we're going to take it."

Cheek resting against his chest, I nodded, breathing in his citrus scent. "I love you," I said, the reminder falling freely.

"I love you, too, Eliza."

He led me down the hallway and opened the door to his bedchamber before depositing me inside while he lit and stoked the fire. I stood nervously in the center of the room as I watched the orange flames flicker and grow, filling the spartan space with warmth and glowing amber light.

Nicolas returned to me, cradling my jaw and kissing me. There was no preamble, no hesitation. He kissed me like it was long past due.

I clutched greedily at the lapels of his white waistcoat while I raised up on tiptoe to return his kiss. I didn't want to be passive in our lovemaking. I refused to deny myself this man ever again. While worries for the future and fears of the past may have lingered, they couldn't fight for dominance in this moment. This was about us and what we deserved.

Our kisses stayed deep and consuming. I was suddenly quite desperate to feel more of Nicolas's warm skin. I slipped the buttons free from the fabric of his waistcoat and used my hands to lift his shirt out of his trousers and away from his skin.

Nicolas's hands moved along my neck and wound around my back to begin the arduous task of undoing the buttons of my gown. He growled in frustration, lips receding. "Would you be terribly distraught if I simply cut you out of this dress?"

I smiled against his mouth. "My lady's maid might have something nasty to say about that."

Despite his complaints, he was making decent progress. My beaded bodice had loosened and was starting to droop.

"Well, your lady's maid nearly always has something nasty to say," he teased as his lips journeyed along the column of my neck. "And for some reason you're missing the bottom third of your dress, so I consider this one—lovely as it may be—somewhat of a lost cause already."

As I relished in my exploration of Nicolas's smooth chest and stomach, the fabric of my gown finally gave way and he was able to push the material down to the floor. He spun me around and loosened my corset while I mourned the loss of his skin until I felt his breath and lips and tongue on the back of my neck. Nicolas was exceptionally good at managing multiple tasks. He sucked and nipped and lavished attention on the sensitive skin there while he continued disrobing me.

Once I was finally clad in only my thin embroidered shift, I faced Nicolas once more and returned the favor. He was patient with me as I removed his cravat. Nervous fingers loosened and removed his shirt, but he didn't rush me or hurry me along. He simply allowed me to explore the riches I unveiled.

Smooth skin stretched taut over muscle and bone. I knew the names of all these body parts, had studied them in medical texts and on many patients over the years. But this body—Nicolas's body—meant something different, something more. He wasn't a collection of scientific words and phrases. This was the shape of my heart, tall and strong and infinitely mine.

With slow, methodical movements, Nicolas raised my remaining undergarment up and over my head. His arms pulled me in close and then he was kissing me once more. "You are so beautiful," he murmured while pressing his lips all over my face. Cheekbones, brows, the corner of my mouth.

His bare skin against mine felt like heaven. I sighed from the force of it. How utterly decadent this was.

I disentangled myself and took Nicolas's hand to lead him toward the bed. Once I positioned him seated on the edge, I sank to my knees and attempted to remove his boots.

His eyes widened as he grabbed my arms and gently lifted me to standing. "Don't do that. It's too—ah—tempting. Just come here. I'll get my boots."

When I finally surmised his meaning, a small shocked laugh escaped me. Nicolas's head snapped in my direction. "Oh, do you find that humorous?"

"A bit," I admitted. "Perhaps I could attempt … to remove your boots," I said with emphasis. "Some other time."

Nicolas's eyes narrowed before a wicked grin took over his features. "Perhaps I shall help *remove your boots*."

"But I'm not wearing boots," I deadpanned.

With a surprised squawk, I landed on the bed with a highly amused Nicolas hovering over me. "Well, for our purposes, pretend you are."

His mischievous green eyes sparkled as he began his descent to the center of my body to deliver on his threat. He stopped along the way to administer hot open-mouthed kisses at various points. My shoulder, the curve of my waist, the under-side of my breast. The feel of his lips on the rosy peak of my nipple had me taking in a shuddering breath. Nicolas noticed and repeated the action on my other breast. Once he'd satisfied his curiosity and catalogued my reactions, he finally lowered himself between my spread legs and released a cool stream of air right over my core.

Looking down, I watched his dark hair as his mouth finally—*finally*—made contact. The flat of his tongue pressed to the bundle of nerves at the apex of my womanhood. My head dropped back as the canopy overhead came into view. Desperate to watch—to see Nicolas nestled between my thighs, I looked down once more. The sight of him was painfully erotic. And god, the sounds his body made with mine had me cringing inwardly and simultaneously tightening deep within.

He was still licking and sucking and kissing my center. The promise of release felt very close at hand. As he focused more and more of his attention at the peak of my entrance, I knew it wouldn't be long. My skin felt tight and constricting. My hands fisted in the blankets at my side.

Suddenly, Nicolas's hands were on mine. The next time I looked down he stared back, up along the length of my body, deliberate in his gaze. With unhurried movements, he loosed my hands from the bedding and placed them on his head, anchoring me there.

And then he went back to work, lips and tongue torturously intent. I ran my fingers through his hair and felt myself grasping and clutching him to me, pulling his mouth in close. As I moved against Nicolas, desperate and inelegant, he sucked and lapped. And then I was falling. The pleasure moved from my core to my limbs and back again. It felt like it might swallow me whole.

When I came back from the delirious fog of my climax, I could feel Nicolas plying my lower lips with tender kisses. I moved my eyes once again from the canopy overhead to watch his very satisfied smile grow wide and knowing. Finally unclenching my death grip on his scalp, I smiled in return. I couldn't find a single mortified or embarrassed cell in my body. That had been … amazing.

Nicolas lifted himself onto all fours, muscles flexing pleasantly as he began his slow return up my body.

"I know you're used to the sound, but I feel as if I should offer a round of applause for that performance," I said, nearly incoherent. I felt boneless with content. At least I did until I noticed Nicolas had removed his trousers at some point and the tip of his manhood dragged along my thigh as he crawled up my body. Then the relaxed and comfortable feeling coiled tight with anticipation. That sensation increased tenfold when Nicolas settled his lean hips in the cradle of my own. His heat and hardness pressed me into the mattress, and I was suddenly alert and expectant.

Nicolas held his upper body aloft as he gazed down at me, smile still firmly on his face. "Feel free to applaud. I like encouragement for a job well done."

I laughed, unable to believe that my nerves had fled so abruptly. I was comfortable here and now. Being in his arms felt like I was right where I belonged. I no longer feared what was to come because I knew Nicolas loved me. He'd already shown me he was willing to put my needs and desires first. And the hollow ache low in my belly told me that my body was ready for more.

When Nicolas finally pushed within, he brought his lips to my ear. His whispered promises cast aside the pinch and pressure, the initial ache and discomfort. His quiet *I'm sorry* and *oh, god* soothed the tension in my limbs. As Nicolas paused to let me adjust to his sizeable invasion, his mouth formed *you're mine* against the skin of my neck, gentling my ragged breaths. And later when his movements stuttered and became frantic driving beats, the strained voice that said *I'll never let you go*, fueled the love singing in my veins.

Eighteen

Nicolas and I exchanged letters for the remainder of the week, but between the clinic and the theater, we'd both been too busy to meet. His correspondence made me smile while drinking my tea or rereading before going to bed. My thoughts strayed to our night together and the future before us.

I'd made love with Nicolas. While we had yet to discuss the future or how our new reality looked moving forward, I knew that would come. Nicolas wasn't one to ignore difficult or awkward situations. He was so honest and forthright, I sometimes worried for his feelings. I didn't know what our joining had meant to him, but I was sure, sooner rather than later, he would tell me. I simply hoped that he would allow me some time to come to terms with us, as a unit. Something I'd been unable to claim in my youth and powerless to deny any longer.

I didn't know if we were lovers in name only. Was I the mistress of Silas Viso, one of the most sought-after performers in London? I had no idea what our future entailed. But I knew I needed time to consider it—to avoid all those worries I had and all the reasons I'd fought our connection for so long. I required time to settle into whatever this was, mostly because I expected disaster to strike at any moment. The last time I let myself hope for a future with Nicolas, I'd been a seventeen-year-old girl who didn't know her world was about to fall apart. Those memories could never be completely forgotten.

A mutual acquaintance, Lady Nethercutt, was hosting a spring ball tonight, and the majority of my social circle was attending. Yet, I'd found myself unwilling to accept. I knew Nicolas wouldn't be there. He had a performance this evening at the Collins. I considered the questions that awaited me with Jane and Cassandra and the others. I could almost envision Fiona's attempts to smooth over and distract from the pervasive tension. Attending tonight's soiree was a reality I wasn't quite ready to face. I was desperate to keep Nicolas and our love private and sacred—just for a little while longer.

Along with the arrival of Nicolas's latest letter at breakfast this morning, the reminder of his evening performance made my decision for me. Therefore, I made my own plans to attend the theater and, as previously instructed by the man himself, prepare my critical remarks for Nicolas following his performance. I smiled to myself at the thought of teasing him. And perhaps more.

Seated alone in my father's box several hours later, I watched the action unfold on stage. There was a portion of the play in which Nicolas's character spoke Italian, and it was my very favorite part. I didn't speak the language and in the scene, another character interprets what is being said—clearly incorrectly translating for the other characters and the audience judging by Nicolas's exaggerated reactions. All part of the show. It was one of the funniest portions of the theatrical comedy. But something about his voice and the way his mouth formed the foreign words, made me lean forward in my seat. Eager was the most accurate way to describe myself when I heard those words fall from his lips.

I needed to ask Nicolas about his use of the language—if it was merely for the role or if he was actually fluent in Italian. I wondered what he looked like up close with those intriguing sounds rolling off his tongue.

I startled out of my warm and wayward thoughts when a small figure settled herself beside me. Angelica beamed, and I found myself smiling back in confusion.

"Tommy told me you were up here, so I came to join you."

I assumed she meant the young boy who acted as messenger and escort among the performers and staff.

"Is that alright?" Her quiet uncertainty made my chest ache.

"Of course," I replied. "As long as you're safe and whoever is meant to be watching you knows where you are."

She nodded eagerly. "I told Miss Pippa and Tommy."

"Alright then."

Angelica leaned forward, unable to resist the pull of the performance. "It looks different from up here."

"It's quite magical, isn't it?" I agreed.

Her delighted smile widened as her eyes sparkled in the dim light. "Will you stay after and visit with us?"

"I must. Nicolas bid me to tell him all my favorite parts and to note whenever he does anything wrong."

She nodded earnestly at my undertaking. "I'll help." And then Angelica turned back to watch the remainder of the performance, her little legs swinging beneath her seat. I watched in amusement as she busied herself with the seriousness of our task.

I wondered idly if her mother was somewhere nearby. Once again an understudy had been utilized in Melinda's place. Perhaps the new arrangement with her marquess provided more security than her role in the play. She seemed to abandon her child as easily as her duties at the Collins. How long would it take before she lost her position and was ejected from the property as a result?

My heart clenched at the implications and the uncertainty Angelica would face if those events came to pass.

She looked over then, smiling her amusement at whatever had transpired on the stage. I pasted on a happy expression to cover the worry swimming below the surface.

When the performance ended, Angelica and I waited a moment while the theater emptied of patrons. And then she took my hand sweetly and led me backstage. On the short walk-through corridors and behind ropes for employees only, Angelica kept up a constant chatter telling me her favorite parts of the play and ways in which Nicolas could improve. I resisted the temptation to laugh at her honest appraisal.

As we neared the dressing area and voices became louder, I slowed our progress as I peeked around the final corner. I would not be well received if Melinda was anywhere in the area. With a curious tug, Angelica laughed as if we were playing a game. Releasing my hand, she took off in the direction of Tommy and Celia who were gathered near the actors. I quickly scanned those assembled but my eyes snagged on a smiling Nicolas. His hair was damp with sweat and he was still in costume from his final scene in the play. My shifting around the corner likely drew his attention and he smiled a brilliant grin, tiny indentions in his cheeks on full display.

When I didn't immediately move from my position, he wandered my way without excusing himself. "Eliza, what are you doing?"

I immediately shushed his overly loud question and ducked back into the hallway.

A moment later, Nicolas's head appeared around the corner. "Are you a spy?" he whispered. "Are we being watched?" He looked pointedly around the corridor as if waiting for unknown danger to present itself.

"No," I hissed. "I wanted to see Angelica safely backstage following the show, but I shouldn't linger in case her mother sees me here."

Nicolas straightened and stepped fully into the hallway, playful demeanor gone. "I told you not to worry about Melinda. You are welcome here and in my home. She has no right to dictate your whereabouts."

"She does when I'm spending time with her daughter," I objected. "Angelica joined me in my box for the latter half of the performance. I wasn't going to let her wander off afterward."

"Come." Nicolas held out his hand. "Melinda isn't here. It's been days. She missed a matinee yesterday and her performance again tonight. Although I wish you'd just let me handle the situation."

My answering glare provided all the response he was going to get.

"Fine. We'll keep hiding in passageways." He rolled his eyes. "I accept the role of handsome operative. I'm afraid your performance could use a little work."

I whacked him on the shoulder with my reticule as he laughed and laced our fingers together before propelling us forward. By now the dressing rooms and backstage area had cleared. I assumed the actors and staff would return to the residence and gather for drinks as they'd done previously.

"Will you stay?" he asked as we walked arm in arm. "I expect a full reporting of my performance as well."

I considered the ramifications of my presence here tonight, but the simple truth was this: I wanted to see him. I wanted his hands on my body, to feel the intimacy he'd ignited so thoroughly days ago. And so I nodded my agreement.

Nicolas led us to his rooms. He deposited me in his cozy sitting room while he changed into fresh clothes. When he returned, he brought with him the scent of citrus and I greedily took in his form in a lavender patterned waistcoat and matching cravat. His dove gray trousers fit snugly to his muscular legs and I did my utmost to swallow against the sudden dryness in my mouth.

His smile was the very opposite of sheepish as he held out his arm and murmured a low "My lady." As we moved to the doorway, Nicolas tugged me back against him. With his nose buried in my neck, I arched reflexively, my head falling back and eyes closing.

"I missed you," he said with a hot, open-mouthed kiss to my neck. "I missed this."

I groaned against his ministrations. When his left hand absently reached down to gather and raise my skirts, voices from the hallway beyond had him pausing.

With a sigh, Nicolas said, "We should go, or I'm liable to drag you to bed instead."

Attempting to regain my composure, I pressed the back of my hand to my flushed cheeks and took a deep breath before taking Nicolas's arm once more.

We made our way to the large parlor—the appointed gathering area for post-performance celebrations. The room was full and loud.

He was constantly hailed and greeted. Hearty backslaps and foisted drinks were delivered with ease. I realized Nicolas was the equivalent of the belle of the ball, and it made me smile.

"Oi, there she be. Dr. Eliza, innit?" The rough voice came from a slightly grizzled man behind Nicolas.

"It's actually La—"

"Dr. Eliza it is," I interrupted before Nicolas could correct the man. I had no need of an honorific here. These people were likely already aware of my profession. Better to cling to that title than any other. "How do you do?"

"I don't see a drink in your hand. Are doctors not allowed to partake?" the man asked. The volume of conversation had dropped nearby. With a quick glance I could see that we'd garnered some measure of attention.

I made a decision then. These people were part of Nicolas's life. Perhaps I'd misjudged them before, and maybe Melinda's vitriol extended to deception about where I was and was not wanted. Mayhap these workers from the Collins just didn't know me. But that didn't mean I couldn't make an effort. I could attempt to be friendly and charming. For Nicolas, I could.

I held out my hand toward his glass. "I'm a physician, sir. Not a nun."

Laughter erupted from those gathered, but it was the pleased grin on Nicolas's face that had me smiling in return.

"Get the good doctor a drink!" bellowed my new friend.

And for the rest of the night, conversation and beverages were never far away. The other actors and backstage staff took great delight in sharing stories about Nick. They were surprised and elated that I had many of my own. My cheeks grew sore from laughter.

Nicolas never left my side. His presence fueled my bravery among his friends and colleagues. I was a version of myself I hadn't been in a very long time. I felt like I was watching this playful and extroverted Eliza from down the exceedingly long lens of a telescope. A discovery that felt both very far away and oddly familiar, like a well-acquainted constellation in the night sky.

The stories continued, likely due to my presence as the newly acquired audience member for their antics. I didn't mind. Where before the obvious kinship and familiarity had cast a resentful light on my previous visit, now I felt included. Not so much an outsider looking in, but someone worth confiding in. I felt like I'd been found worthy of these people who loved my Nicolas so. And I couldn't begrudge them their affection. I knew how difficult he was to resist.

Once it was very late, the eight or so of us remaining were all settled in the sitting area of the parlor.

Nicolas was in a relaxed sprawl beside me on the navy blue velvet settee. His grin was lazy and his cheeks were flushed from jubilant conversation and a fair amount of ale. I was inebriated enough to be exhausted but still managed to remain awake in order to hear those assembled teasing Nicolas for having so many fans and unparalleled popularity. There was quite a bit of ribbing for having his likeness used as an advertisement in the newspaper.

He took it all in good humor, the smile rarely leaving his face.

The heat of his thigh pressed against my own and I thought I could sleep quite comfortably right here with Nicolas's warm body supporting me and his lemony scent filling my lungs.

"Dr. Eliza," my name from the lips of Hugo Bentley—one of the other main actors—drew my attention from the far reaches of encroaching daydreams. "You should join us for the next demimonde ball. It would be far more enjoyable than a soiree with all your toffs in Mayfair. Bring her, Nick," Hugo demanded as the remaining performers and stagehands voiced their support as well.

"That sounds like an excellent idea," I agreed as a small cheer went up and glasses clinked in a toast.

I let my head loll to the side from where it rested on the back of the sofa. Nicolas's did the same, mirroring my position.

I smiled, full of warmth and unexpected acceptance. "Will you bring me to a demimonde ball?"

Nicolas looked entertained. "Do you want to attend?"

And I found I did wish for this scenario in my loose, intoxicated state. I could allow myself to admit that I'd enjoyed tonight immensely. I felt happy and free with my affection in a way that I prayed would remain with the light of morning and the return to reality.

But for now, I could answer in truth. So, I nodded. "Wait, are there rules at these events? Can we dance together six times if we wish?"

Nicolas's green eyes crinkled in amusement. He leaned closer as if to impart a secret, and I forgot for a moment that we weren't alone. His nearness became my sole focus. The light dancing in his gaze, the flush on his cheeks, and the very proximity of his lips to my own made remembering our surroundings a challenge.

"We could even dance seven times, if we so desired," he whispered, the words breathed into our secluded little space.

"I would. So desire," I admitted with a loopy smile.

"So would I," he agreed.

My eyes strayed once more to his lips. I was too comfortable, too at ease in his presence to maintain the distance required for polite company, no matter how informal. With my inhibitions lowered, Nicolas's proximity was dangerous. This night likely would not end without my lips and hands seeking his own.

"What is she doing here?" The angry screech from the middle of the parlor was enough to banish my improper thoughts.

The volume of the words and the venom behind them expunged the fatigue from my brain. I sat up abruptly. All eyes were on Melinda in elegant attire who had paused—I assumed—at the unwelcome sight of me. Before anyone could speak, Nicolas was up and moving toward her, intention and determination in his stride.

"Let's have a chat," he gritted out before ushering Melinda through the open doorway at the far end of the parlor.

I rose on unsteady legs. Nicolas didn't need to fight this battle for me. I was convinced—even now—that his intrusion would only make things worse.

Easing closer to the hallway, I paused behind the threshold when I heard Nicolas's furious voice.

"—what are you even doing, Melinda? Abandoning your child and your position here. Angelica doesn't understand how utterly selfish you are. She just misses her mother. Eliza has done nothing but try to help her, and for whatever reason you feel compelled to threaten her. She cares about Angelica and Angelica cares about her for that matter. So do I. She has every right to be here. Every right to be by my side. She is my future. So get used to her being at the theater and in my home."

She is my future.

God. What was I going to do?

Nicolas had painted a target on my back as thoroughly as his own. I could hear the hysteria in Melinda's tone as she shrieked her rebuttal, but I couldn't make out the words.

Backing away slowly, I caught fragments of Nicolas's reply. "—get your life together—" Nicolas's words came back into focus as my gasps turned to deep inhalations. "—before you lose your job and you can no longer care for your child."

My mind was awash with worry. My presence here—and my intimacy with Nicolas—could have a negative impact on Angelica as well as Nicolas's position. It surely was not good to be involved in such blatant confrontations with the other performers. I realized that Silas Viso was beloved and highly regarded, but I still did not wish for Melinda to cause trouble for him.

Nicolas reentered the parlor, and upon seeing me so unexpectedly close to the entrance, paused in his hurry back to the seating area. "Don't worry. She is leaving. She only returned for some of her things. Her daughter not being one of them," he sneered.

I approached and grasped the front of his waistcoat. "I do not want to cause trouble for you or Angelica."

"I know." Nicolas loosened my hands from the fabric and held them firmly in his own. "It will be alright. She can't make threats or demands of us. If she doesn't stop neglecting her duties here, she'll be sacked any day now."

My breath hitched at the implications for Angelica if that were to come to pass. But I couldn't think of that right now. The altercation with Melinda had me feeling alert and uneasy.

Nicolas squeezed my hands and garnered my attention. His green eyes were troubled, but his tone was light. "Come, let's go and say goodnight to your new fan club." He smiled. "And then you'll stay?"

I appreciated that he asked and didn't assume. While our relationship had progressed and felt very much like it was moving toward ... something, I didn't yet have answers for the future. Expectations were difficult to manage when more than one person was involved.

She is my future.

I wanted that. I loved Nicolas and wanted to be his future. But what that future looked like, I hadn't a clue.

I nodded and managed a small smile. "Yes. Of course, I'll stay."

Nineteen

Knock. *Knock. Knock.*

Nicolas groaned. His arms tightened around me reflexively. "No. What is that? Make it stop." His grouchy sleep-roughened voice made me smile.

The knocks persisted and my amusement fell away. I'd been on the receiving end of summons enough to know that middle of the night intrusions were typically very serious.

I sat up abruptly, pulling the sheet around myself. "Nicolas," I said, shaking his shoulder and dislodging his arm where it had banded snugly across my hips. "You need to get the door. It could be an emergency."

The fire was down to glowing embers. I couldn't find a clock to know the time.

"Fine," Nicolas grumbled. "But then we're going back to bed."

Three more knocks sounded while Nicolas pulled on his trousers and quit the room. Some instinct had me exiting the bed and sliding my shift over my head. I heard the front door open and a frantic whispered voice.

A short while later, a still shirtless Nicolas came rushing into the bedchamber holding the shoes I'd abandoned in his foyer. "Come, it's Angelica."

"What happened?" I asked quickly.

He strode over to his wardrobe and retrieved a robe before helping me shrug it on. His lemon scent washed over me, helping me find calm when panic threatened. "The girls sneaked out of Pippa's apartment where Angelica has been staying. She told Celia that she was sad and missed her mother and wanted to go home. So they waited until Pippa was asleep and went to Angelica's room. Celia admitted she read stories to Angelica until they fell asleep by accident in her bed. Celia woke up to Angelica coughing and gasping and got scared. She didn't seek her mother because she knew they'd be in trouble. So she came knocking at my door instead."

Nicolas retrieved his boots while he spoke, and we made our way quickly to Melinda and Angelica's quarters.

I rushed toward the narrow bedchamber I knew was Angelica's. Celia was crouched beside her friend, worry evident on her tiny face. Angelica was wheezing on the bed, leaning against a mountain of feather pillows. There was no wool blanket in sight, nor the cotton blanket I'd given her for that matter. Angelica's ever-present blue security blanket was equally absent. But something else about this situation was different as well.

"Celia, dear, where did all these pillows come from?" I asked as I lifted Angelica into my arms and sat in the rocking chair.

I'd asked the question gently, but the girl of no more than six years reacted as if struck. She burst into tears. Nicolas lowered himself beside her and spoke in a kind voice. "It's alright, Celia. No one is upset. Doctor Eliza just needs to know about the pillows to help Angelica."

I took the edge of my shift and wiped Angelica's watering eyes and drippy nose.

Finally, Celia answered, "They was in the wardrobe in Miss Melinda's room. We piled them up to sit on and read our stories."

I nodded and smiled. "Thank you for telling me. Now, can you go back to your mother, Celia? I'm going to try to help Angelica. Nicolas, can you bring me the basin and water I see in the other room and a cloth?"

Celia left, still sniffling. And Nicolas rose to do as I requested.

I looked down to the little girl in my arms. "It's going to be okay, Angelica. Can you try to breathe like I am?" With deep inhales and exhales, we attempted to regulate her breathing.

Nicolas returned and wetted a cotton square for me. As I began wiping Angelica's face and hands with the cool water, I asked him to go to Pippa and check the pillows in Celia's bed. I had a theory. I also asked if he could retrieve some boiling water from Pippa's kitchen as well. The steam would help soothe Angelica's airway.

After a time, the wheezing abated. I assisted Angelica in breathing the warm moist air as I braided the hair back from her face. Her inhalations regulated and she became drowsy from all the early morning excitement. Nicolas carried the nearly sleeping child to Pippa's rooms while I removed every feather pillow from the vicinity.

"The girls are resting. Pippa said she'd keep an eye on them." Nicolas watched me from the doorway. "You think it's the pillows?"

"Yes," I agreed. "The ones in Celia's bed are simple cotton batting. Depending on what sort of foul feathers are used in these, Angelica could have developed an affectation over time. Certain allergens plague the body for no rhyme or reason and can present suddenly after months or years of exposure. And she often had her little blue blanket spread across her pillow. That likely lessened her contact and subsequent reaction. The girls pulled out several down pillows this evening. It likely created the severe reaction we witnessed." I sighed. "You'll need to tell Melinda to keep the feather bedding away from Angelica. I don't know how you'll convince her or tell her you reached the conclusion but it's imperative for Angelica's safety."

"Let me worry about that." Nicolas approached, placing his hand on my shoulders to still my nervous fidgeting.

"I checked Melinda's room—looking for more pillows," I admitted.

"I know." It was his turn to sigh.

I looked at Nicolas with a worried frown. Angelica's mother's room had been nearly barren. A trunk was open in the middle of the floor, full of gowns and undergarments. The wardrobe stood open, practically empty. There had been no pillows in sight nor any bedding, linens, or drapery of any sort. "Do you think she's coming back?"

"I don't know."

"She can't simply abandon her daughter. It's unconscionable. I don't care if she found some rich lord to offer her protection."

Nicolas rubbed his hands up and down my arms in a soothing gesture. I was irrationally angry with Melinda for her reckless and irresponsible behavior. She didn't deserve a child as sweet and kind as Angelica.

Sighing, Nicolas laced his hand through mine, leading me toward the corridor. He blew out the candles before saying, "I know. It's not fair. But we'll figure it out. Perhaps she plans to bring Angelica with her."

That possibility turned my stomach as well. If Angelica was stripped from her home and the support system she relied on, how would that affect her? I couldn't imagine that Melinda would assume the role of responsible mother simply because she'd landed a townhome in a fashionable area of the city or a cottage in the country. None of those advantages spelled acceptance for a mistress's daughter.

With a reassuring arm around my shoulder, Nicolas closed the door to the apartment behind us. "Let's go back to bed, my sweet Eliza. With any luck, you've helped immeasurably and Angelica will have no further episodes."

Back to bed.

With the unexpected interruption from Celia and the frightful situation with Angelica, I hadn't had the time or capacity to consider the implications of my presence in his residence so very late at night.

I also hadn't had more than a passing moment after intimacies to consider how wonderful and complete I'd felt before passing out from exhaustion.

However, tonight—here and now—I wanted nothing more than to return to his bed. So I tucked my arm around Nicolas's waist and let him lead me toward our future.

AWARENESS CAME SLOWLY. I didn't open my eyes just yet. I could feel the sunlight brightly warming my face though. Our limbs were tangled beneath the covers. Nicolas's body heated my skin where we were anchored to one another. He was awake. I could just tell.

"I can feel you staring at me," I accused, lids still shut against the morning.

"It's called gazing. And it's romantic."

I smiled before opening my eyes and bringing him into focus. Nicolas was facing me on his side, elbow bent, head propped on his hand. His jade green eyes sparkled with amusement, a brilliant grin gracing his full lips.

"Is it romantic to stare at an unconscious woman? Is it really?" I teased.

And in a rare moment, he abandoned the easy banter he typically favored for honest solemnity. "I just can't believe you're really here. I fear that if I take my eyes off of you for even a moment that you'll disappear like a dream upon waking."

I swallowed. His admission made guilt rise uncomfortably. I hadn't stayed the night in his bed after the first time we'd made love. I'd been nervous and worried, so I'd returned home despite Nicolas's obvious disappointment. Waking up together now and spending the remainder of our busy night in each other's arms was a revelation. I wanted to sleep with Nicolas every night.

Nicolas leaned forward and dropped a lazy kiss on my shoulder. "Can I kiss you?"

"You already have," I said, both relishing the sensation of his warm lips and the rough scrape of his morning stubble.

After another sensual kiss to my collarbone, he replied, "Can I kiss you more?"

I nodded my agreement.

Nicolas brought his free arm to my waist and rubbed his thumb against the soft skin there. His mouth descended once more to my neck, my shoulder, my chest. He murmured words of praise between kisses, telling me how soft I was, how sweet. He breathed the compliments into my skin where they heated and ached. I squirmed beneath the bedlinens before bringing my hand to his back, nails scoring and encouraging his attentions.

His whispered words continued—lyrical and poetic—as his curious lips meandered to my breasts, lowering the white bedsheet as he progressed.

Before coherent thought abandoned me entirely, I considered something. "Are you speaking Italian?"

A pause from above my sternum. "Perhaps. I hadn't noticed."

I craned my neck to meet his gaze. "You're fluent? I assumed you just memorized the lines for the play."

"I studied years ago for a part in a different show. It was something I enjoyed, so I continued. I'm passable, barely fluent." Another pause, considering. "Why?"

"Oh, um … just curious." I tried and failed to keep the interest out of my voice.

Nicolas's features turned positively roguish. "Do you like it?"

I didn't answer. I didn't need to.

Nicolas returned his attention to my breasts, crooning endearments between bites and kisses in a language I didn't understand. I groaned my appreciation for both his touch and his voice as he slowly and painstakingly made his way down my body.

A short while later, when he finally eased inside me, his face open in wonder at the connection between us, a single *finally* escaped before he resumed the pace of this thrusts and his Italian monologue.

I didn't need to know what the words meant to comprehend. They spoke of devotion and adoration, of love and belonging. Inevitability.

It was somehow still morning as we lazed in bed. Following our unhurried lovemaking, I was snuggled against Nicolas, my head resting on his chest. We'd been talking and touching leisurely. I wasn't quite ready for reality to intrude so I remained here, stroking the smooth skin of Nicolas's chest and stomach while he talked about the play he was writing and how his seemingly random meeting with Quinton had yielded an investor.

"I'll have the spring to finish writing before auditions will need to be held and sets built, but the prospect of it is all coming together."

I smiled against his skin. "I'm happy for you."

"And that means we can spend at least a portion of the summer in Wiltshire. Mother will likely wish to plan the whole wedding herself. And I'm sure my siblings will remain in residence with their families for a long holiday."

I stiffened at his words and the assumption therein.

Sensing my unease, Nicolas questioned, "Eliza?"

"You—you—mean *our* wedding?"

The thumb stroking the length of my arm stopped its ministrations. "Yesss. Of course, I mean our wedding."

With a huff of laughter that conveyed neither hilarity nor amusement, I said, "Well, how was I to know? It's not as if we've discussed getting married. You didn't exactly ask for my hand, Nicolas."

The thumb and hand attached to it fell away entirely. "Is this—a—secret for you, Eliza? Am I a secret you mean to keep?"

"No, Nicolas. Of course not. We simply haven't talked about the future yet. This —you and I—literally just happened. When have I had time to think about a marriage you haven't asked me for?" Pressure was constricting my lungs. I didn't understand why we needed to discuss this right now. Obviously Nicolas and I had a future. There was a chance we'd created a new life with our love-making. I wasn't naïve or averse. I simply needed to consider the implications and what all of this meant moving forward.

"You think you and I—us—that this all began just this week? Because we were intimate?" His tone was incredulous.

I needed to see him. I couldn't continue this conversation lying in his bed. Sitting up, I secured the sheet beneath my arms and turned to face Nicolas. "That's not what I meant. You just surprised me is all. I'm sorry."

No longer reclining, Nicolas shifted to the side of the bed, feet braced and resting on the floor. "It's fine. We don't need to figure this out right now. You're right."

Inexplicably, my nose stung as if tears were threatening. I was messing this up already. "I'm sorry—"

"It's alright, Eliza," he cut me off from further apologies, further attempts to restore our equilibrium. "You're correct. It's wrong to assume something as certain. It would be nice to be asked, to be chosen without doubt and without pause."

Speaking to his back, I tried to explain. "Nico—"

"No," he interjected. "It's alright. All is well. I apologize for rushing you with my suggestion. I believe I'm nearly late for rehearsal, however. I shall talk to you later."

The first of my tears started to fall as I watched Nicolas gather his trousers and quit the room. My neck was wet by the time I heard his front door open and close with a quiet snick. I would have preferred he slam the door in frustration. Cold indifference from someone like Nicolas felt worse somehow than the full range of his emotions.

I dressed in a state of disbelief. We'd had less than one week before I'd ruined things—again. I wiped my tears and debated whether I should follow after Nicolas. I didn't want him to constantly feel ahead in this relationship. If he was always waiting on me to catch up—emotionally and physically, then he'd start to resent me. Perhaps he already did.

However, rushing after and confronting him when he was clearly wounded would only lead to angry lashing out. I knew Nicolas well enough to know that, and I knew any anger he elicited in me would just make me feel worse. We'd always been good at fighting—Nicolas and me. I supposed that's what happened when you loved someone. They had a way of knowing all your weak spots, the vulnerable heart within. The trust was in hoping they would protect those secret places instead of using them against you.

Resolved to give Nicolas the time and space he'd clearly needed, I continued dressing and pulling myself together. My long blond hair was a snarled mess so I plaited it and finally went to retrieve my slippered heels.

A soft knock came at Nicolas's door and my heart stalled in my chest. Perhaps he'd returned. But no, he wasn't likely to knock on his own door.

Attempting to settle myself, I straightened my skirts and moved to the entryway. My tiny visitor smiled up from her place in the hallway.

I opened the door wide. "Good morning, Angelica. How are you feeling?" I quickly catalogued the residual redness around her eyes, but otherwise she appeared well.

"Good," she said simply. "Thank you for helping me. Miss Pippa says my pillows made me sick."

I nodded, grateful that Celia's mother had already explained the conclusion I'd reached. "That's right. I believe your body doesn't like feathers in your pillows so you have to be careful about breathing them in and sleeping upon them."

She nodded solemnly, still standing mostly in the corridor.

"Would you like to come in?" I asked.

She shook her head. "I'm going to the rehearsal with Celia. I wanted to come see you first though."

"I'm glad you did. I'd much prefer to see you smiling and happy than when you're sick."

Her happy grin was infectious. "You know, Celia is my very best friend even though I'm four and she is six. I'm used to having friends who are older than me. You could be my very old friend if you wanted to, Miss Eliza."

I laughed. "I would be very happy to be your very old friend. You would be my youngest friend. Would that be alright?"

She nodded eagerly, smile firmly in place until a shrill angry voice shattered the peace of the moment.

"What are you doing with my daughter?"

"Mama!" Angelica called and made to move toward her mother, but the anger and derision on Melinda's face stopped her forward progress. The conflict evident made my heart ache for the girl. She so desperately wanted her mother, but everything about Melinda pushed her away.

The woman moved swiftly down the corridor toward us, dressed in her finery. A silk brocade gown with lace at the hem molded to her figure. She donned an elaborate coiffure, but her features were twisted in fury. "I warned you to stay away from my child," she snarled.

Angelica had backed into the front of my skirts. I could feel the pressure of her small body seeking refuge from the ire her mother displayed.

In a quick motion, Melinda lurched forward and grabbed for her daughter's hand. She caught the edge of my sleeve in her mad attempt and the distinct sound of tearing fabric rent the air as she jerked Angelica away from me. I stumbled back in an effort to remove myself from her grasp and Angelica made a terrified squawk as her mother pulled her roughly by the arm to her side.

The air was cool on my skin where the material had been torn by her desperate hand. I took in Angelica's frightened face and looked calmly to Melinda. I had no desire for the anger she felt for me to be transferred to her child. Melinda was obviously too upset to consider the strength of her hold.

"Why are you trying to steal my daughter from me?"

With a steadiness I didn't quite feel, I endeavored to control the situation. "Angelica loves you very much. I know that she is your daughter. I wouldn't try to steal her from you."

"Then why are you here?" she spat the words, accusation ringing in her tone.

"I'm trying to help Angelica," I said, using my best physician's voice, direct and with authority. "Her body has a negative reaction to her feather pillows. She needs to keep away from them so she doesn't have trouble breathing. I've just been trying to keep her from feeling so unwell as a result."

"What?" she frowned. "That's preposterous. I think I know what's best for my own child. You keep coming here and embarrassing yourself for *Nicolas*." She hissed his name. "But you're nothing. You're disgraceful. You'll never be anything to him." Her volume rose steadily and by the end of her pronouncement she was fairly shouting.

Angelica's wide eyes met mine before she spun out of her mother's grasp and ran, panicked and terrified down the corridor in the direction of the stage.

Melinda shouted after her, but turned her accusing gaze on me. "You did this. If you had stayed away like I told you, none of this would be happening."

I raised my hands in a placating gesture. I needed to leave. I had no idea if Melinda was angry enough to be violent. She seemed desperate as it was. And if Angelica got to the stage and interrupted rehearsal, Nicolas would come. I didn't want to consider the trouble that would cause and the reaction it might elicit from Melinda.

"So, I'll go," I offered. "I'll leave, like you asked. I won't trouble you anymore and I'll stay away from Angelica." I pulled Nicolas's door closed behind me and edged my way around Melinda. She didn't say a word as I backed down the hall in the direction of the rear exit. Her dangerous glare followed me nevertheless.

It wasn't until I'd made it down the stairs and into the very alleyway she'd originally confronted me in, that I breathed a sigh of relief. I didn't know what to do. Melinda was clearly disturbed. And after everything that had happened this morning with Nicolas, perhaps it was best to put distance between myself and the Collins.

Since I'd bid my driver return home last night after deciding to stay, I exited the alley onto the Strand and hailed a hackney. The midday sun shone warm and bright overhead, and I couldn't believe all that had transpired in the span of an evening. I felt worn, body and soul.

The future seemed a nebulous thing, so delicate and fragile. I didn't know how to reconcile what I wanted with the path before me. I had to hope that my hesitancy hadn't driven Nicolas away, after all.

Faith required courage.

I would do my utmost to be both brave and worthy.

Twenty

I watched the rain descend in a steady torrent. The windows in Fiona's drawing room near Hyde Park were streaked with moisture and the world beyond was murky and gray.

It had been three days since I'd seen Nicolas.

Perhaps I'd worked for too long to isolate myself and remain independent in nearly everything I did. The horrible decision to dance with Dr. Miles had been solely my own, and if not for a last minute change of opinion and a timely interruption, who knew where that disastrous choice could have led.

Perhaps it was time to seek help from my friends. I didn't want to feel miserable. They were here and they were eager to support me, as evidenced by the sorrowful gaze Fiona tried to hide and how Ashleigh occasionally looked in my direction and shook her head sadly. Allowing myself to rely on others or worse, to inconvenience them, hadn't been something I'd permitted in the past. But where was the harm in seeking out one's friendships? In honoring your circle by considering their opinions and advice?

This wasn't getting any easier on my own. Whereas before, I'd done everything to resist the connection I'd felt to Nicolas, now I felt brave enough to try. We'd crossed a line, he and I, and I didn't want to live a life without him.

And yet, my fears were being realized. I'd already hurt him with my hesitation, my indecision. How could I convince him that I was ready for a future together while also being cognizant of the past?

The complications didn't feel unsurmountable insomuch as they felt complex and varied. But I needed help putting it all into perspective. I could admit that.

I returned my attention to the ladies and away from the foul weather. Everyone was quiet and looking at me carefully.

"Are you ready to talk now?" Jane asked hopefully from her place across from me.

I nodded, frustrated tears filling my eyes unexpectedly.

"Oh, dear," Cassandra murmured from beside me. "I'm going to embrace you now. Just allow it to happen."

I snorted a watery laugh as two arms wrapped around my shoulders, the force of which surprised me.

The tears didn't fall. Rather, I regrouped admirably and recounted the events of the last week. I admitted my spur-of-the-moment intentions for Dr. Kenneth Miles, and how Nicolas's surprising presence at the ball had caught me unawares.

Mary gasped and covered her face. "I'm so sorry, Eliza," she said through muffled fingers before meeting my gaze. "I invited Nicolas to the ball when he attended our meeting last week with Jane. I assumed I was doing a good thing for you. I had quite forgotten about my father's physician and your—erm—association."

I had been curious as to Nicolas's attendance at the Huffleton ball, but in light of all that had transpired, I'd forgotten to wonder about why he was there that night. "It's alright, Mary. I know the invitation was extended with good intentions in mind." My friend still appeared miserable by the implications of her hasty decision, so I smiled at her. "It worked out for the best, actually."

And then I proceeded to describe how I'd pursued Nicolas to the Collins, desperate to explain. I recounted the events of the evening with more vague suggestion than detail but Cassandra still muttered a "Well, well, well," when I indicated that Nicolas and I had confessed our mutual affection. I admitted to attending another show and spending a lovely evening with all of his friends. It felt necessary to mention Melinda's argument and confrontation with Nicolas, and how I'd remained at the theater's residence for the night.

Moving quickly to the following morning, I explained how Nicolas had surprised me with his talk of the future and impending marriage in the country with his family. And how I'd hurt him with my confusion and hesitation. The ladies' reactions ranged from wincing to sympathetic grimacing.

I felt it necessary to catch my friends up on Angelica's progress as well and how I'd tended to her in the night and hopefully isolated the cause of her malady. I also shared the frightful encounter I'd experienced with Melinda before I'd fled the Collins.

"I told ye that woman was a jealous harpy." Ashleigh broke the silence at the conclusion of my tale.

I felt a guilty pang in my midsection. I still didn't know what to do about Angelica and her mother. I worried for the child.

"Eliza." Fiona's voice drew my attention to her compassionate brown gaze. "I can see how troubled you are about Angelica. But you've risked your safety to help her as much as possible. You've improved her quality of life already through your dedication and efforts to her health. One never knows what the future will bring for Angelica and her mother. But it's not for you to blame yourself over."

Recognizing the wisdom of her words didn't absolve me of the conflict in my heart, however. But I offered a nod for her well-intentioned support.

"So, what will you do about Nicolas?" Cassandra asked once all the relevant facts had been relayed.

With a sigh, I said, "I don't know what to do. He hasn't visited the clinic." With Mr. Stanley standing guard, I'd stayed even later on Monday night on the off chance Nicolas would seek me out as he'd done before. "He hasn't written. He seemed to want some space from me."

"Do you want that?" Kathleen asked quietly, embroidery paused in her lap.

"No," I answered adamantly. "I feel like I've just found him again and at the same time discovered myself. I've been trapped in the past for so long. I cannot lose him now. I don't want Nicolas to push me away. Or to be without him. We've been separated long enough. He just surprised me is all. I regretted my reaction immediately. But it was too late to call it back. He'd seen it. I want to show him I'm actively choosing him. I want to make a statement."

Kat offered my honesty a sympathetic smile. I was thankful she'd asked the question because until now, I hadn't let myself say all those things out loud, much less think them.

"So marry him," came Cassandra's abrupt declaration from my side.

We all turned to look at her.

"What?" She widened her eyes dramatically. "You should marry Nicolas. Have his babies. Take his name. Be Mrs. Silas Viso," she teased. "Or don't. Be Dr. Eliza Morgan or Finley. Claim whatever name you wish just as long as you claim Nicolas for yourself."

"Yes," agreed Ashleigh with feeling. She straightened in her seat and eyed me from across the table laden with cakes and tarts and all manner of refreshment. "Ye need to find him and tell him exactly what ye want and make him listen to ye. No more space. No more wasted time. Force him to hear ye and don't let him escape until—"

"Alright," the duchess interjected. "Threats of kidnapping aside, I think what Ashleigh is trying to say is that love won't wait for you, Eliza. And neither should Nicholas. He's been honest and open about what he wants from the beginning. And what he wants is you," Fiona finished with a gentle smile.

"What about his family? How could they possibly wish to welcome me as a daughter into their family once more?" Despite our physical union, Nicolas and I still had a painful past. My relationship with his family was one of the many hurdles I felt ill-equipped to traverse.

"Let them love you, Eliza," Cassandra said in exasperation before biting quite forcefully into a biscuit.

"They seem to want to," Kat offered. "Things went well with Nicolas's mother, did they not?"

Before I could answer in a wary affirmative, Jane spoke. "It doesn't sound like the Morgans have a problem with you. Of course, there may be some initial awkwardness as you reacclimatize to each other. But they probably hope for your happiness just as fervently as Nicolas's."

"Why wouldn't the rest of them fall eagerly in line to love you? You're very lovable, you know," Cassandra insisted, amusement causing her green eyes to sparkle.

"When you aren't fighting us," Mary chimed in, smiling behind her teacup.

"Or yerself," Ashleigh concluded.

I considered my remaining concerns as I fidgeted with the embroidery hoop in my lap. I'd long since abandoned my efforts, too morose and distracted to continue stitching. In fact, it didn't appear as if any of the ladies in attendance were on task. They were too absorbed with my troubles. Too dedicated to helping me reach a solution. These were good friends I had. The best in all of London. Most women couldn't claim as much. *Ton* relationships were fraught, but the friendships in this room were genuine, and I counted myself very lucky indeed.

Further reflecting on the fickle nature of the *ton* and finally giving voice to my insecurity, I said, "What if an association—a marriage—with me, hurts his career, his dream of being a playwright?"

Jane frowned. "How could you possibly? His play is backed by Quinton. It will happen. You needn't fear."

"And in an effort to sound realistic," Fiona said from her patterned armchair by the fire. "But the day in which a woman negatively impacts the reputation of a man—and not the other way around—is very far off indeed."

Heads nodded all around the drawing room in agreement.

Cassandra's red curls were still bobbing when she turned to me on our shared settee. "Let yourself be happy, Eliza. Stop looking for excuses and stop allowing your past to dictate your future. Trust yourself. Not every decision will end in misery and disaster. You were a seventeen-year-old girl trying to do the very best she could. You should not be trapped in your painful past forever. You deserve a future—a good one. And if Nicolas makes you happy … then *that* is the future you must seek."

I took in Cassandra's earnest features and met the gazes of the other ladies in the room. I saw nothing but encouragement and love reflected back to me. "How do I make the decision for both of us? How do I choose him definitively and without question?"

"Nicolas is a man of the stage," Ashleigh said. Her blue eyes threatened mischief. "He'll appreciate proper theatrics."

Cassandra's smile widened. "That is an excellent idea."

"We'll need a plan!" Mary called.

"Wait, what plan? What is happening?" My confusion was evident as I took in the flurry of women and raised voices in the drawing room.

Jane sat placidly, calm within the storm of sororal support. She smiled at me—a knowing sort of smile that I didn't know quite what to do with.

And then a moment later, Ashleigh's Scottish brogue announced to the room, "Jane, call for yer carriage. It's the largest. We're going to need it."

Carriages were not intended to transport quite so many people.

We'd ended up with two more in addition to our seven following the events at Fiona's London home. It was determined that attending Nicolas's performance at the Joc Collins theater that evening to profess my love and promise myself in matrimony necessitated some precautions. With the threat from Melinda, not only to myself but to Angelica and Nicolas as well, the ladies had summarily decided that Lord Sullivan and Mr. Daniel O'Connor should accompany us all to the theater.

Once the plan was set—with very little input from myself—we had been joined by Quinton and Daniel.

I looked around the cramped space noting Jane draped across her husband's lap in an effort to conserve space, I was sure. Kathleen was wedged rather close between the wall of the carriage and Mr. O'Connor. She seemed nervous and wide-eyed but Daniel didn't appear to mind their forced proximity at all. I smiled as I watched him relay some story with large animated movements, concluding with a hearty laugh.

Mary, Cassandra, Fiona, Ashleigh, and I were all squeezed into the opposite side as the Sullivan carriage rumbled toward the Strand. Skirts and underskirts were shoved toward the center of the space and we'd long since resigned ourselves to being in each other's pockets. But this was friendship. This was support in its finest form. I was equal parts nervous and terrified to face Nicolas. But this overflowing carriage meant I had people who cared about me and fought for my happiness—even when I refused to fight for myself.

"Remind me why we couldn't have taken more than one carriage," Quinton asked, glacial blue eyes taking in the calamitous scene before him.

"Because, my lord, Eliza is undertaking a monumental endeavor." Cassandra answered Sullivan but gave me a wink. "And she requires support, from all of us. At the same time. Not separately and arriving at different intervals."

Quinton looked unconvinced but the ladies and Daniel all nodded their agreement.

"Are you actually complaining?" Jane asked sweetly from her perched position.

"Not at all," Quinton replied, meeting his wife's gaze while his lip twitched the tiniest bit to indicate his amusement—or possibly his irritation. It was hard to tell with Lord Sullivan.

"So, what do we do once we arrive?" Daniel asked. He was clearly invested in this plan and for that, the man had endeared himself to me even more.

"I'm so glad you asked, Mr. O'Connor," Cassandra replied grandly. "Eliza has a box at the theater. We should all be able to fit in there."

"About as well as we all fit in here, I imagine," I mumbled.

Cassandra shot me a look and then proceeded as if I hadn't spoken. "Nicolas will see us during the performance and then afterward, Eliza will declare her intentions for their upcoming union. And then they shall live happily ever after. Oh, and should Eliza's angry nemesis be in residence, you and Lord Sullivan might be called upon to protect her."

Daniel nodded as if that all made complete sense.

In all honesty, it *was* rather simple. As Ashleigh had not so delicately put it, I would make him hear me. I was eliminating the hesitancy and the space between us. The prospect of announcing my feelings and hopes for our future was decidedly less simple. I felt nervous down to my bones. What if Nicolas rejected me? What if this short time apart made him realize that he was better off without me? I wiped my sweaty palms on the skirt in front of me, hoping it was my own.

"Aye," Ashleigh said, focused on the embroidery she'd insisted on bringing. "And if for some reason, that dinnae work, one of us can yell 'fire.'"

"No!" both Quinton and I barked at the same time. Our eyes connected and a moment of shared commiseration passed between us.

"Oh, look," Jane said with a smile, elbowing Daniel in the shoulder. "They're getting along."

Mr. O'Connor snorted a laugh as Quinton and I exchanged a glare before breaking eye contact.

I peeked out the window and saw we were nearing our destination. The nervous energy that threatened seemed to amplify tenfold. Forcing my mind to consider Nicolas's hypothetical reaction did nothing to quiet the anxiety I felt. He could reject me in so many ways. I could be too late.

However, I couldn't turn back. Nicolas needed to know that I was invested in him—in us—and a future together. If he wanted to get married and spend the summer with the entire Morgan clan, I'd be by his side. I would face the inevitable awkwardness, and we would confront the remnants of our past together.

It was doubt that had gotten me into this mess with Nicolas in the first place. Time and space had done nothing but further my resolve. We belonged together. I refused to allow the worry I felt in my frantic heartbeat and my roiling stomach to sway me from the decision I'd made. I would talk to Nicolas. I would fix this.

It was nearly half an hour later that all nine of us were settled in my father's box in the theater. The show was starting soon. I was desperate to see him.

I felt someone squeeze my gloved hand and looked over to see Jane's encouraging smile. "It will be alright."

Nodding tightly, I wrapped my gloved hand firmly around hers, accepting the support she offered.

As the lights began to lower, I allowed hope to suffuse my limbs. Courage and faith wrapped themselves around my fortress of a heart, and I watched as my future took the stage.

It wasn't until nearly intermission that my optimism started to dwindle. Just a bit. And even then, it was more frustration than any real hopelessness.

Nicolas hadn't glanced toward our seats once. His gaze hadn't strayed to the audience nor anything or anyone beyond the stage.

"This isn't working," I growled as theater patrons milled about below. The heavy curtain was drawn as the performers and musicians took their leave before the next act. "He hasn't seen me. He doesn't know I'm here."

"Could you go backstage now—during the intermission?" Cassandra asked from her seated position behind me.

"No—I—I need time to talk to him. We'd only have a short while before he'd need to be back on stage."

"Should we send a message then? Let him at least know that yer here?"

Ashleigh's idea had merit, but before I could answer, Quinton parted the fabric at the entrance to the box and stepped forward. I hadn't realized he'd been gone.

"Let's go," he ordered, looking in my direction.

I frowned in confusion. "What? Where?"

"I *encouraged* a couple I know on the second row to give up their seats. Get you closer to the stage so that Morgan will notice you," Quinton said with exasperation, as if he didn't have time to deal with my questions.

"Why did you say *encouraged* like that?" I inquired.

"He means they owe him money," Jane chimed in helpfully. "And he probably threatened to call in their debts if they didn't turn over their seats."

I looked from Jane to her husband, shock likely written all over my face.

"Sullivan, I—thank—"

"Let's go before the next act begins," he interrupted my attempt at gratitude. Well, I wouldn't be trying again. And I wouldn't refuse this favor.

I rose on unsteady legs as the ladies and Daniel offered me words of encouragement. I placed my hand on Quinton's arm and let him lead me down to the lobby. However, once we arrived, it was a crush as men and women made to return to their seats.

"I'm fine," I assured the looming gentleman at my side. "I can slip through easier without you on my arm."

Sullivan's unamused glare met my own, but he relented and spoke in a low voice before retreating. "Second row, the seats on the very end of the left aisle." I nodded. "Good luck, Finley."

I would need it.

After starting and stopping and carefully navigating my way toward the stage. I settled myself in the interior seat in the appointed row. The gentleman next to me nodded in greeting, seemingly unperturbed to be joined by a stranger—definitely not the person he'd been sitting next to for the first half of the play. He took a casual sip of some amber liquid in his glass before focusing his attention on his companion.

The house lights flickered their final warning, and I took a deep breath. I had hope. A thread of it wrapped tightly around my heart. *Let him see me*, I thought to myself. *Let this work.*

I couldn't help the smile that came over my face as Nicolas waltzed on stage, full of confidence and the supreme knowledge that hundreds of eyes were trained on him. I'd never been so close to him during a performance. But from this distance, I could see the jade green of his eyes and the curve of his smile I loved so well. I could see the differences, too. This was Silas Viso. There were parts that were my Nicolas, but something in his voice changed when he was entertaining the masses. His countenance shifted to the famous performer, and the man I loved receded.

Something in me softened at the thought. Nicolas—the true Nicolas—was someone special, someone separate, someone secret from his fame and his career. I wanted him to be mine and mine alone. Reckless claiming and possessive tendencies had never much appealed to me. But I could understand it now—seeing this man on the stage made me ache for all the intimate moments when he was wholly mine.

The chair on the aisle beside me jostled suddenly, drawing my attention. Surprised, I turned, expecting Sullivan despite my assumption that he would have returned to Jane and the others. But it wasn't the earl pushed up next to me.

It was Melinda, and her expression spelled violence nearly as much as the knife she had pressed to my side.

Twenty-One

"Don't move," came the hissed demand right beside my ear.

The urge to flinch away was instinctual but I did my best to remain motionless in my seat. Melinda was pressed close, right up against me. Her breath was sour and her kohl-smudged eyes were wild. This was a far cry from the fashionable, well-appointed woman I'd occasionally crossed paths with. She emanated desperation and appeared unhinged.

The pressure from the knife bit into my corset just behind my ribcage. Knowing the details of my own anatomy didn't help the situation. This woman and her weapon could kill me easily with a well-placed thrust.

With my breathing elevated, I continued facing the stage while my eyes failed to take in the performers and the action therein. My mind was churning, racing through scenarios and a way out of this mess.

"Are you happy now?" Melinda's harsh whisper wafted over my neck. "I've been sacked from the play. And the Marquess Whistlethorpe is no longer content with our arrangement. Angelica and I have nowhere to go."

My stomach clenched painfully. I had anticipated this turn of events, but I hadn't wanted it. I didn't wish an uncertain future on Angelica. How could this woman think that?

"And now," Melinda continued, unconscious of the stares and frowns pointed in her direction by theater-goers nearby, "you're impeding my future with Nicolas. Our future—mine and Angelica's. He loves her like a daughter. We could have been a happy family together, the three of us. But you keep showing up. How dare you waltz into this theater with a gaggle of women and act as if you belong?"

I vaguely registered that Nicolas was offstage for this portion of the play. I felt grateful suddenly that he'd failed to notice me in the audience thus far. He was safe backstage. There was no doubt in my mind that he'd do anything to protect me. If he'd seen Melinda—disheveled and unbalanced—practically on top of me in the second row, he would have likely inserted himself into the drama playing out beyond the stage. That realization—that no harm would come to him— allowed me to inhale a fortifying breath and start to plan.

Melinda was fully invested in her monologue. The ladies and gentlemen nearby were casting her aggrieved glances for her continued whispers, but none moved to intervene. And they couldn't see the weapon she wielded, pressed so close to me as she was.

"You don't belong here," she hissed. "You don't belong in our lives."

With a quick downward glance, I eyed the drink in my neighbor's hand. I needed a distraction, some way to put distance between Melinda and myself.

I thought of Nicolas and my father and my friends here with me tonight. When I felt my hands steady, I took a bracing breath and snatched the crystal glass from the man on my right. Twisting away from the knife, I splashed the golden liquid in Melinda's face. She reared back, coughing and sputtering as I stood suddenly during the middle of the performance. If we caused enough of a scene, surely someone would intervene, alert the theater employees, and have us forcibly removed. That was all I wanted—to get Melinda away from all these people and away from Nicolas.

Melinda rose, wiping her eyes and expression fierce. She blocked the aisle and I didn't know what to do. All heads had turned in our direction but the performers continued on stage, reciting their lines unaffected.

And then a moment later, I heard Cassandra, voice clear and strong from the second floor. "FIRE!"

The result was instantaneous. Patrons stood as the sounds of chairs scraping and women screaming rent the air. Melinda's furious gaze met my own and she launched herself at me. As her momentum carried us to the ground, I landed hard on my right shoulder amid scattered chairs. My own frantic breathing mixed with the sounds of panicked audience members as I fought to push Melinda off of me. I knew the knife was still in her hand, and that knowledge fueled my desperation. I forced and shoved and bucked my hips to dislodge her any way I could, but she had the advantage of rage. She fought like a woman possessed, a desperate mother with no more options, and a vested interest in wounding a perceived threat.

Amid all the screams and shuffling of bodies frantic to escape the Collins, I could very clearly hear my name. And as my forearm pressed into the vulnerable skin of Melinda's neck, I gave a hard shove that had her retreating momentarily, sitting back on her heels as she straddled my waist.

Nicolas bellowed my name from the direction of the stage once more. Odd that I could recognize it and pick it out over the noise and disorder around me. In my distraction, Melinda raised her hand and the knife with it. But before I could think to do anything, movement streaked from the side and forced Melinda from atop me.

I scrambled back from the tangle of limbs as Daniel O'Connor wrestled my attacker to the ground and disarmed her before my very eyes. He rolled Melinda onto her stomach and secured both of her hands behind her back in one of his own. She was still kicking and flailing wildly, testing the limits of her restraint.

Daniel seemed unconcerned by the thrashing woman in his grasp. "Dr. Finley, are ye alright?"

I sat up, rubbing my shoulder and nodded. "Yes. I—I—think so. Thank you."

"I would have been here sooner, but *someone*," he said without malice but obvious disapproval, "thought yelling 'fire' in a crowded theater was a wise decision."

Melinda had finally stopped moving, whether resigned to her fate or preparing for another barrage, I couldn't presume.

"Are ye sure yer alright?" Daniel moved to stand and dragged Melinda with him. At my nod of assurance, he said, "I'm going to turn her over to the bobbies."

Before I could offer any opinion on the woman's fate, Nicolas was moving toward me, face flushed with panic. He'd already cleared the stage and was tossing chairs aside as he forced his way across the rows of seats.

Sliding to a stop beside me on the floor, he grasped my face in his hands before moving them down my neck and to my arms. "Eliza, are you hurt? Did she hurt you?"

I sought to slow his frantic movements and clutched his seeking hands. "I'm well. She didn't harm me."

But his breathing was labored and his eyes kept scanning me, searching for an injury that wasn't there.

"Nicolas," I attempted once more, "I'm fine. I assure you."

Finally, registering my words, his tortured green gaze met my own. And then I was hauled into his arms, clutching him back just as desperately. "I'm so sorry," Nicolas murmured against my hair, half of which had fallen from its pins.

"No—" I began before he interrupted.

"I'm sorry, Eliza. I brought this on you. I foisted this danger upon you. I never should have involved you in Angelica's life. I just—I never thought she'd do something like this. I didn't realize what Melinda was capable of and how easily she could get to you." He squeezed me tighter somehow. "I'm so damn sorry."

"Stop, Nicolas. The actions of a madwoman are not your fault. Irrationally, she blamed me for her problems. You couldn't have known the lengths she would go to."

Appearing far more calm and collected, Nicolas pulled back, taking in my tousled state—dark blue dress a ruin on the theater floor. "I'll do anything to make it up to you. Please—Eliza—please forgive me."

I thought about telling him there was nothing to forgive. But then I remembered why I'd come here in the first place. Before being derailed by Melinda and her attack, I'd come here to win Nicolas back. To show him I was serious about our future and ready for it to start now.

So I met his earnest stare and said, "There is one thing you can do."

"Anything," he declared, clutching my hands.

"Marry me."

Nicolas frowned, looking confused and lost. But his hands gripped mine a little tighter.

"That's why I came here tonight," I admitted. "I choose you. I choose us. I needed you to know that I was ready for everything. For all of it. Holidays in the country. Being a doctor and a wife. Having a family. Being part of one again. I know we need to talk more but I needed you to—"

My words ended abruptly as Nicolas's lips interrupted the remainder of my speech. He wrapped me in his arms. When my surprise had faded, I returned his kiss. Eagerly and enthusiastically.

Nicolas pulled back suddenly. "Yes," he said before pecking a hard kiss on my startled mouth. "Yes," he repeated his words and his movements. "I'll marry you." Kiss. "And we'll have a family." Kiss. "And we'll be happy."

I smiled against his lips as they descended once more.

Not long after, I felt Nicolas shaking against me. His laughter reached my kiss-muddled ears as I registered the clapping and hollering from the balcony above.

I rested my forehead against Nicolas's as I admitted, "I brought all my ridiculous friends with me for moral support."

He was still laughing. "And was that Lady Cassandra who yelled fire in a crowded theater?"

I sighed. "It was indeed."

"Well, let's not keep our public waiting, my betrothed." With a wink, he dropped a final kiss on my temple before hopping nimbly to his feet. Nicolas extended a hand and pulled me up gently with him. Careful with his movements, he spun us to face the direction of my father's box where my ladies—and a reluctant Lord Sullivan—were raving madly. The rest of the theater was empty.

Nicolas threw his free arm out to the side and clutched my gloved hand to his chest as he executed a dramatic bow. The cheering from my friends intensified. Still pressed forward, Nicolas looked back and up over his shoulder. After an expectant yank on my arm, I rolled my eyes. Leaning over, I gave an exaggerated bow that had Ashleigh giving a loud whistle and Nicolas laughing.

With a final wave and without releasing my hand, Nicolas began leading us toward a doorway near the front of the stage. "Come. Let's get you cleaned up and we can talk more about your proposal."

"Are you upset that I asked?" I could feel the soreness throughout my body making itself known as I walked carefully beside Nicolas.

He frowned in obvious concern and slowed his pace. "No, of course not. I like knowing that you wanted it for yourself."

I swallowed painfully against the doubt I'd caused.

We finally arrived at Nicolas's apartment. He led me straight to his bedroom and bid me to lie down. "Don't worry. I'll take care of you," he promised as I lowered myself atop the coverlet, wincing from acute discomfort in my limbs.

Nicolas returned with a wet cloth and began wiping away whatever filth had accumulated on my face. He peeled away the fabric of my gloves and placed tender kisses on my knuckles and the center of my palms. "Where does it hurt?" he asked softly.

I pointed to my jaw where a glancing blow had landed during my tussle with Melinda. Nicolas leaned in softly pressing his lips to the place I'd indicated.

"Where else?" he whispered.

We continued this way for some time. Me pointing out the tender places on my body while Nicolas administered his affection. After I directed him to my aching shoulder, he loosened my gown and my stays and pushed the dark blue fabric away to press a line of lingering kisses across my collarbone and down the slope of my shoulder blade.

"I'm sorry, you know," Nicolas finally said. "I shouldn't have made assumptions about our wedding. I surprised you and pressured you. And I should have given you a moment to collect your thoughts. I reacted badly and allowed my selfish fears of losing you—and this very new version of us—to override rational thought."

I cupped Nicolas's stubbled jaw in my palm. "It's alright. I made you fearful and untrusting with my skittishness. I'm sorry, too."

He nuzzled into my hand before placing a soft kiss on the delicate skin of my inner wrist. "I'll do better to trust you, Eliza. I'll think the best of you. Always."

"I am ready to live this life together," I announced, voice firm and unwavering. "I don't want to waste any more time being afraid of my instincts and paralyzed by my fears. The past will always be there. But I'm done running from it. And from you."

Nicolas nodded solemnly. "We deserve happiness."

I brushed his dark hair back over his ear and traced the line of his skin down his strong neck, looking for any excuse to stay close, to feel him warm and solid beneath my touch. "I've learned it's alright to make mistakes. Especially when you have someone who loves you enough to forgive you."

OVER A WEEK later and fully recovered of any lingering aches from Melinda's attack, Nicolas and I found ourselves on a dance floor at last. It was our second waltz of the evening in this particular ballroom. Jane and Sullivan were hosting —their first event since marrying. My friend had taken some time to settle into her role as hostess. The event was lovely however.

I smiled to myself, thinking how far Jane and I had come. Three years prior would have found us adhered to the wall in the farthest corner of any ballroom. Now we were dancing, mingling, and conversing with friends. The desire to hide ourselves away no longer seemed the easiest nor the best option.

Nicolas grinned. "Why are you smiling?"

"Just happy," I said honestly.

As the song came to a close and dance partners bowed and curtsied to one another, Nicolas asked, "Are you ready to leave?"

I laughed. "We've only just arrived. I can't leave Jane's event so soon."

"Yes, but I'm ready for more dancing. And we can't do that here."

I gave his arm a warning squeeze as Nicolas escorted me to where our friends were gathered. Jane and Quinton were still greeting guests, but Fiona, Mary, Ashleigh, and Cassandra were all chatting in a circle near the open balcony archway. The ladies looked beautiful in their formal wear. Fiona's petite frame was accentuated by her gold brocade gown. Mary was attracting admiring gazes from all around the ballroom tonight. Ashleigh's elaborate coiffure suited her ensemble as her strikingly beautiful face was in full view. And Cassandra's pale yellow gown gave my exuberant friend a radiant glow.

"Good evening, my ladies. Your Grace." Nicolas greeted my smiling friends with an efficient bow.

"Good evening, sir," came the chorus in response.

A very tall footman approached with a tray of champagne. The powdered wig he wore didn't particularly suit his expressively stern features. Rather than inserting himself into our circle to serve our drinks, he skirted the edge of the group and offered refreshment to each individual.

I plucked a drink from the tray as Nicolas hesitated, casting me a glance. "So, we're staying?"

"Yes!" I laughed. "You're terrible. We'll greet our hosts before we make our exit."

Only after he'd confirmed that we were, in fact remaining, did Nicolas lift a glass from the footman's tray. He nodded his thanks and the servant moved on. He continued distributing refreshment until he reached Cassandra's side. We all watched in astonishment as the tall, broad-shouldered man spun away with his wares before Cassandra could acquire her glass.

We all exchanged confused glances while Cassandra's glare fixed firmly to the back on the footman, hand still outstretched for her beverage. "Did that really just happen?" she asked.

My friend appeared ready to stomp off after the unsuspecting servant in a huff, but Jane and Quinton choose that moment to join us. We were all distracted with greetings, and Cassandra appeared to put the awkward moment behind her in favor of addressing the newcomers.

"Lovely ball, Jane dear," Ashleigh complimented.

"Thank you," Jane replied. "There is so much involved in planning. I was oddly nervous."

"We're all having a lovely time," I rushed to assure her.

"Where did all these servants come from?" Cassandra asked apropos of nothing. We all turned to stare. "Are they normally here at Randolph House?"

Jane, unfazed by seemingly random topic changes, answered easily, "Oh, no. We hired additional servers for the event. Most of our regular staff isn't in the ballroom tonight."

"Do you know who he is?" Cassandra pulled Jane closer so she could follow her line of sight while pointing across the room at the footman who'd refused to serve her. "I swear I've seen him several times now."

I noticed Fiona's gaze narrow on the livered servant. She and Quinton shared an odd look. What was that about?

Jane frowned. "No, I don't recognize him. I admittedly delegated the task of hiring temporary servants to our housekeeper. Mrs. Hooper was a tremendous help." Belatedly picking up on Cassandra's odd questions, Jane finally asked, "Why? Did something happen?"

Jane's alarm seemed to snap Cassandra from her fixation on the footman because she turned to our hostess with a wide smile. "No, of course not. Now tell us where you got these beautiful flower arrangements because this is the loveliest ballroom I've been in all season."

Jane launched into a discussion on flowers, growing seasons, and greenhouses in London.

Nicolas leaned in to whisper, "Can we go now?"

I looked over with an indulgent grin. "Fine. Once Jane finishes her lecture on horticulture." His answering smile was unrepentant. Dratted Nicolas.

Several minutes later, the discussion topic shifted to a recent theft from Lady Helm's private jewelry collection. Impatient and unrepentant, Nicolas smoothly cut in, "Well I'm afraid Eliza and I must be off."

"You're leaving already?" Mary asked, voice confused.

"I'm afraid so, Lady Mary. We have more dancing ahead of us this night."

"If you're so eager for more practice, Mr. Morgan, you could always dance with one of us," Fiona said with a sly grin, indicating herself and the rest of my friends.

"While I would welcome a turn about the dance floor with you anytime, Your Grace," Nicolas affected an exaggerated whisper, "It is not *I* who requires additional practice."

The ladies laughed delightedly, as they so often did in Nicolas's presence.

"Ha. Ha," I intoned. "I'm a perfectly adequate dancer, I'll have you know."

Green eyes twinkling, Nicolas gathered my gloved hand and placed a kiss to my knuckles before replying more seriously than I would have expected, "Yes, you are. More than adequate. You simply require the right partner."

Epilogue

Several months later

The summer sun warmed my skin as I gathered my burgundy skirts and made my way to the site of our gathering. The staff had readied the area with blankets, covered dishes, linens, and beverages. Several large trees shaded our picnic area and various members of the Morgan clan were already seated and conversing easily.

Newly married, Nicolas and I had spent the last fortnight in Wiltshire in his family home with a steady stream of siblings and nieces and nephews. With his older brother Miller's arrival this morning, we were all finally in residence. Today's outdoor luncheon was a casual belated celebration of our rather hasty marriage in London this spring. Most of the Morgans had been in attendance, but not all. And that was a story for another day.

"Eliza! Come join us," Roberta called from her position on the thick blankets near the trunk of the tree. Roberta was Nicolas's eldest sister. She was seated beside her husband Victor Edmonds, the Earl of Westwicke, but none of their five children were nearby. Actually, only adults were reclining in the shade. Considering Nicolas's absence, I could deduce where all the children would be.

I made my way to sit on the closest blanket and warmly greeted those gathered. "Are all the children with Nicolas then?"

Francesca grinned from her spot across from me. "Of course. He is the best form of entertainment after all."

Francesca was the second eldest Morgan and such a vital fixture from my youth. While Roberta had been in London and married for most of my childhood memories, Franny had been part of our youthful escapades early on. While ten years my senior, she had been lovely and kind and had never made me feel like an interloper or tagalong. I'd admired her greatly and, as an adolescent, longed for a friendship with Nicolas's elder sister. Now, in her mid-thirties, married with three adorable children, the prospect seemed wholly attainable.

A chorus of squeals rang out from the distance.

"Perhaps you should go and save him, Eliza dear." Rosemary Morgan, Nicolas's mother, approached our small gathering from the main house and seated herself on a thick cushion near her eldest daughter. She gave me a brilliant smile.

I waited for the devastation of being in the midst of this family—the inevitable awkwardness I'd anticipated and feared for so long—to squeeze and choke. But it never came. I returned Rosemary's smile and allowed myself the small ache in my chest that spoke of memories and loss. Taking in the scene before me didn't overwhelm. I could call forth happy times with beloved Thomas and our missing patriarch Robert Morgan. They would have loved our time spent together this summer. It was a dull edge of loss, wrapped in fondness and a bittersweet ache. But it no longer made me question my place here in Wiltshire nor my belonging with Nicolas and his family.

We had three more days in the country before Nicolas needed to return to London for rehearsals. We'd departed following the auditions for his upcoming play. It was all coming together, and I couldn't be more proud of my husband. Nicolas had worked hard to make his dream a reality, and his first production would premiere in the autumn at the Joc Collins Theater.

"That is an excellent idea, Rosemary."

I aimed to retrieve my husband and all the children so that our luncheon could begin. A gloved hand entered my field of vision and I used it to rise gracefully from the blanket.

"Good day, sister," Miller, the current Viscount Fritterton, said with a charming smile. My heart warmed at his greeting.

"Hello, brother. How was your journey?" I inquired with a smile of my own.

"All was well," he answered, green eyes sparkling. Miller and Nicolas looked very much alike despite their nearly thirteen year age difference. The man before me smiled easily and often, and if not for the slight curl in his hair and the gray at his temples, Miller and Nicolas could be twins.

"And do you know how your journey could be improved, Miller?" Rosemary called. Miller groaned but didn't answer. "If you had a wife to accompany you."

My wide eyes met Miller's, and I bit my lip to keep from laughing at his expression. Rosemary had long been encouraging her son to settle down. As the only remaining Morgan who was unattached, I feared he'd be under constant assault from his matchmaking mama. He was the current viscount and without a wife and an heir, his position was often criticized. I fully expected him to capitulate if for no other reason than to stop the constant barrage from his mother.

"Go," he mouthed. "Save yourself."

I looked down quickly to hide my laugh and set off in the direction of the litany of squeals.

Walking quickly toward the gardens, I turned the corner and found Nicolas under attack from nine children ranging in age from two to twelve. He'd abandoned his coat somewhere and his skin was flushed from exertion. They each held a stick aloft and Nicolas was spinning dramatically in an impromptu sword fight. Every parry and thrust earned him cheers and shrieks of delight. I smiled wide, my heart nearly bursting at the sight.

"Pardon me, brave knight!" I called.

Nicolas turned. His smile was so quick and earnest that I took an involuntary step toward him.

"Greetings, wench!" he called, and I rolled my eyes as the children all laughed.

With his attention turned to me, Nicolas failed to notice an oncoming attack. The sword from Francesca's youngest caught him deftly in the side. With theatrics befitting a stage performer, Nicolas collapsed to the ground in a fit of wails, claiming he'd been vanquished dishonorably. His eager audience took in the spectacle, and honestly, I couldn't look away either. That was just Nicolas. Endlessly engaging and charming.

Finally, with a loud groan, he shouted, "I need a doctor!"

"That's my cue." I clasped my hands in front of me and began a slow stroll toward my patient writhing on the ground. "The rest of you brave maidens and knights have refreshment waiting for you."

With hands still clutching their sticks, the children ran toward the food and family awaiting them. Nicolas remained on the ground, committed to his role.

Before all the little legs could run past, one small girl with a crown of dark hair and wide brown eyes made her way to my side.

"Are you having fun?" I asked.

Angelica flung her tiny arms around my waist and said "Yes, Eliza!" with her sweet, excited voice.

My throat tightened, and I pushed some sweaty strands of hair back from her forehead. "Rosemary has some luncheon for you. Are you hungry?"

She nodded eagerly and with a final squeeze to my waist, took off after the other children in search of Nicolas's mother.

Angelica had been with us since shortly after the incident at the theater. Following the attack, Melinda had been arrested and imprisoned. And with no other family, Angelica had remained with little Celia and her mother Pippa for a short time. It was but a temporary solution. Pippa wasn't able to support two children on her own. Nicolas and I discussed the prospect of bringing Angelica to live with us, and following a short betrothal and a hasty marriage, we acquired a home together and brought Angelica to stay. It hadn't been perfect or easy, but Angelica was growing more comfortable all the time. The stability and regularity of her life with us made the transition easier, however. She missed her mother and probably always would. But she had a safe and steady home now, and we would love her and care for her like our own.

The trip to Wiltshire had been a step in the right direction. We were establishing ourselves as a family unit, and Angelica had been embraced wholeheartedly. And with Nicolas's production this fall, we'd be splitting our time between our home in Mayfair and the apartment in residence at the Collins. Angelica would be able to experience the comforts of the theater with the acquired family she'd known since birth. And occasionally, she could join me in the clinic with my father and Meg. We had plans and a future, and I was thankful that Angelica could be a part of that.

"Are you coming to tend me, wench?" Nicolas asked from his place in the grass. He had his hands beneath his head and was squinting toward me as the sun shone brightly on his handsome face.

"I suppose I should," I said, reaching toward him.

Nicolas slipped his warm hand into mine, as he sprang lightly to his feet.

Lacing our fingers together, he leaned forward. "I'm going to steal a kiss before we return."

He received no complaints as I rose up on my toes to receive him. Nicolas's free hand cradled my jaw as his lips met mine. The kiss was warm and sweet. It spoke of summer days and country air and contentment. Of young love's past and a future, bright and hopeful.

After a time, our affection slowed and gentled. Nicolas pressed his forehead to mine.

With my eyes closed I said on a sigh, "We should return. Your mother will be stuffing Angelica full of pudding."

Nicolas nodded and pulled back. Keeping our hands locked tight, he led me back toward the house—back toward our family and the merriment there.

As the others came into view, I could see the chaos of children, drinks being poured, and food being served. Angelica was settled happily next to Rosemary, conspiratorial smiles on both their faces.

Without slowing, I asked Nicolas quietly, "Did you ever think it could be like this?"

He slowed his gait before finally pulling me to a stop. And then while wearing a serious expression, he admitted, "Yes, I did."

I looked away from the scene of familial commotion and unconditional love. Turning to Nicolas, I said, "Thank you … for believing when I didn't know how."

Nicolas smiled gently. "Are you happy, Eliza?"

The question echoed in my thoughts from months ago. "You asked me that once before, you know."

"I did," he acknowledged.

I took in his lovely face, green eyes soft and earnest. Smiling tenderly, I leaned forward and grasped the lapels of his waistcoat. I opened my expression, cast aside the serious, somber woman who'd clung to me for so very long. I wanted him to see. I wanted him to know. "And what do you think? Am I happy now?"

His grin was quick and devastating. "Nearly." Leaning close, he whispered against my lips. "You just need a little reminder."

I clung to his waistcoat as his arms engulfed me. I laughed lightly as he rained kisses across my cheekbones, my chin, my nose, and finally my lips.

It was only moments later that Miller's loud whistle and the responding hollering from those assembled had us breaking apart and smiling at one another.

I knew that happiness wasn't dependent on the man at my side. Joy wasn't conditional or reliant upon one another, but rather we were enhanced by it. Our story wasn't only happy—it couldn't be just one thing. There were bits and pieces and chapters of … everything in between. We were the sum of our parts, and I was finally able to enjoy the good without being overwhelmed by the past.

For the first time in a long time, the future was more than I'd ever dreamed.

Author's Note

Even though this story is firmly in the **fiction** category, I felt like I should warn you … I took some liberties with Eliza's profession and training and historical acceptance. At the time, in London, she would not have been a socially acceptable practicing and licensed physician. But, for the purposes of *Well Acquainted*, I needed her to be a doctor. So here we are. 🩶

Acknowledgments

To Piper and Karla: This book was written while deep (so deep) in the Dramione pit of obsession, and I feel like I really only have you two to thank (see also: blame).

About the Author

Laney Hatcher is a firm believer that there is a spreadsheet for every occasion and pie is always the answer. She is an author of stories that have a past, in a language of love that's universal. Often too practical for her own good, Laney enjoys her life in the southern United States with her husband, children, and incredibly entitled cat.

Find Laney Hatcher online:
Facebook: https://bit.ly/3s6KnuY
Newsletter: https://bit.ly/3sUGwAk
Amazon: https://amzn.to/3IaOwU7
Instagram: https://bit.ly/3s4IRcS
Website: https://laneyhatcher.com/
Goodreads: https://bit.ly/3BD0Gme
TikTok: https://www.tiktok.com/@laneyhatcherauthor

Find Smartypants Romance online:
Website: www.smartypantsromance.com
Facebook: https://www.facebook.com/smartypantsromance
Twitter: @smartypantsrom
Instagram: @smartypantsromance
Newsletter: https://smartypantsromance.com/newsletter/

<h1 style="text-align:center">Also by Laney Hatcher</h1>

London Ladies Embroidery Series

Neanderthal Seeks Duchess: A Smartypants Romance Out of This World Title

Bartholomew Series

First to Fall

Second Chance Dance

Third Degree Yearn

Also by Smartypants Romance

<u>Green Valley Chronicles</u>

<u>The Love at First Sight Series</u>

<u>Baking Me Crazy by Karla Sorensen (#1)</u>

<u>Batter of Wits by Karla Sorensen (#2)</u>

<u>Steal My Magnolia by Karla Sorensen (#3)</u>

<u>Worth the Wait by Karla Sorensen (#4)</u>

<u>Fighting For Love Series</u>

<u>Stud Muffin by Jiffy Kate (#1)</u>

<u>Beef Cake by Jiffy Kate (#2)</u>

<u>Eye Candy by Jiffy Kate (#3)</u>

<u>Knock Out by Jiffy Kate (#4)</u>

<u>The Donner Bakery Series</u>

<u>No Whisk, No Reward by Ellie Kay (#1)</u>

<u>The Green Valley Library Series</u>

<u>Love in Due Time by L.B. Dunbar (#1)</u>

<u>Crime and Periodicals by Nora Everly (#2)</u>

<u>Prose Before Bros by Cathy Yardley (#3)</u>

<u>Shelf Awareness by Katie Ashley (#4)</u>

<u>Carpentry and Cocktails by Nora Everly (#5)</u>

<u>Love in Deed by L.B. Dunbar (#6)</u>

Dewey Belong Together by Ann Whynot (#7)

Hotshot and Hospitality by Nora Everly (#8)

Love in a Pickle by L.B. Dunbar (#9)

Checking You Out by Ann Whynot (#10)

<u>Architecture and Artistry by Nora Everly (#11)</u>

<u>Scorned Women's Society Series</u>

<u>My Bare Lady by Piper Sheldon (#1)</u>

<u>The Treble with Men by Piper Sheldon (#2)</u>

<u>The One That I Want by Piper Sheldon (#3)</u>

<u>Hopelessly Devoted by Piper Sheldon (#3.5)</u>

<u>It Takes a Woman by Piper Sheldon (#4)</u>

<u>Park Ranger Series</u>

<u>Happy Trail by Daisy Prescott (#1)</u>

<u>Stranger Ranger by Daisy Prescott (#2)</u>

<u>The Leffersbee Series</u>

<u>Been There Done That by Hope Ellis (#1)</u>

<u>Before and After You by Hope Ellis (#2)</u>

<u>The Higher Learning Series</u>

<u>Upsy Daisy by Chelsie Edwards (#1)</u>

<u>Green Valley Heroes Series</u>

Forrest for the Trees by Kilby Blades (#1)

Parks and Provocation by Juliette Cross (#2)

<u>Story of Us Collection</u>

My Story of Us: Zach by Chris Brinkley (#1)

My Story of Us: Thomas by Chris Brinkley (#2)

<u>Seduction in the City</u>

<u>Cipher Security Series</u>

<u>Code of Conduct by April White (#1)</u>

<u>Code of Honor by April White (#2)</u>

<u>Code of Matrimony by April White (#2.5)</u>

<u>Code of Ethics by April White (#3)</u>

<u>Cipher Office Series</u>

9 781959 097235